Also By Brenda Hasse

<u>An Afterlife Journey Trilogy</u>
On The Third Day
From Beyond The Grave
Until We Meet Again

<u>Adult</u>
The Cursed Witch
A Victim Of Desperation

<u>Young Adult</u>
The Freelancer
A Lady's Destiny
The Moment Of Trust
Wilkinshire

<u>Picture Books For Children</u>
My Horsy And Me, What Can We Be?
A Unicorn For My Birthday
Yes, I Am Loved

Leaving You Behind

~

Brenda Hasse

Leaving You Behind

978-1-7347786-8-7 (pbk)

979-8-9864383-0-6 (ebk)

To Petey and Max, my furry felines, who healed my heart after the loss of Jackson.

Chapter 1

Elise opened her sapphire eyes to the sound of a toilet flushing. She watched her husband enter the bedroom dressed only in his boxer briefs and admired his well-built, tall physique.

Freshly showered, Gabe selected a shirt from the closet. He hung a tie around his neck before grabbing a pair of dress pants from a hanger. Glancing at his wife's face, which lacked color, he paused. "How are you feeling this morning?" He shoved his foot into the leg of his pants.

Elise took a silent inventory of her body. "About the same. My stomach is a little queasy." She looked at the alarm clock on her nightstand. Her appointment with her doctor was in an hour. "Dang flu just won't go away."

"Maybe you'll feel better after you take a shower." Gabe tucked in his shirt, zipped his pants, and buckled his belt. He leaned over and gently placed a kiss on her forehead. "Happy Anniversary, Babe."

Elise brushed his damp charcoal hair away from his hazel eyes and forced a grin on her face. "Happy Anniversary."

"Let's go out for a nice dinner tonight," he suggested but then took her illness into consideration, "or I can bring home take out."

Stretching her arms over her head, Elise yawned. "Take out? Not very romantic for our first wedding anniversary."

Gabe grinned as he tied his tie. He turned toward the dresser mirror to ensure it was centered correctly in his collar. "Babe, we have been together since high school and celebrated incidental dating anniversaries over the years." He hoped to ease her guilt. "This is just our first official anniversary, with many more to come. So, we'll make do."

Elise nodded slightly, disappointed her illness was ruining their special occasion.

Gabe read her mind. "Whatever way we celebrate will be memorable." He leaned toward her and kissed her on the forehead again. Aware of her fear of doctors, he offered. "Do you want me to call into work and go to the doctor with you?"

Elise masked her face with bravery. "No, that's OK."

He clasped her hand and gave it a slight squeeze. "I've got to get to work. Give me a call after you see the doctor."

Elise closed her eyes as the apartment door clicked shut. She heard the engine of Gabe's motorcycle come to life and fade into the distance as he drove away. Reluctantly, she threw back the covers and rose from the bed.

The hot shower failed to make her feel any better. Elise dressed in a pair of jeans and a cotton shirt. Even though the mid-summer temperatures were sweltering, she kept the bookstore airconditioned at a refreshing temperature for her customers and dressed accordingly. "Maybe a little vitamin C would do me some good." Retrieving an orange from the refrigerator, Elise pushed her thumb into the peel and pulled it away from the fruit. The repulsive citrus aroma squirting into the air caused her to wrinkle her nose and turn away. She put the orange back into the refrigerator and washed her hands. Elise dropped her cellphone into her purse and left the apartment without eating.

When she called yesterday, Elise was thankful there had been a cancellation for an early morning appointment. If there were no delays, she would have time to see the family doctor quickly before hurrying to the bookstore to open it on time.

The patients in the lobby stared at Elise as she entered. She scribbled her name on a clipboard and sat in a vacant chair. Then glancing around the small waiting room, she cringed inwardly as a woman blew her nose, an elderly man spat something into a handkerchief, and a young mother tried to comfort her crying baby.

"Elise Messenger."

Elise sprang from the chair, eager to be away from the infectious people.

A middle-aged woman dressed in burgundy scrubs smiled as she held open a door. The medical assistant held a folder in her hand. "Hello, I'm Heather. How are you today?" She motioned for Elise to pass through the doorway.

"Hi. Not to be sarcastic, but if I felt great, I wouldn't be here." Elise heard the woman snicker behind her. She waited for Heather to lead the way to a small room where her vitals were taken and recorded.

"Right this way." Heather escorted Elise to another room and closed the door for privacy.

Poised with her readied pen, Heather looked at Elise, who sat in the only chair in the room. "What are you seeing the doctor for today?"

"I haven't been feeling well lately. I'm fatigued, and my stomach is queasy."

"How long have you been feeling like this?"

"A week or so."

"Are you on any medications?"

"No."

"Date of your last period?"

Elise scolded herself for not checking her calendar. "I think it's due by the end of this week, maybe next week."

"Ok. Doctor Griswold will be right in."

"Thank you."

Heather opened the door and placed the file in the clip on the hallway wall. She closed the door, isolating Elise, who rhythmically twitched her foot as she glanced at her watch, wondering how long she would have to wait.

She saw a faded print on one wall, a few typed instructions posted on the back of the door, and a hazardous waste dispenser. Elise recognized the outline of a used syringe through the opaque plastic. Her heart began to race as she recalled the event that started her phobia of doctors.

Her father's words of encouragement echoed within her memory. "It's just a baby pinch." Even though he downplayed the injection, he held her hand and promised to get her ice cream afterward. She glanced at her watch again. "The ice cream shop probably isn't open this early."

Recalling him fondly, he always greeted her with a smile and a warm bear hug as she entered the bookstore after school. He was kind, patient, and educated her well, for she knew every facet of operating the family business. When he died shortly after she graduated from high school, Elise honored her father by continuing to run the bookstore instead of going away to college as planned.

It was a sad time in her life. Gabe, her best friend during high school, was supportive throughout. When he went away to college, her heart ached as if he took a part of it with him. As promised, he called her often, and they exchanged letters. After completing his first year, the hum of his motorcycle echoed from the front of the bookstore announcing his arrival. He entered carrying a single red rose and told her he loved her. Once he graduated from college and secured a job, he asked her to become his wife on her twenty-fifth birthday. A year later, her mother escorted her down the aisle. She grinned as she recalled Gabe wiping the tears from his eyes. "I'm such a softy," he kidded, trying to lighten the moment's emotion.

The door opened, and middle-aged Doctor Griswold entered. Elise's smile faded.

"Hello, Elise. Not feeling well, huh?"

"Not really. Tired and upset stomach."

"Let me take a look." Doctor Griswold scanned the entries in the file. "No temp." She put the paperwork on the counter next to the sink, washed her hands, and placed her palms on Elise's neck. "No swollen glands." She examined her patient's nose and throat. "Probably the flu. I've seen a few cases this week." The doctor inserted the otoscope in Elise's ears. "Looks good." She warmed the end of the stethoscope in her hand before placing it on Elise's chest and hearing her patient's heartbeat. "Good." The doctor moved the instrument to Elise's back. "Take a deep breath." She listened as Elise took several deep breaths. "Sounds clear." Placing the stethoscope around her neck, she sighed. "I'm not seeing anything. You could have a virus."

Elise exhaled and looked heavenward. She knew she was ill. 'It's a virus,' was just another way of saying, 'I don't know what's wrong with you.'

Doctor Griswold sat on a stool and lifted the file from the counter. "You may have caught something from one of your customers. How is the bookstore doing?" She flipped through several papers in the file.

"It's doing well."

"And your mom?"

"She's fine too." Elise watched as the doctor scribbled something in the file.

Doctor Griswold handed the check-out form to Elise. "I'll have Heather swab you to see if you have the flu. For now, rest, and sleep when you're tired. If you aren't feeling better in a week, come and see me.

Elise looked at her watch. "Do I have to wait? I need to open the bookstore."

"I'll have Heather call you once the test comes back."

"Thank you, Doctor Griswold."

"You're welcome. I hope you feel better." The doctor exited, closing the door behind her and placing Elise in solitude again.

Chapter 2

Elise made a quick stop at a drugstore to purchase some antacids. Her stomach grumbled as she popped two into her mouth and lethargically walked back to her car. "What I need is coffee." She drove her car to the nearest fast-food restaurant and ordered a large decaf and breakfast sandwich. When she pulled forward to pay at the first window, the employee indicated the previous customer had paid for Elise's food. She thought it was only fitting to forward the kind gesture.

"How much is the next order?" She pointed toward the vehicle behind her.

The cashier checked the computer screen and announced, "$37.46."

Elise looked in her rearview mirror to see a van with several people inside. "Oh, my, that's a little out of my budget. Maybe next time." She pulled up to the next window and accepted her order from the employee. "Thanks. Have a good day."

Parking her car in the reserved spot of the alley, Elise unlocked the deadbolt of the old brick building's back door and entered. With her coffee and brown paper bag containing her breakfast sandwich in one hand, she turned on several lights, went to her office, and switched on her computer before settling into the chair behind her desk. As she unwrapped the sandwich, a shadowy movement near the floor caught her attention. "Hello, Petey." The feline's nose sniffed upward, detecting the sausage. "Ok, I'll share, but you have your own food." She pinched off a small portion for the resident cat. "Here you go." She placed the morsel on the floor. "I'll get your canned cat food when I'm done." Elise stroked the cat's silky long black hair as the feline sniffed the sausage, questioning if it was edible. "Good thing Dad isn't here to see how chubby you have gotten."

She watched Petey swallow and look toward her for another bite. "I remember when I came into the bookstore after school one day. Dad had you wrapped in a dust rag. You were so tiny. Do you remember meowing for help from beneath the dumpster?"

The feline stared at her with his yellow eyes, patiently waiting for another bit of sausage.

"You had blue eyes then. Between Dad and I, we fed you morning and night. Dad would put you in your carrier and take you back and forth to work with him."

Petey tilted his head to one side, trying to understand what Elise had told him.

She patted Petey on the head and looked at her dad's framed photograph on her desk. "If you could only see our little Petey now. Making him the official bookstore cat was a good marketing decision. The customers ask for him when they visit."

Her stomach seemed to settle with each bite she ate. She began scanning through her emails when her cell phone rang. Elise removed it from her purse and smiled as she read the caller ID. "Hi. Miss me already?"

Gabe chuckled. "You know it. What did the doctor say?"

She deleted an email, rotated her chair away from her desk, patted her thigh, and Petey jumped into her lap. "I think the doctor doesn't know what's wrong with me. She said I have a virus." Elise heard Gabe sigh as she gently scratched the cat beneath his chin.

"Are you feeling any better?"

"A little now that I ate something."

"Should I make reservations for tonight?"

Elise detected the hesitancy in Gabe's voice. It was a special occasion, and she did not want to ruin it. "Sure. Where shall we go?"

Petey rose onto his back legs, headbutted her chin, and arched his back against her chest. Elise turned her head to avoid the collision with his tail.

"How about the restaurant we went to on our first date?" Her husband suggested.

Elise looked at the clock on the wall. It was almost time to open. "You remember our first date?" She smiled and could tell he was smiling too.

"Our first official date after I told you that I loved you, yes, I remember."

Elise tried to remember their first official date. Over the years, they had visited many of the restaurants in town. "Oh, Johnny's, right? We had pizza." Elise chuckled. "So romantic."

"It was for me," Gabe admitted.

Elise nodded. "Me too."

"Great, I'll meet you at the apartment at 6:30."

"Sounds great. See you then."

"Oh, Elise."

"Ya."

"I love you. I can't imagine sharing my life with a better friend, wife, partner, and lover than you."

Elise considered herself lucky beyond belief, truly blessed. Some people search their entire life, hoping to find that special someone. To think their paths had crossed a dozen years ago, years filled with happiness, good times, and enduring bad times together. She smiled. "I love you too. See you at 6:30."

She put Petey on the floor. "I know. You want your breakfast." Elise retrieved a can of cat food from the closet, opened it, and dumped the single serving onto the feline's dish before leaving her office to open the bookstore.

Chapter 3

Marge, a retired English teacher and Elise's only employee, worked a day or two a week to help check in new merchandise, wait on customers, and shelve books. Since her employee was not scheduled to work today, Elise managed to plaster a smile on her face and help customers in her lethargic condition.

Late afternoon, Elise received a call from the doctor's office with the test result. Negative, probably a virus other than the flu.

Drained of what little energy she had by day's end, Elise clicked off the 'open' sign to end her busy day, locked the front door, and shut off the lights.

After cashing out the register drawer, she filled out the bank deposit slip, turned off the computers, and ensured the cat had food and water. "See you tomorrow, Petey." As was her habit, Elise kissed and patted him on his head as he lay curled in her desk chair, sleeping.

With little energy and her stomach feeling queasy once again, she drove to the apartment and climbed the stairs to the second floor. After tossing her purse on her dresser, Elise collapsed on the bed and drifted off to sleep.

"Elise."

She heard her name called, but her eyelids were too heavy with sleep to open.

"Elise, wake up."

She opened her eyes, blinked them several times to focus on a blurry redness held before her, and inhaled the fragrance of roses. Elise looked up at her husband's smiling face.

"Happy Anniversary." Gabe leaned forward, pressing his lips to her forehead.

Elise leaned against the headboard as the bouquet of roses was placed on her lap. "Oh, Gabe, they're beautiful." She raised them to her nose and inhaled their fragrance again. "Thank you, but I didn't get you anything."

"It doesn't matter." He consoled her as he lifted her chin with his index finger to meet his lips and kissed her tenderly.

The buzzer sounded, announcing someone at the front door of the apartment building.

The gold flecks in Gabe's hazel eyes sparkled mischievously. "Dinner's here."

Elise looked confused. "I thought we were going out for dinner." She glanced at her alarm clock. "7:30?"

"You were snoring quite loudly. Obviously, you needed the rest."

"I don't snore."

"Yes, you do. I'll go get the pizza. Be back soon."

Elise heard the apartment door close as she rose from the bed. She took a large vase from the kitchen cupboard, filled it with water, and arranged the roses. After placing the flowers in the center of the kitchen table, she set each place setting as Gabe entered with the pizza.

Guilt tugged at her consciousness as Elise glanced at the pizza her husband set on the table.

Gabe opened the box and looked at her face for approval.

She cringed. "Not much of a romantic anniversary, is it?"

"I think it's perfect, just like our first date." Gabe pulled out her chair and gallantly motioned for her to sit. "Do you want any wine?"

"No, thank you. Just water, please." Elise sat as he pushed her chair forward.

Gabe took a beer from the fridge and filled a glass with ice and water. "Here you go." He sat across from her. "So, still not feeling well?"

Elise wrinkled her nose. "About the same. Sorry to ruin our evening." She took a slice of pizza from the box, ate a bite from the pointed tip, and placed it on her plate.

"It's not going as we planned, but we'll make the best of it." He selected a slice. "Maybe we can find a good movie to watch on TV."

"If we can agree on one." Elise enjoyed comedies and romance, while Gabe was all action, espionage, and war movies.

"Since you're feeling crappy, you get to pick the movie, but don't be surprised if I fall asleep during it." Gabe smiled before biting into his slice.

"Deal, but the way I'm feeling, I may fall asleep too."

"Then we better watch the movie in bed."

"Sounds good."

Gabe raised his can of beer. "To us, happy anniversary, Elise."

She raised her glass of ice water. "Happy anniversary, Gabe."

Chapter 4

Elise blindly extended her hand toward her alarm clock. She shut off the annoying sound, rolled over, and reached for Gabe. His side of the bed was empty. "He left without saying goodbye?" She sighed, quite assured he had kissed her before leaving the apartment. "He probably wanted to let me sleep."

Rising from the bed, Elise curled her lips as her stomach reminded her of its current condition. Cursing herself for leaving the antacids at the bookstore, she took a box of saltine crackers from the kitchen cupboard, grabbed an opened sleeve, and shoved an entire cracker into her mouth. Elise entered the dining room and selected a second cracker. Even though she was not feeling very well, she grinned as she saw the bouquet of roses. At the base of the vase was a note from Gabe. She picked it up and read it.

> I kissed you goodbye, but you didn't wake up. So, I sat on the edge of the bed and watched you sleep. My beautiful wife, I love you so. See you tonight. Gabe   PS – I hope you are feeling better today.

"Aw, I love you too, Gabe." She placed the note on the table, shoved another cracker in her mouth, and looked out the balcony's sliding glass door. It was raining. "My day will go one of two ways; either we will be swamped at the bookstore, or no one will visit at all."

Elise dressed, grabbed the wrapped leftover pizza from the fridge and her purse, and drove to the bookstore.

~

Petey sat near the back door anticipating Elise's arrival. He tilted his head to the side and listened as the key was inserted and rotated in the lock. The eager feline rose on all fours and stared at the door as it opened. His bulbous belly waddled as he walked toward his owner with his tail raised. His long black fur was mussed as if he had put his paw into an electrical outlet.

"Good morning, Petey. I'm sorry I didn't stop for breakfast this morning, but you are more than welcome to some ham from my pizza." She brushed the feline's silky fur before turning on the lights and stepping toward her office. Petey nearly tripped Elise as he wove between her legs. After turning on her computer, she took several tiny pieces of ham from her pizza and placed them in Petey's dish. "When you finish that, I'll give you your canned food." She put her lunch in the small refrigerator and hung her purse on the coat rack.

"Coffee, I need coffee." She inserted the one-cup container into the machine, placed her mug beneath the dispenser, and pushed the button. Her cell phone buzzed. Retrieving it from her purse, she glanced at the text. "Another spam." Elise blocked the number and put the phone in her back pocket. She felt a tapping on her leg and looked down at her hungry cat.

"Finished already? My goodness." She picked up Petey, cuddled him close to her chest, and kissed the top of his head while she waited for her coffee. He wiggled in her arms. "You win. I'll feed you first." Elise retrieved a can of cat food from the closet and dumped it into his bowl as the last of her coffee sputtered into her mug. "There you go, Mr. Chubbycat."

The echo of a book slamming to the hardwood floor in the next room startled Petey. He crouched near the floor, looked at the open doorway of the office, and chewed what was in his mouth.

Elise was accustomed to the common occurrence in the old building. With her coffee cup in hand, she reassured her cat. "Petey, it's fine. Just the dang ghost again." She left her office searching for the wayward novel leaving the cat to finish his breakfast alone.

The book was indeed on the floor in the center of an aisle. Elise bent over, picked it up, and read the title. "An interesting topic you have chosen, Mr. Ghost." She glanced at the dingy wooden floor. "Looks like it needs to be mopped." Returning the book to its proper place, she ran her finger over the shelf. "And this needs dusting."

Insisting the bookstore remained spotlessly clean, her father's words of wisdom rang true. "No one wants to visit a store that is filthy." So, she would have the store dust-free by the end of the day, or she hoped.

Elise looked at the clock on the wall. "Time to open." She turned on the open sign in the display window before unlocking the front door and planned to clean between the customer's visits.

Marge arrived just before lunch for her five-hour shift. "The restaurant next door sure has become popular. I read a review in the paper that it now has a gourmet chef who creates many of its signature sandwiches."

Elise looked up from the computer screen as her employee approached the counter. "So, I've heard. They're quite large and a little too expensive for my pocketbook."

"They must be quite busy today. I had a difficult time finding a parking spot. I guess our small city needs more parking." Marge waited on the few customers who came into the store throughout the day, allowing her boss the time she needed to clean.

Her employee's blue eyes framed by graying brunette hair peeked around the endcap of the aisle where Elise was replacing the books onto a dusted shelf. "Would you like me to stay the extra hour until closing?"

Elise glanced at the clock. "Thanks for offering, Marge, but there has been so little foot traffic today, you may as well go home. I should be able to finish this shelf and mop the floor before locking up for the night."

"Ok. I'll see you tomorrow. Goodnight."

"Goodnight." Quite pleased with her progress, Elise placed the last book on the dusted shelf as the back door shut. She wheeled the empty cart into the closet and went to the utility room.

After drizzling oil soap into the bucket, Elise lifted it into the washtub. The bell to the front door rang before she could turn on the water. Peeking her head out of the door, she smiled as a familiar silhouette came into view. "Hello, Aileen." Joining her customer, she glanced out the front display window. It had stopped raining. The sun glistened off the damp green leaves of the mature trees lining the street. "What can I help you with today?"

Everyone in town knew the widowed Aileen. The sweet elderly church lady remained active in the community, always willing to lend a helping hand.

Aileen turned and looked at Elise. Her ever-present smile was displayed on her face. "Hello,

Elise." Her white hair was neatly curled as if she had just visited the beauty shop. She had a book in her hand, a current bestseller, and scanned the cover. "I don't think I've read this author before, but it looks interesting."

Elise peeked over the stooped woman's shoulder. "Ah, yes, she writes suspense. I read it last week. It's a good one. I think you will like it."

Petey brushed against Aileen's leg, causing her to look down. "Well, hello, Petey."

The curious feline stretched his front legs up the elderly customer's thigh. He flexed his tiny toes before pulling himself toward her outstretched arthritic hand.

Aileen scratched Petey under his chin. She watched the cat close his eyes, appreciating the attention. "You're such a good boy. I used to have a cat like you. Sammy, he was a good boy too. I miss him. But it's always nice to visit with you, Petey."

Elise posed the question on her mind. "Why don't you get another cat?"

"Oh, it would be unfair to get one at my age. I would probably die before it did, and where would it end up?" Aileen petted Petey's head. "My children and their families have dogs. I would hate for it to go to a shelter and be put to sleep."

"Have you thought of fostering an elderly cat? It would make the last years of its life pleasant before it crosses over the rainbow bridge?" Elise had suggested the same to her mother, but she had refused.

"I'll give it some thought." Aileen tucked the book in the crook of her arm, picked up another from the shelf, and examined the cover.

Elise looked at the clock. She would need to lock the front door in fifteen minutes. Assuming Aileen would shop during that time, she called over her shoulder as she returned to the utility room. "Take your time browsing. I'm going to mop the floor. Let me know when you are ready to check out."

"Oh, don't mind me, just go about what you need to do." Aileen turned the book to the back cover and read the synopsis.

Elise filled the bucket with hot water, lifted it from the sink, and grabbed the mop as she exited the room. She glanced at her customer to ensure she was still shopping and began to mop. After washing the back third of the floor, she placed her mop in the bucket, walked to the front, turned off the open sign, and locked the front door.

With two books in her hand, Aileen looked at Elise. Her deep blue eyes had faded to nearly gray over the years. "Are you closing?"

"Not yet. Take your time." She reassured

With a nod of her head, Aileen returned a book to the shelf and selected another one.

Gathering the rugs from the front door and counter, Elise exited the back door. Since the door locked automatically, she propped it open with a brick kept near the wall. She shook the rugs until they were dust-free. Elise finished mopping half of the floor when Aileen went to the counter, indicating she was ready to check out.

"I see you found three books. They look quite interesting." She scanned the first barcode.

"Yes, you always have a good selection." Aileen took her credit card from her wallet and waited.

Elise picked up the next novel in the trio. "Oh, I have yet to read this one, but it looks like a good one." She scanned it.

"I'm looking forward to tucking myself into bed tonight and reading until I fall asleep."

"Having trouble sleeping?" Elise picked up the last book.

"A little. Old age is no friend of mine. It would be nice to sleep through the night."

"Well, you may be staying awake until you finish this one." Elise teased as she picked up one of the books and put it in the paper bag. She stated the total and watched Aileen insert her credit card into the machine.

"Then I better start reading when I get home." The elderly customer smiled before returning her credit card to her wallet.

Elise printed the receipt, put it in the bag with the purchased books, and handed it to her customer. "Here, I'll walk you out."

"I'm certain I'll be in next week for more books," Aileen assured as Elise unlocked the front door and held it open.

"I look forward to seeing you again. Thanks for coming in today. Goodbye."

"Bye, Elise."

Elise looked at the clock on the wall. It was nearly a quarter past the hour. She texted Gabe, letting him know she would be late coming home and why. Shoving her phone into her back pocket, she continued to mop until the floor was spotless. Returning to the utility room, Elise dumped the filthy water down the sink and put the cleaning tools in

28

their proper place. Pulling her phone from her pocket, she checked to see if Gabe had replied. He had not. "He's probably driving home." Elise counted the money in the register, prepared the bank deposit slip, and went to her office to shut down her computer. Grabbing her purse, she began shutting off the store lights as a knock sounded on the front door. "Ugh, I'm closed," she said under her breath as she saw Officer Morton standing on the stoop.

Living in a small town had its advantages and disadvantages. Everyone knew everyone. Everyone knew the happenings, good or bad, too. Officer Ed Morton was a member of Elise and Gabe's high school graduating class. He was a trusted and respected officer.

Elise sighed as she put the strap of her purse over her shoulder, went to the front door, and unlocked it. "Hello Ed, shoplifters again?"

His face was gaunt, unsmiling. "No, I wish. It's Gabe. He's been in a motorcycle accident with another car."

Chapter 5

Elise had enough wits about her to lock the front
door. "Is he hurt?"

Ed did not answer.

"Ed?"

"I'll drive you to County where they've taken
him."

"I can drive . . ." She began.

"Elise, my car is right here." He opened the
passenger door. "I insist."

She glanced at the empty seat, the concerned
expression on the officer's face, and complied. Ed
closed the door, hurried to the other side of the car,

and slid into the seat, slamming the door shut. He turned on the siren and sped away.

The blaring noise hurt Elise's ears. She wanted to cover them with the palms of her hands but thought she would look silly. Holding her breath, they dodged around a car in an intersection and continued. "Why wasn't Gabe taken to General Hospital? Isn't it closer?"

Ignoring her question, Ed knew why they were going to the County Hospital but did not want to tell her. "I called your mother and Gabe's parents too. So, they're meeting us there."

Elise looked at Ed as a sinking feeling settled within her chest. "My mom?"

He simply nodded. What seemed like an hour's drive was only minutes. Ed turned into the hospital facility and directed his car toward the emergency entrance.

Janet paced near the double glass doors. She breathed a sigh of relief as she recognized her daughter in the front seat of the police car. She tried to calm herself, but her face, masked with worry, revealed her concern.

Elise stared at her mother's sepia eyes. Their haunting hollowness looked similar on the day her father passed away.

Ed turned off the siren, parked the car, and opened the passenger door for Elise to step out.

"Mom, how's Gabe?"

Janet embraced her daughter. "They won't let me see him. We must wait in a consultation room until a doctor can give us an update."

Gabe's parents hurried to the entrance to join them. "What happened?" Douglas looked at the police officer and then at Elise.

"Gabe was in an accident." Elise turned to Ed. "Thanks for the ride."

"If you don't mind," he escorted the group through the automatic doors, "I'll be in the waiting room after." He patted Elise's upper arm, giving her the confidence and strength to hear the doctor's report.

She nodded to the officer before her mother ushered the small group into their assigned room. A clerk came in and asked for her health insurance card, which Elise took from her purse and gave to the woman, who turned and left the room.

Janet sat in the chair next to her daughter.

Within minutes, Father Herold entered with a doctor. Staring at the priest's black and white-collar, an uneasy feeling crept into Elise's heart.

The doctor sat in the vacant chair beside Elise. "Mrs. Messenger," he began.

Both Elise and her mother-in-law, Barbara, replied. "Yes."

Glancing up at Barbara, the doctor turned his attention to the younger of the two.

"Elise." She corrected.

He sighed. "Elise, your husband was in an accident with another car. The medic detected a weak pulse as he was taken by ambulance and transported here. Unfortunately, when he was brought into the hospital, he was unresponsive. We tried to revive your husband but were unsuccessful."

Elise's eyebrows raised in question. Had she heard him correctly? "He's dead?"

Barbara's eyes began to well. Douglas put his arm around his wife.

The doctor nodded slightly. "We did everything we could. I'm sorry for your loss."

Elise looked at her mother, who helplessly wept, unable to take the hurt away from her daughter.

"Do you have any questions?" The doctor looked at the young widow.

"I don't understand. What happened?" She needed to know the truth.

"A witness indicated your husband was looking at something in his hand, possibly his cellphone, when he ran a red light. Another car hit him."

Elise went numb, staring at nothing. "My text." Tears cascaded down her cheeks. "He was looking at his phone at my text."

Janet put her arm around her daughter's shoulder. "Honey, you don't know that."

Elise looked at her mother. "I do know. It's true. I sent him a text, and he never replied. So, I assumed he was on his way home and couldn't answer because he was driving his motorcycle." She closed her eyes. "He shouldn't have looked at his phone."

Barbara's hazel eyes narrowed as she glared at her daughter-in-law.

~

Gabe stared at his body as it lay on the stainless-steel table. He watched the nurse wash away the blood from his face.

"I don't want his wife to see him in such a mess." She explained to her coworker as she dipped the paper towel in the basin and wiped the dried red smudges from a scuffed cheek.

"It never is easy to lose a patient," the middle-aged nurse straightened the broken and contorted leg and placed both arms next to the body, "especially one so young." She pulled a white sheet over Gabe's body and tucked it beneath his chin.

The young nurse tossed the bloody towel in the trash. "That's about the best I can do."

"I'm dead?" Gabe looked down at his face. His hair was mussed, and several red abrasions were on his face.

"Yes, sir, you're dead alright."

Gabe looked behind him to see an elderly man in the corner of the room. His ebony face was framed by a beard sprinkled with gray whiskers.

"No, I can't be. I'm too young. My wife and I have only been married for a year."

The man shrugged his shoulders. "It's the luck of the draw. You died for a reason."

"What reason?" Gabe scowled.

"Beats me. I guess that's for you to find out." The old man looked over his shoulder. "Gotta go and greet another one. Best of luck to you." The man disappeared through the wall.

Alone in the room, Gabe tried to remember how he died. "I was going home after work, eager to see Elise and see how she felt," Gabe remembered the distraction. "My phone vibrated as I approached an intersection, and I withdrew it from my shirt pocket to see who was calling me." He closed his eyes, recalling the echo of screeching tires, the impact of the car with his motorcycle, and being thrown into the air. He shook his head. "I've driven that road hundreds of times. Complacency breeds danger." It cost him his life and future with the woman he loved.

~

A nurse opened the consultation room door with a clipboard in hand, looked at the doctor, and nodded her head once.

Understanding the silent signal, the doctor looked at Elise. "I know this is difficult for you to grasp. It feels a little surreal. I often suggest that the deceased's loved ones spend some time with the body before its taken to the morgue. It is a way to come to terms with what has happened. Father Herold will accompany you. He will give Gabe his last blessing." The doctor stood. "Whenever you are ready. Take your time." He nodded to the priest, handing off the responsibility of the grieving family to the man of the cloth before exiting, signing the clipboard the nurse presented to him and closing the door.

Elise whispered to her mother, who clutched her hand. "I don't know if I can do this." Her bottom lip quivered.

"I think it's important we say goodbye," she reassured, "I'll be by your side."

Elise nodded as she looked at the tile floor.

Father Herold, silent until now, offered his words of wisdom. "Elise, this is a lot for you to comprehend."

"It's just so sudden. Gabe left this morning without saying goodbye." She looked at the priest's kind face as tears trickled down her cheeks. "He didn't wake me up to say goodbye."

Father Herold sat in the chair vacated by the doctor. "The next few days will be difficult. Let's begin by giving you a few moments alone with Gabe."

"Days?" His words gave her little comfort. How could he only say 'days'? She would spend the rest of her life without her husband.

"Yes, we will walk this path one day at a time. Let's begin by blessing his body and soul and spend these precious moments with him." The priest explained.

Janet pulled several facial tissues from a box on the table and handed them to her daughter. "Take a deep breath." She watched as Elise dabbed the tears from her cheeks. "Are you ready?"

Elise blew her nose, nodded her head, and stood.

The sorrowful group walked to where Gabe's body lay.

Father Herold tried to justify why one so young would be called away to God. Firm in his belief, he knew Gabe was in a better place. However, conveying that belief was of little comfort to those who grieved. To allow the grieving family some privacy, he stopped shy of the room where the lifeless body lay on a table. "I'll wait here and give all of you some time alone with Gabe."

"Thank you, Father." Janet guided her daughter into the room. Douglas and Barbara followed.

Elise stood transfixed, almost afraid to approach the table. On it lay her husband covered in a white sheet as if he were sleeping. A clear plastic bag was on the seat of a chair. She saw Gabe's shoes, helmet, wallet, and cell phone inside. The room was lined with monitoring devices, tubes, and hoses. Elise tried to control her breathing, but her anguish and despair could not be contained. "Gabe."

A whimper escaped from Barbara's lips. She covered her mouth with her hand.

Father Herold turned away from the doors and cringed as Elise's cries of grief echoed from within the room. He touched the sign of the cross on his body and began to pray.

Elise's hands trembled as she reached for her husband, laid her head on his chest, and cradled his head within her arms. Her tears fell onto the white sheet, representing her love that had nowhere else to go, for he was no longer there to receive it.

Gabe stood on the opposite side of the table. He looked at his wife's trembling body as she cried. "Elise, I'm right here." He placed his palm on her head to stroke her flaxen hair, but his hand passed through her locks without feeling them. Holding his hand before his face, he rotated it, staring. He touched the table. Again, his hand passed through it. "Interesting."

Barbara and Douglas reached out and touched their son's body. They wept silently.

Elise quieted as she listened for a heartbeat. Her ear was met with silence. A hollowness crept into her heart as she faced the truth. Her husband was indeed gone from her life. "Why? Why did you have to go?" She looked at his face, sleeping in eternal rest, and placed her hands on his cheeks. They were cold to the touch.

"I don't know why Elise. maybe it was just my time to go?" Gabe guessed, uncertain if it was the correct answer. He began to ponder the question as well. "Why have I died? I'm only twenty-seven years old, newly married, and had so much of my life ahead of me. Why?"

Elise brushed her deceased husband's charcoal hair, putting the wayward strands back in place. "You have been a part of my life ever since I can remember. How am I going to go on without you?" Her bottom lip quivered. "I hope you know that I love you and always will."

"I love you too, Elise. I'll stay by your side for as long as I can. I promise." Gabe looked at his mother-in-law as she rubbed her daughter's back, silently supporting her.

The door to the room opened, and Father Herold entered. He went to the end of the table near the deceased's head, made the sign of the cross, and began to bless the body.

Chapter 6

Gabe watched as Father Herold anointed his body with oil and prayed. His wife, mother-in-law, and parents huddled together with their hands clasped and heads bowed. He hoped the simple ceremony would give them comfort.

When the priest finished the blessing, he went to Elise and clasped her hand between his palms. "I'm sorry for your loss." Father Herold looked each mourner in the eye to convey his sincerity. "If any of you need anything, please call me."

They nodded as Douglas stepped forward, shook Father Herold's hand, and thanked him.

"You're welcome. Someone will be in to speak to you soon." The priest explained as he went to the door.

"Thank you, Father." Janet dabbed her eyes with facial tissue. She took a deep breath, hoping to find the strength to see her daughter through this difficult time.

Moments passed lethargically as they waited for someone to come and talk to them.   Barbara leaned toward her son's expressionless face. She placed her hand on his cheek, bent toward his ear, and whispered her sentiments. As she stood erect, she glared at Elise before looking away.

Elise turned to her mother. Her voice was barely audible. "Now I know how you felt when Dad died." She patted the sheet where her husband's arm lay beneath.

"A feeling I wish you didn't have to experience so early in your life." Janet rubbed her hand on her daughter's back.

Gabe began to pace. It disturbed him to see Elise in such an emotional state. He wished to hold her, tell her that everything would be all right, and let her know he was fine. Instead, he looked at his wife as she spoke.

"What now?" Elise wanted to prepare herself for what lay ahead.

Janet thought for a moment. "If I remember correctly, Gabe will be taken to the morgue where the funeral home will pick him up. After that, you will have to make some decisions."

"Like what?"

"Details of the funeral and such." Janet was fully aware of the decisions Elise would have to make. Would Gabe be buried or cremated? Which readings would be read at the funeral? Unfortunately, her daughter was too distraught to go into a full explanation.

"We never talked about something like that." Elise looked at her in-laws. Douglas was an older version of Gabe in personality and physical resemblance. He was pleasant, kind, and always welcoming. However, Barbara was a different matter. Elise was under the impression her mother-in-law looked down upon her as if she was not good enough for her son. Would his death make amends for any past discretions she may have made? Elise offered. "Maybe it's something we should decide together."

"Yes, in fact, we insist," Barbara demanded.

Thoughts invaded Elise's mind like a gang of unwanted intruders. "I need to call Gabe's boss and tell him . . ." She was unable to complete the sentence. Taking a deep breath, Elise brushed a tear from her cheek. "And call Marge to ask her to cover for me tomorrow."

The door to the room opened. Everyone watched as the same woman from the consultation room entered.

Elise looked at the clipboard in the woman's hand. "Paperwork." She whispered.

The woman removed the health insurance card from under the clasp. "Here is this back." She handed it to Elise.

"Thank you."

"Now, I understand this is overwhelming and a lot to comprehend. If you have any questions, please feel free to ask." The woman instructed.

Elise nodded.

"For tonight, go home and make any necessary calls. Your husband's body will be taken to the morgue where it will be picked up by whichever funeral home you notify."

Elise looked at her mother, who read her mind. "I'll call the funeral home where Dad was taken," Janet informed, easing the burden from her daughter.

The woman went on to explain. "From there, you will work with the funeral home and decide the type of funeral you wish to have for your loved one."

Elise looked at her mother for clarification.

"Cremation or casket," Janet explained.

"Casket, and we will pay for our son's funeral." Douglas insisted.

The woman presented an ink pen. "I just need you to sign here. Men from the morgue are waiting outside the door. They will not enter until you have left the room."

Elise numbly scribbled her name on the paperwork. The words spoken by the woman had yet to register within her mind. She handed the pen back and accepted a receipt of some sort.

"Mrs. Messenger, I'm sorry for your loss."

"Thank you." Elise watched the woman exit and the door close. She sighed. "This seems like a bad dream. If only I could wake up, everything would be back to normal."

Janet wished it was a bad dream. But unfortunately, she knew the following days, months, and even years would be difficult for her daughter.

Elise went to her husband's side. "I guess it's time we part ways. Goodbye, Gabe." She leaned toward his face and paused for a moment wishing her husband would open his eyes. She stared at the features of his handsome face, casting it to her memory. Elise kissed his forehead and brushed his hair with her fingertips, ensuring it was perfect. The young widow could not control her tears as she went to the chair and picked up the plastic bag containing her husband's belongings. She waited for Gabe's parents to bid farewell to their son before turning toward her mother. "Let's go."

Elise watched the men wheel a gurney through the open doorway as she exited the room.

Gabe followed his wife. He looked over his shoulder at his body's means of transportation as it wheeled by him.

Officer Morton rose from his seat as the four mourners entered the waiting room. He noted Elise's swollen, bloodshot eyes. "The doctor told me of Gabe's passing. I'm sorry."

Elise tried to grin, but the ends of her mouth failed to respond. "Thanks, Ed, and thanks for the ride here."

"You're welcome. Would you like me to drive you home?" He glanced at Janet, who smiled at the officer's kindness.

"Thank you, Ed, but I can take Elise home." Janet indicated. "We appreciate all you have done today."

"You're welcome." Ed followed the mourners out of the emergency room. "You know how to get a hold of me if you need anything."

Elise nodded. "Thanks again, Ed."

Ed tipped his hat at Gabe's parents before going to his car.

Gabe passed through the side of Janet's car and sat in the back seat.

Elise opened the passenger door and looked at Gabe's father as she heard her name called.

Douglas stopped before her. "We will call you in the morning," he stated before joining his wife, who waited by their car.

Elise sat, closed the door, and looked at the emergency room's double doors.

Janet joined her daughter. She glanced at Elise's profile as she turned the key in the ignition

Recalling her husband's death nearly a decade ago, the tragedy shattered her soul. Even though Elise was still living with her, there were times when Janet was alone, and memories crept into her mind. Walking from room to room, she inhaled his aftershave that lingered in the bathroom. A pair of pants he intended to wear a second time was draped over the chair in the bedroom. After sharing a bed with him for twenty years, his vacant side was as hollow as a portion of her heart. She welcomed the smell of him lingering on the sheets and his pillowcase. Perhaps that was the reason she did not wash them for some time. She recalled standing in the living room and staring at the old coffee table. Her husband had insisted on repairing the broken leg instead of purchasing a new one.

Janet knew all too well that loneliness was a terrible companion. She hoped to cushion the emptiness for her daughter. "Do you want to go to your apartment or come to my house for the night?"

Elise sat frozen, numb to reality, weighing her options. The thought of being in her apartment alone was a disheartening challenge. However, going to her mother's house would only delay the inevitable. "I want to go to my apartment."

"I really don't think you should be alone tonight. Do you want me to stay with you?"

"No, but thanks. I need to call Marge. Gabe's employer can wait until tomorrow." Elise reasoned. "My car is at the bookstore. Maybe you should drop me there."

"I don't think you should be driving. I can come by and pick you up in the morning, and you can get your car then." Janet turned her car onto the main street.

Elise remained silent during the remainder of the drive.

Pulling into the parking lot of the apartment building, Janet put the car in park. "Do you want me to walk up with you?"

"No, thanks, Mom. I can take it from here."

Janet got out of the car and embraced her daughter. "If you need anything, even just to talk, call me."

"I will."

"I love you."

"Love you too, Mom." Elise apprehensively opened the door to her apartment building and entered.

Janet stared through the glass entry and watched her daughter climb the staircase with the plastic bag of her husband's possessions in one hand and her purse over one shoulder. Elise rounded the corner and disappeared from her sight.

Chapter 7

Elise turned the key in the lock. The mechanism clicked.

Gabe stood behind her. Peering over her shoulder, he heard her sigh and momentarily rest her forehead on the door. "Come on, Elise, you can do this."

She pushed the door open, flipped the switch on the wall to illuminate the lamp, and closed the door behind her. She stood, unfeeling, and listened to the silence. "Oh, Gabe. How could you leave me?" Elise inhaled, trying to catch her breath as she slid down the wall and crumbled onto the floor. The plastic bag with Gabe's belongings fell from her grasp as she pulled her knees to her chest and wrapped her arms around them. Tears cascaded down her cheeks. "You shouldn't have looked at your phone."

"I know." He confessed. "I'm sorry, Elise."

She rested her forehead on her arms and continued to shed her tears of grief. Her queasy stomach reminded her that she had yet to eat dinner. Regaining control of her emotions, Elise rose and put the plastic bag on the coffee table. She slipped her purse from her shoulder and tossed it on the kitchen table as she passed by. Opening the fridge, she stared at the leftovers. Curling her lip in disgust, Elise closed the door and grabbed some graham crackers from the pantry.

Unable to withstand the quiet apartment, she sat on the couch, pushed a button on the remote, and turned on the TV. After eating nearly half a sleeve of crackers, she looked at the plastic bag of Gabe's belongings, leaned forward, and opened it. With a shaking hand, she reached inside and began extracting items.

Elise lifted the helmet, touched the deeply grooved scratches on its side, and imagined her husband's body skidding a great distance along the pavement. Her eyes welled with tears. She ran her finger over the cracked shield before setting it on the coffee table and taking his black dress shoes out next. They were scuffed. "You always kept them polished." Placing them on the floor, Elise took out his coiled black belt and wallet next. She recalled giving both to him for Christmas. Placing his belt on the table, she ran her hand over the fine ebony leather of the wallet, opened it, and stared at a photo of the two of them taken on their honeymoon. Tears cascaded down her cheeks.

Gabe sat on the couch next to her and looked at the picture. "One of my favorite photos of us. Even though we only went up north for a few days, our honeymoon was great."

Elise thumbed through the credit cards, business cards, and money before setting the wallet aside. Picking up his phone, she stared at the shattered glass. She took her phone from her pocket and called Gabe's cell. Much to her surprise, the face of his phone lit up, and Beethoven's *Für Elise* began to play.

"Yep, the same ringtone as always," Gabe admitted.

Elise grinned as she wiped the tears from her cheeks and ended her call, silencing Gabe's phone. She could not remember his password but hoped she could take it for service and have the photos downloaded. Maybe she would display some of the pictures at the funeral home.

She removed his clothing from the bag. It was tattered and had been cut by the hospital staff. Elise set it aside. Peeking into the bottom of the bag, she saw one last item in a sandwich bag. "His wedding band." Tears cascaded down her cheeks as she opened the bag and removed the symbol of their pledge to each other. Elise inspected it. The ring was in perfect condition. Setting it in her lap, she unclasped her necklace and added the wedding band to her silhouette diamond, his wedding present. She returned it to its proper place, ensuring the clasp was secure, and momentarily grasped the ring.

Elise picked up Gabe's ruined shirt, pressed her nose to the fabric, and inhaled. It smelled of his cologne. She clasped his wedding ring in her hand and curled up on the couch as her tears fell again.

Gabe knelt next to his beloved wife. He wished he could take her sadness away, ease her mind of the choices she would have to make, and more than anything, let her know he was nearby.

His shirt fell to the floor as Elise rose from the couch. She got a drink of water from the kitchen faucet, finished the graham crackers in the sleeve, and took a shower. Elise plugged in her phone to recharge it and tucked herself into bed. Gabe lay down beside his wife and watched helplessly as she cried herself to sleep.

Chapter 8

As the indigo night sky began to turn light blue, Gabe sat admiring his wife's face. "You're so beautiful, Babe. I'm glad you could sleep." He looked at her hand resting atop the comforter and wondered how long she would wear her wedding ring. Gabe brushed his lips against hers, confident she would not wake.

Elise's eyes snapped open. She inhaled a familiar fragrance. "Gabe?" She listened, lying still as if frozen, but her husband's rhythmic breathing was absent. Stretching her arm blindly, Elise confirmed his side of the bed was vacant. Tears welled in her eyes, trickled from the corners, and disappeared into her hairline. She looked at her alarm clock. The bookstore needed to open in two hours.

Throwing back the covers, Elise sat on the edge of the bed. She ran her hands through her hair, pulling it away from her damp cheeks, and mentally reviewed a list of items she needed to address. First and foremost was calling Marge, an oversight from last night. Elise unplugged her cell phone from the charger and pushed the call button.

"Hello."

"Hello, Marge." Her voice came across as small, weak, and shaky as Elise tried to keep her composure.

"Oh, Elise, your mother called me last night. I'm so sorry."

The sympathy expressed by her employee was enough to open the floodgates of her tear ducts. Elise was too distraught with grief to speak as she sobbed.

"I wish I could crawl through the phone and hug you right now." Marge consoled.

All Elise could do was nod in agreement.

Marge waited for her young boss to regain her self-control.

Elise wiped away her tears and took a deep breath. "I need you to open the store. I'm not certain if I will be in today. There are so many things . . ." She could not finish her statement.

"Take as many days off as you need."

"Thanks." Her phone began to click. The incoming call was from her mother. "I have another call. Gotta go. Thanks, Marge."

"Bye, sweetie."

Elise sighed as she answered the next call. "Hi, Mom."

"How are you feeling this morning?"

"Tired. Drained." She placed the palm of her hand on her stomach. "Still like I have the flu." Elise sighed. "It all seems surreal, as if I'm in a bad dream."

"I know."

"Ah, when Dad died," Elise whispered, realizing her mother's implication.

They were silent for a moment, reflecting on a past time when he was alive.

"We can't be professional mourners now, can we? They wouldn't want that. So, we will carry on." Janet stated, hoping to give her daughter some emotional strength. "And we will make them proud."

Elise nodded as she sat a little taller on the edge of the bed. "Yes, we will."

"But first, we must arrange to say goodbye to Gabe. We're to meet his parents at the funeral home at ten o'clock. I will pick you up at 9:45."

Elise glanced at her alarm clock on the nightstand. "Sounds good. And Mom..."

"What?"

"Thanks."

"You're welcome. See you soon."

Gabe waited nearby as his wife showered and chose something to wear. He wished she would have eaten more than a granola bar and a cup of coffee before leaving the apartment.

As the buzzer announced Janet's arrival, Gabe accompanied his wife and mother-in-law in the car to the funeral home. Scanning the parking lot, he did not see his parent's car. "Running late, as usual." He turned and followed Elise and Janet into the building.

"My condolences." The director greeted, dressed in a nicely tailored black suit.

"Thank you," Elise replied.

Gabe strolled through the office and the two viewing rooms. "Nice place." He looked behind him as he heard his wife's reply from a doorway.

"I don't know if I can afford that."

He peeked through an office door to see the four sitting before a large mahogany desk.

The director leaned forward. "Do you know if he had any life insurance?"

Douglas and Barbara entered the office and sat in chairs behind Elise and Janet.

Elise shrugged her shoulders. "I don't know. We never talked about it."

"He may have signed up for it with his employer."

"I'll have to call and see what benefits he enrolled in." Elise pulled a facial tissue from the box on the desk before her. She dabbed the corners of her eyes.

"Will the insurance company need a death certificate to file a claim?" Janet inquired as she rubbed her daughter's back.

"Normally, no." The funeral director confirmed.

Gabe ran his hand through his hair. "Dang, I don't remember what I signed up for at work. There may be a policy for $10,000, just enough to put me in the ground."

Douglas had listened to enough. "We'll pay for Gabe's funeral." He looked at his daughter-in-law as she turned around. "Whatever insurance money there may be, you should keep it for yourself, Elise."

"Thank you." She simply nodded.

"What type of funeral would you prefer for your loved one?" The director picked up his pen, ready to jot down Elise's request.

Barbara lifted her chin and spoke. "Since we're paying for it, we should decide." She insisted on having only one day for visitation at the funeral home, a Mass at the church the following day, followed by Gabe's burial, and a small reception at the church hall.

The director looked at the young widow. "Is there anything you wish to add?"

Elise glanced at her mother, who remained silent. She did not want to argue with her mother-in-law, so she decided to add her own personal touches to her husband's funeral later without Barbara's knowledge. "I think it sounds lovely."

Gabe leaned against the wall with his arms crossed over his chest. "No sense in dragging things out. Short and sweet, just the way I like it."

Chapter 9

Over the next few days, Elise, Janet, and Gabe's parents prepared for a proper sendoff. Elise presented three of Gabe's suits to her mother-in-law, who chose the one she preferred her son to wear. Elise compiled several poster boards of photos and informed friends of her husband's passing and the visitation hours.

    The young widow masked her face with bravery as she greeted each visitor at the funeral home. When their sympathy became more than Elise could bear, she sought the solitude of the small room provided for the family and nibbled on the prepared food.

As visitation hours ended, Elise stood before one of the poster boards.

"How are you holding up?" Janet placed the palm of her hand on the small of her daughter's back as she stepped beside her.

"As well as to be expected." Elise took a deep breath and looked toward Gabe's closed casket; a framed photo of his smiling face placed where his head lay beneath. The bouquets of flowers were too numerous to count. "I'm going to visit with Gabe for a moment before I drive home."

"I'll see you tomorrow." Janet embraced her daughter before respectfully giving her a moment alone with her deceased husband's body.

Elise nodded as her mother's arms released her. "Goodnight, Mom, and thanks." She scanned the visitation room to ensure she was alone before approaching Gabe's casket. She stared at his photo and sighed, releasing the stress she had withheld throughout the day. "Even though I know your soul is not here, it comforts me to be close to your body. That may sound morbid, but it's all I have left of you, other than memories."

"Yes, Elise, lots of memories." Gabe agreed.

"Mom said I can't become a professional mourner, but at this moment, I don't see how I can become anything else. You've been a part of my life for such a long time."

Gabe smiled. "Many years, many wonderful years. I treasure each and every moment."

"I really don't see how I'll be able to love anyone else. My heart will always belong to you." Elise placed her hand on the casket and wiped a tear away from her cheek.

Gabe's smile faded. "What are you going to do? Become a nun? You must move on, Elise. I don't want you to grow old by yourself."

"Goodnight, Gabe." Elise kissed the casket before leaving the room and heading home.

~

The sun peeked over the horizon, greeting Gabe's soul with open arms. Within hours, Elise watched solemnly as her husband's casket was loaded into the back of the hearse. Her mother and in-laws stood behind her like loyal sentinels. Their arrival at the church and the unloading of the casket was observed by a standing-room-only congregation. The flowers from the funeral home decorated the altar filling the church with a floral fragrance, each sender expressing their grievous sentiment.

Marge closed the bookstore to attend the funeral and pay her respects. It pained her to see her young boss grieving.

Elise shouldered the ceremony, mumbling the prayers insensibly as she drew them from her memory and stood silently as Gabe's casket was loaded again into the hearse. The funeral director handed her a single red rose for her to place on her husband's casket. Tears escaped her eyes and cascaded down her cheeks as the priest said a final blessing at the gravesite. When cued, she stood from her seat, placed the single flower on Gabe's casket, and watched as it was lowered to its final resting place. Back at the church, Elise greeted guests in the hall. Even though her upset stomach continued to remind her that she was not well, she tried to eat some of the delicious food the volunteers had prepared.

It was a relief to have Gabe's public farewell behind her. Elise entered her apartment clutching Gabe's framed photograph to her chest, looked at it longingly, and placed it on the kitchen table next to her purse. She planned to put it on her office desk in the bookstore to view it often.

The day after the funeral, Elise slept until nearly noon. She had decided to take the remainder of the week off. Marge would keep a sense of organization and run the bookstore proficiently during her absence.

Elise second-guessed her decision to remain home for the week as she wandered around the apartment with her morning coffee in hand. She wondered what she could do to stave off her boredom and distract her mind from grieving. "Is it too soon for me to donate Gabe's clothes?" Entering her bedroom, she stared at his clothing hanging in the closet. They conveyed a false hope that he was away at work and would return. It was comforting yet also a painful reminder he was gone. He would never wear them again. She clasped his ring on her necklace. Wiping a tear from her cheek, Elise looked at their wedding photo on his dresser and grinned. "My only regret is not marrying you sooner."

"Mine too." Gabe reflected. He began to wonder why he had not moved on. Where was the white light? Not that he minded. It was nice to remain near Elise. He watched as his wife closed the bifold door on his side of the closet and walked away.

After three days, Elise was tired of isolating herself from the world. Her upset stomach did little to improve her melancholy mood. She had never been one for being idle. Growing weary from crying, Elise needed to distract her mind from her grief. Even though she had several more days off from work, she decided to return to the bookstore the next day.

A thought entered her mind. "Maybe I should bring Petey home in the evenings to keep me company."

"Good lord, you'll bring that alley cat home every night?" Gabe glanced at the ceiling. "You know pets aren't allowed in the apartment. What if you get caught?" He scowled and shook his head. Gabe had objected to having Petey spend Sundays at the apartment. But now that he was no longer in residence, so to speak, he had little to say in the matter.

Even though her stomach was queasy upon rising the next morning, Elise made a slice of toast with lots of butter and clenched it between her teeth as she put Gabe's photo in a cloth bookbag, grabbed her travel coffee mug and purse, and left the apartment.

Marge looked toward the back door as she heard it unlock and watched her boss enter. She smiled. "Elise, I'm glad you came in."

"Me too," she replied while chewing her last bite of toast and setting her bookbag, purse, and coffee next to her office door. "I couldn't stand to be alone in the apartment anymore."

Petey rubbed against her leg and meowed.

"Well, hello, Petey." She reached down and stroked his silky black fur. "I've missed you too. In fact," she picked him up and held the feline close to her chest, "you will be coming home with me every night to keep me company."

Marge scratched the cat beneath his chin. "As you can see, he has been well cared for, none the worse for wear."

Elise kissed the top of the cat's head before placing him on the floor. "Marge, I can't thank you enough for putting in the extra hours over the past few days."

"I'm more than happy to do so."

"Well, catch me up. Any shipments? Special orders? Advanced reader copies for me to review? Local authors asking us to stock their books?"

Marge grinned. "All of the above and more."

Gabe toured the small bookstore. "I haven't been here in so long. Not much has changed, though." The aisles remained as Elise's dad had arranged them, with their genres clearly marked at the top of each bookcase.

Petey waddled toward his favorite upholstered chair in the children's section. His bulbous stomach swayed back and forth with each step. He froze, turned his head toward Gabe, and arched his back. His fur stood on end. Petey hissed.

Elise and Marge looked at the cat.

"My goodness. I wonder what has gotten into Petey?" Elise went to the cat, picked him up, and stroked his fur until it lay flat. "You're fine, silly boy." She settled him on his chair. "Time to assume your throne, your majesty." Elise chuckled before looking at Marge. "Let me put my things in my office, and then you can give me an update." She retrieved her items from the floor, put her purse in her desk drawer, and placed Gabe's photo on her desk. "Right where you belong, Gabe. Always watching over me."

The day went by quickly. Elise welcomed the distraction, but her stomach's ever-present queasiness made it challenging to smile throughout the day. Elise turned off the 'open' sign and locked the front door at closing time. After cashing out the drawer, she took the cat carrier from the closet.

Petey spied the rectangle cage, hopped down from the chair, and hid beneath it.

"Come on, Petey. I'm tired and want to go home." Elise knelt and peeked under the chair to see his wide yellow eyes staring back at her. "I'm not taking you to the vet. I promise." Reaching under the chair, she pulled the chubby cat out from beneath and tried to shove him headfirst into the carrier.

Petey spread his back legs, making it impossible to pass through the opening.

"See, the dang cat is better off staying at the store," Gabe confirmed. "Smart cat."

The timid feline was stronger than Elise estimated. She held the cat under one arm while tipping the carrier on its end. "Let's try it this way." She dangled the cat over the opening and lowered him inside, bottom first.

Petey reached his front paws toward the opening. His claws curled around its edge, and he tried to escape. Elise placed her hand on his head and closed the door quickly. "That was a struggle." She sighed and peeked through the holes in the door as he meowed. "You're fine." Laying the carrier on its side, she picked it up by the handle. "My goodness, Petey. We will have to start monitoring how much you're eating." With her empty travel mug balanced on the top of the carrier and her purse slung over her shoulder, Elise shut off the lights, exited the back door, and drove home. Petey continued to voice his displeasure.

Chapter 10

The following month, Elise received a check for Gabe's life insurance policy. Unfortunately, it was barely enough to cover the medical expenses that trickled in through the mail. Without her husband's income, it was only a matter of time before she could no longer afford the apartment.

Downhearted, Elise sat at the kitchen table, transferring money to pay another bill.

Petey hopped onto the table and lay down next to her laptop. His tail swished back and forth on the keyboard.

She lifted the feline's tail and rotated his body away from her computer. "What do you think, Petey?

I'm between a rock and a hard place. Should I sell the bookstore and find a real job?"

The fat feline put his head on his paws and closed his eyes.

Gabe paced behind her chair. "Don't sell it, Elise. You love the bookstore. Something will come along."

Elise sighed. She took another saltine from its sleeve and ate it. Unfortunately, she was no longer covered under Gabe's medical insurance and was forced to purchase her own policy. Another monthly expense. Elise looked at the balances in her checkbook and savings accounts. "Something has got to change."

Concerned she was still feeling unwell, Elise made an appointment to see Doctor Griswold the following day. Marge agreed to open the bookstore in case she ran late.

After a good night's sleep, Elise rose early. She entered the nearly empty waiting room and was ushered into the examining room.

"So, still not feeling well?" Doctor Griswold scanned the paperwork in the file as she entered.

"No, I still feel like I have the flu," Elise admitted.

Gabe stood in the corner of the room. His arms crossed over his chest, concerned.

"No temp. Pulse is good." Doctor Griswold looked over the top of her reading glasses. "No period yet?"

Elise shook her head.

"Well, that's understandable." She sighed, aware of her patient's recent loss. "Let's get a urine sample. Draw some blood as well and check your thyroid." The doctor left the room and placed the paperwork in the bracket on the hallway wall.

Moments later, a nurse entered, took a sample of Elise's blood, and guided her to the restroom. The woman explained how to urinate in a cup and place it in the cubby that resembled an old-fashioned milk box on the wall.

Allowing his wife her privacy, Gabe waited in the small examining room. He looked at the open doorway as she returned and closed the door, sat on the table with the retracted stirrups, and waited.

Elise inhaled, convinced she caught a whiff of Gabe's favorite aftershave. Her thoughts drifted from puzzlement to concern by the doctor's request. *Urine test? Does she think I have a UTI? I've never had one.* Elise looked at her entwined fingers in her lap. *I completely forgot about my period. I've never been regular, and I've been late before.*

The door opened, pulling Elise from her thoughts.

Doctor Griswold sat on the stool, scanned the entry on the paperwork, and looked at her apprehensive patient's face. "Since your life has been turned upside down lately, I'm not certain how you will take this news."

"Is there something terribly wrong with me?" Elise scooted to the edge of the table.

"Oh, there's nothing wrong with you, Elise. If it were me, I would think everything is perfectly right. What you have been experiencing is morning sickness. You're pregnant. By my calculations, you are about eight weeks along."

Gabe unfolded his arms and took a step toward the doctor.

Elise stared at the doctor's face. Her eyebrows raised in question. "Excuse me?"

Doctor Griswold smiled as she nodded. "Yes, you heard me correctly. You're expecting a baby."

"A baby?" Gabe clapped his hands as he jumped into the air. "Yes! A baby!"

Thoughts of panic raced through Elise's mind. How would she take care of a baby and run the bookstore too? How would she afford daycare, diapers, baby clothes, etc.? Her eyes were downcast to the floor as she exhaled. "Gabe isn't here to help me raise the baby. He won't be there to see its birth. He won't see the baby's smile, its first tooth, first step, first word, its first everything." Tears began to well in her eyes.

The doctor placed the palm of her hand on her patient's knee. "It's a lot to digest. I'm certain you're in shock."

Elise nodded slightly, unable to speak.

"Shock? This is great!" Gabe wished his wife shared in his enthusiasm. He looked at the droplets cascading down her cheeks. His smile faded.

"How am I going to manage as a single mom?" Elise confessed as she wiped the tears from her cheeks.

"I'm right here," Gabe assured but realized he would be of little help.

"Other women have found themselves in the same situation and have managed it quite well. I'm confident you will too." The doctor scribbled something on a slip of paper before handing it to Elise. "I refer all my patients to Doctor Martin. She is an excellent OBGYN. I'll have my receptionist call her office and set up your first appointment. Does that sound OK?"

Elise nodded her head, uncertain what question was posed.

"Good. Congratulations, Elise. Even though your pregnancy is unexpected, I believe that life is to be celebrated. If you have any questions, feel free to contact me. Have a good day." Doctor Griswold handed a second paper to Elise to use to check out with the receptionist.

Once seated in her car, Elise leaned her forehead on the steering wheel. "How am I going to do this? I can no longer afford the rent, and now I'll have doctor and hospital bills."

"Elise, if you only knew how happy I am. A part of me will always be with you." Gabe grinned. "A legacy. It gives my soul peace."

She started the car but had yet to put it into drive. Elise looked at her cellphone and was pleased Marge could cover for her until she arrived. She made a call to the bookstore and let her employee know she would be in after lunch. Then she called her mother.

"Hello, Elise."

"Hi, Mom."

"What's wrong? I can tell by the tone of your voice."

"I know it's a bit early, but have you had lunch yet?"

"No, but I can throw together sandwiches when you arrive."

"I'll be right over."

"This sounds serious."

Elise sighed. "I'll explain when I get there."

Janet went to the back door as she heard her daughter's car arrive. Anxious to listen to whatever news Elise cared to share, she opened the back door to the garage. "I thought I would make grilled cheese and tomato soup for lunch. Does that sound good?"

"Sounds amazing. Thanks, Mom." Elise stepped into the kitchen and inhaled the familiar fragrance of home. She watched as her mother pulled the ingredients from the cupboard and refrigerator. "I'll get the drinks and set the table." She volunteered, uncertain how to break the news to her mother.

Within minutes, Janet placed freshly grilled cheese sandwiches and steaming bowls of soup on the table. Sitting across from her daughter, she waited patiently for Elise to divulge what was troubling her. Janet filled her spoon with soup and blew on the steaming liquid to cool it. As she was about to insert it into her mouth, Elise spoke.

"I'm pregnant."

Janet froze with the spoon nearly touching her lips and looked at her daughter. "Are you sure?"

"I just came from the doctor. She confirmed that I'm pregnant, believes I'm eight weeks along, and has referred me to an OBGYN." Elise inserted her spoon into her soup but only moved it around in the bowl as she waited for her mother's reply.

"How do you feel about the news? Janet knew the pregnancy would change her daughter's life immensely.

"I'm not quite certain how to feel. Sadly, Gabe isn't here. That he never knew I was expecting his child. I'm scared. I can't afford the apartment once the last of Gabe's life insurance money runs out. I'm happy about the baby, but raising a child is a big responsibility. I just wonder how I'm going to do it and run the bookstore."

Janet reached across the table and placed her hand on her daughter's hand. "Well, since your dad passed, it's pretty lonely here. I think you should move back home. You can sleep in your old bedroom, and we can decorate the third bedroom for the baby."

"I would have to talk to the apartment manager. I don't know if he would let me out of the lease."

"If you can't afford to pay the rent, it would be better if he found another renter who could." Janet reasoned.

"True." Elise sighed. "There are so many unknowns. For example, who will watch the baby while I'm at the bookstore working?"

"We have seven months to figure that out." Janet grinned. "A baby, a granddaughter or grandson. This is happy news." Janet squeezed her daughter's hand.

"Yes, it is. I just don't know how I'm going to manage." Elise dipped her sandwich in the soup and took another bite.

"We will manage." Janet imitated her daughter and let the excess soup drip from the sandwich. "We'll manage."

"Yes, we will," Gabe confirmed.

Chapter 11

After the encouraging conversation with her mother, Elise saw the future in a more positive light. She went to the bookstore eager to share the news with her loyal employee.

Marge could hardly contain her excitement. "Oh, a little one! I'm so happy for you." She hugged Elise. "When are you due?"

It never occurred to Elise to ask for her due date. "I don't know. Doctor Griswold told me I was eight weeks along."

"We can look it up online." Marge, a woman in her early 60s, was proficient with navigating the internet. In no time at all, she discovered the information. "Let's see, you are eight weeks, making your due date April 17th."

Gabe peeked over the woman's shoulder to see the date for himself.

"A spring baby," Elise whispered as she looked at Marge. "Gabe's favorite season. He could hardly wait to ride his motorcycle after having it in storage all winter."

Marge recognized the melancholy tone in her boss's voice. "And he would be pleased to know his little one will be born then.

"And proud," Gabe added.

Elise nodded. "Mom suggested I move back home."

Marge thought it was a good idea, but preferred Elise come to that decision without her influence. "Are you going to?"

"I may have to because I can't afford the apartment much longer."

"It'll be good for you to have someone to help you with the baby."

Elise was unsure. She sighed, knowing she must change the course of her life.

Gabe glanced under the counter and saw the books sent by the publishers for each bookstore owner to review. Elise usually brought several books home every week. He helped her evaluate them. He would offer his opinion of the storyline and writing, and she would decide whether to stock the book. "I guess you will have to find someone else to help you read the publisher's advance copies." He scanned the titles. "Oh, that one looks interesting." Gabe reached for the book, pulled it from the shelf, and watched as it fell to the floor. It landed on its spine and its pages parted.

Elise and Marge looked at the open book on the floor.

"Oh, that silly ghost is at it again." Marge picked up the book and returned it to its proper place.

"I need to take those home to review. When you get a chance, can you pack them into a bookbag and set it next to my office"

Marge chuckled. "Sure."

Gabe looked at his hand, rotating it. "How did I do that?" He had not touched the book, yet it moved on its own as if possessed. "I read a book once about energy and the imprints we leave behind when we die. Perhaps whatever energy I may possess enables me to move objects?" He reached for another book as Marge stepped away, pulled it from the shelf, and allowed it to fall to the floor.

Marge turned around. "That's enough now. You've had your fun. Let us get to work." She picked up the book and put it back in its place.

Gabe watched as Marge returned to Elise's side.

The pair began shuffling books, checking them into inventory, filling special orders, and reviewing what stock needed to be replaced. When they finished, Marge collapsed the empty cardboard boxes. She placed them by the back door before waiting on a customer.

Elise went to her office to see what emails needed her immediate attention. Gabe entered behind her before she closed the door. He was drawn to the photographs on her desk. Gabe saw a photo of her father, another of their wedding, and a third that caused him to pause. He stared at the framed photo of himself. It was the one she had used for his funeral. Gabe wished he was still alive. He noticed the picture of the two of them pinned to the memo board above her desk. "When was this taken?" He was wearing a suit, and Elise was in a dress donned with a corsage. "Someone's wedding? Maybe our engagement party?" He was captured, staring at her with an intensity that conveyed his deep love and affection for her. It dawned on him then that the same photograph was in their apartment. "You must like this photo a lot, Elise. It's a good one." He was about to leave the office when he heard crying behind him. Turning, he watched as his wife's shoulders shook up and down, and she dabbed her cheeks with a facial tissue.

Her sobs were heart-wrenching, more than he could bear. "Elise, you've tried to remain strong. Maybe a good cry is all you need right now." He went to her chair and wrapped his arms around her shoulders, but they passed through her.

Elise shivered as if she had just stepped into a walk-in freezer. She looked at her office door. It was closed. The air conditioning was off at this time of year, and the furnace had not kicked on. "Maybe a customer left the store causing a draft." She glanced at the gap beneath the door.

Elise rose from her chair, placed her hand on her abdomen, and began to pace. "What am I going to do?" Weighing her options, she came to a decision. "I'll tell you what I'm going to do. When I get to the store, I will call the apartment manager for an appointment for tonight after work. I'm going to tell him I can't afford the apartment any longer, and since I have yet to pay the rent for this month, inform him that he can take this month's rent out of our deposit.

I'll move home with Mom, decorate the baby's room as she suggested, well, maybe after I discover if I'm having a boy or girl, and together she and I can raise the baby." She dabbed her cheeks again, turned, and looked at the photo on her desk. "Gabe, I promise I'll do my very best to raise our child." She signed. "You would have made an excellent daddy."

"If you only knew, Elise. You have made me the happiest of men, or should I say spirit, and I'll remain with you for as long as possible."

~

"Sorry, Petey, but I have a meeting with the manager. So, you'll have to stay here tonight." Elise kissed the feline's head as he slept on his chair. She picked up the collapsed cardboard boxes and the bag of promotional books. Elise exited the bookstore leaving Petey for the evening. Arriving at the apartment building, she temporarily set the items outside the manager's office and entered to plead her case.

The manager looked up from the paperwork on his desk as she entered. "Hello, Elise."

"Hi, thanks for staying late."

He motioned to the empty chair before his desk, offering her to sit. "No problem. What's going on?"

Elise sighed. "As you know, my husband passed away."

"Yes, I'm sorry for your loss." He leaned forward and clasped his hands together, placing them on the paperwork.

"Thank you. Since Gabe's death, I've been able to cover my bills with my reduced income. I apologize for my late rent payment this month, but my checkbook is low on funds. I've also discovered I'm pregnant with my late husband's baby."

"Congratulations."

"Thanks. My mother has offered for me to come and live with her. I'm hoping you will allow me to break my lease."

The manager turned to a file cabinet, rifled through the documents, and pulled a manila folder. He placed it on his desk and withdrew a piece of paper. "I see you just renewed last month."

"Yes."

"There are consequences for breaking a lease, but I'll ignore the penalty under your circumstance."

"Thank you. Can you pay this month's rent from the security deposit?"

"Sure. Once you move out and the apartment is inspected for damages, I'll forward any remaining balance. You'll just have to let me know where to send the check once you turn in your keys." He grinned, recognizing the relief in his tenant's face.

"Thank you." Elise rose from her chair.

"And Elise..."

"Yes."

"Let me know if you need any help moving out. Best of luck to you."

"I will. Thank you." Elise climbed the stairs to her apartment. With the click of her key, she entered and leaned the cardboard boxes next to the wall. After propping the bag of books against Gabe's college desk, Elise stood still momentarily in the silence. She grabbed the remote for the TV and turned it on. It didn't matter which station it was on; she welcomed the noise. "Soup sounds like an easy meal for tonight."

Opening the cupboard, she stared at the cans of chicken noodle soup. "Gabe's favorite." After heating her meal in the microwave, Elise grabbed a sleeve of saltines and plopped down on the couch.

She stared mindlessly at the woman chattering about local news.

Elise crushed several crackers and dropped them into her bowl. Spooning a bite into her mouth, she looked around the apartment. "I'll have to bring a lot more boxes home from the store." The wedding photos on the wall stared back at her. Tears welled in her eyes. "I miss you, Gabe."

"I'm right here." He reassured, knowing she could not hear him, but it made him feel better by saying so.

She finished her simple dinner, took a nice hot shower, and dressed in her coziest pajamas.

Gabe's parents had remained distant since the funeral. When she married their son, Elise had hoped they would accept her as part of the family. That hope was no longer possible. Maybe it was for the best.

Uncertain how they would react to the news, Elise needed to let them know about Gabe's baby, their grandchild. She stared at their illuminated contact on her phone, gathered her thoughts, and called.

"Hello," Barbara answered.

Elise cringed. "Hi."

"Do you need something?"

"No, but I have news to share with you."

"Oh."

"I'm expecting Gabe's baby. I'm due April 17th."

Barbara remained silent for a moment. "Are you sure it's his?"

Taken back by the insult, it took Elise a moment to respond. "Yes. I thought you would be happy with the news, but apparently not. Goodbye." She hung up the phone.

Snuggling with a blanket on the couch, she flipped through the stations and settled on a documentary about Mary, Queen of Scots. Even though she was upset by the insinuation, she was sound asleep within minutes.

Gabe stood next to the couch. He listened to her rhythmic breathing. "That baby must be making you tired. You've never slept that much before." He looked at the furniture, bookshelf, and other items in the room. "I hope you hire a moving company. I doubt you should be lifting anything in your current condition." Gabe was glad Elise was moving in with her mother. "At least you will have someone to help you with the baby." He sat on the floor, staring at his wife's face. "So peaceful. I assumed it's normal for you to grieve for a while." He smiled as his wife mumbled something in her sleep. "I want you to be happy, to fall in love again. You need someone to share your life with, to help raise our baby." He sighed. "As much as it pains me, I want you to find someone who will love you as much as I do."

Elise opened her eyes and looked at the TV. "I must have dozed off." She clicked the remote, and the screen turned black. She pushed the blanket aside and stood. "Dang bladder."

Gabe stood as he watched his wife walk toward the bathroom. A few moments later, he heard the rustling of the covers as she got into their queen-size bed.

He entered their bedroom. The closet bifold door on Elise's side was open, a bad habit of hers. Gabe hoped she would donate his clothing before moving. There was really no sense in keeping any of them. Someone less fortunate could use them. He laid down on his usual side of the bed, staring at her face as if casting it to memory.

Chapter 12

Elise's eyelids lethargically raised like a blind on a window. The natural light beaming into her bedroom indicated it was morning. She rolled onto her side and stared until the blurred digits on her alarm clock came into focus. "Dang, I slept in." She flopped onto her back and looked at the ceiling, trying to clear the cobwebs from her mind. "What day is it?" Sunday. "It's Sunday." The bookstore was closed on Sundays until the holiday hours began in November.

Her morning sickness had yet to subside. "I need to eat something." Tossing back the covers, Elise made an urgent trip to the bathroom to relieve her bladder. She looked at her bloated stomach as she stood and pulled up her pajama bottoms. "I wonder when I will begin to show?" Curious, Elise stepped on the bathroom scales and shook her head at the few pounds she had already gained. "Must be baby weight. I haven't eaten much lately."

Brushing her mussed hair away from her face, Elise retrieved her phone from the bedroom before going to the kitchen. She poured herself a bowl of cereal and added milk. Elise clicked on the TV, settled onto the couch, and spooned the cereal into her mouth, hoping to settle her stomach.

The spoon clattered as she dropped it into the empty ceramic bowl and set it on the coffee table next to her phone. Pausing, Elise sensed something was wrong. Darting to the bathroom, she flipped up the toilet seat and threw up the contents of her stomach. The milk was still cold.

"Well, that didn't work." Elise dampened a washcloth and wiped her mouth.

Gabe watched from the doorway. "Sorry, Babe. I'm not even there to hold your hair." He stepped aside as she exited the bathroom and entered their bedroom.

She tossed the covers toward the headboard and put the pillows in their proper place. Elise prided herself in making her bed every day. She took off her pajamas and caught a glimpse of herself in the full-length mirror on the bedroom wall. Turning sideways, she scrutinized her nearly flat belly. "It's you and me, kid." She placed her hand on her abdomen and recalled seeing other expectant mothers post monthly photos of their growing baby bumps on social media. Elise had no intention of publishing them online but adding them to a baby album would be nice. "This will be the only baby I'll ever have." After putting on her bra and shirt, Elise retrieved her phone and returned to the mirror. Turning to capture her profile, she grinned at her reflection and took the photo. "Gabe would have been thrilled to watch my belly grow larger every month." Elise examined the captured picture on her phone and scowled. "Dang, I forgot to make a sign."

She went to Gabe's desk in the living room and pulled a piece of paper from a side drawer. Elise took a black marker from the center drawer. Pausing as she removed the cap, she decided to write '2 months' on the paper even though she was a little further along in her pregnancy. Elise returned to the bedroom and snapped another photo. "Wait, am I further along than two months?"

Wanting to verify that Marge's research was correct, Elise opened the laptop on Gabe's desk and did a quick search. "First day of your last period?" Her eyebrows raised. "Oh, a good question." Hoping she had entered the date in her phone, Elise brought up the calendar and scrolled back to her cycle entry. "July 11." After entering the information into the website, the due date was displayed. "April 17. Nice, Marge was correct."

Gabe clapped his hands together. "Yes, she was. I hope you have a girl just like you, Babe."

Elise entered 'due date' on April 17th on her cell phone calendar. "So, I'm nine weeks along." She withdrew another sheet of paper from the desk, used the black marker to make another sign, and went to the bedroom to take another photo of her non-existing baby bump. Satisfied with the photo, she dressed in jeans and shoved her cell phone into the back pocket.

Elise returned to the living room and looked at the cardboard boxes propped against the wall. She had to move out of the apartment by the end of the month. With limited space in her mother's house, could she bear to part with Gabe's clothes by the deadline?

Tapping her index finger on her bottom lip, Elise wondered if she would be able to wear any of Gabe's clothes to accommodate her growing abdomen. It would be less expensive than purchasing maternity clothes. She took a roll of packaging tape from the desk, selected two boxes from the wall, and went to the bedroom.

After taping the bottom of both boxes, Elise stared at Gabe's side of the closet. "Maybe it would be easier to sort through his dresser first." She opened the top drawer and withdrew a pair of boxer briefs. "Who would want to wear a pair of used underwear?" All of Gabe's underwear was placed in a pile on the floor to be discarded. Any worn, stained, or holey socks went there as well. Those that remained were put into a box for donation.

Elise reached into the back of the drawer and pulled a stack of letters forward. She recognized her handwriting on the top envelope and checked the date of the canceled stamp. Her lips trembled. "Aw, he kept my letters."

"Yes, Elise, I kept them all," Gabe admitted. "Even though we often talked on the phone or texted, I knew you enjoyed receiving letters in the mail. No matter how busy I was with my classes, I always tried to write to you at least once a month. Of course, I wished I could have been at the bookstore to see the surprise on your face when my letter arrived. But please know, it always brightened my day when I received a letter from you."

Elise went to her dresser and withdrew the stack of letters, tied with a pink ribbon, from the back of her underwear drawer. With a stack of letters in each hand, she lowered herself onto the edge of the mattress. Glancing from one pile to the other, a tear trickled down her cheek and fell onto her lap. "I wonder . . ." She rose from the bed, went to the kitchen table, sat in a chair, and took the bindings from the letters. Placing them in order of correspondence by date, she made a stack representing each year Gabe was at college. Elise cupped her hands over her mouth and nose with tears cascading onto her fingers. What lay on the table was dearer to her than any diamond, any amount of money, for it captured their unbeknownst affection, their budding love for each other.

Elise wanted to preserve them for eternity, but how? She looked toward Gabe's desk. "I wonder if he has any of those left?" She searched the desk drawers, shuffling papers, and files. Elise discovered a new three-ring binder and set it on the desk. "Now, if I can just find . . ." Inside a hanging folder was an opened package of page protectors. "Ah, here they are." She thumbed through the remaining protectors in the packet. "There aren't many left. "I'll have to get more."

She returned to the table, opened the binder, and slipped the page protectors onto the rings. Elise removed the first letter Gabe wrote, reminisced as she read each word, and carefully inserted it and its envelope inside the first page of her keepsake. She was able to put their correspondence during his first year into the binder before she ran out of protectors. Setting the project aside, her energy was drained emotionally and physically. Glancing at her phone, it was nearly noon. "My goodness, nothing like getting sidetracked." Her stomach grumbled. "A bowl of soup sounds good. And crackers. Lots and lots of crackers. Ah, it seems I've had a steady diet of soup lately. At least I don't have to cook."

Elise removed the last sleeve of saltines, tossed the box into the garbage, and added 'saltines' to the grocery list hanging on the refrigerator. After heating the bowl of soup in the microwave, she ate her light lunch at the kitchen table while estimating the number of page protectors she would need to purchase.

With her appetite satisfied and praying it remained in her stomach, Elise returned to the bedroom, looked at Gabe's dresser, and took a deep breath. She pulled the handles of the second dresser drawer. It would not open all the way. "My goodness, Gabe. How did you fit all of this in here?" Elise reached her fingers into the drawer, pressed the tee shirts down, and the drawer finally opened. "Goodness, I think you have kept every tee shirt since high school."

Elise pulled each wrinkled shirt from the drawer, held it up to inspect it for stains, holes, and wear, and tossed it in a pile to either throw or give away. She hesitated as she held up his college tee shirt. "This one is a keeper." Elise set the shirt on her dresser and planned to use it as a nightshirt.

After sorting the remainder of the drawer, she stared at the box nearly overflowing with Gabe's shirts. Maybe it was too soon to part with his clothes. But unfortunately, with her impending move, she had little choice but to do so. "I wish I could keep them."

Gabe stood in the corner of the room with his arms crossed over his chest. "Elise, they're just a bunch of tee shirts. Get rid of them."

"I wonder." She began laying them out on the bed. Their various colors resembled a patchwork quilt. "It may work, but I don't know how to sew." Elise pulled her phone from her back pocket and called her mom.

"Hello."

"Hi, Mom. You still have your sewing machine, right?"

"Yes."

"I've been going through Gabe's clothes. Would it be possible to make a quilt from his tee shirts?"

"You mean from the fronts of the shirts?"

"Yes, I guess."

"It's possible. I just don't know how well the quilt would hold up over time."

"Oh."

Hearing the despair in her daughter's voice, Janet offered a suggestion. "Set them aside for now. We'll see what we can do with them once you are moved in."

"OK. Thanks, Mom."

"I have a small roast with carrots and potatoes in the oven. Would you like to join me for dinner?"

A homecooked meal sounded heavenly. "What time?"

"Does five o'clock work for you?"

Elise looked at the dresser drawers she had yet to open and checked the time on her alarm clock. She would need to leave the apartment in an hour. "Sure, sounds good. See you then."

"Great. Love you."

"Love you too, Mom. Bye."

Chapter 13

Elise selected enough shirts to make the quilt and put them into a separate cardboard box. She opened the next drawer to discover sweatshirts and hoodies. Most were tattered and stained from Gabe working on his motorcycle. Elise put all but two in the throw-away pile. The last drawer contained sweatpants in the same condition as the sweatshirts.

With the dresser empty, Elise was pleased with her progress. "Baby steps." She put all the throw-away clothes in a garbage bag and took them to the dumpster in the parking lot. The box containing the donated clothes was taped shut. "Mom probably knows where I can donate them. Maybe church. They have a garage sale at least once a year." With the box of tee shirts for the quilt balanced on her hip, she left the apartment and drove to her mother's house for dinner.

"Hi, Mom." Elise greeted as she entered through the back door. "Here are Gabe's tee shirts for the quilt." She placed the box on the kitchen table.

Janet held up the first shirt and grinned. "I remember him wearing this one."

"Yes, me too."

Janet thumbed through the stack. "You have quite a few here, enough to make a quilt, but like I said, I don't know how well the material will hold up over time."

"Would it be possible to make one for me and a smaller one for the baby too?" Elise struggled to keep her tears in check. Her bottom lip trembled.

"It would depend on how large we cut the squares. We could always use the backsides for the baby's blanket."

Elise nodded as she placed the palm of her hand on her abdomen.

Janet covered her daughter's hand with her own. "I read an interesting fact the other day. Did you know when I was pregnant with you, your tiny body contained all the eggs of the possible children you would bear? So that means not only did I carry you inside of me, but I also carried my grandchild too."

"Is that true?"

"If it is online, it must be true." Janet chuckled, causing her daughter to smile. She smoothed the tee shirts until they lay neatly in the box. "Well, this project can wait for another day." Janet put the box on the floor next to the wall. "It's time to take the roast out of the oven and eat."

With the food on the table and the women sitting in their usual places, Elise glanced at her mom as she watched her butter a slice of bread. It was like old times after her father passed away. "Do you think Dad would be happy about my pregnancy?"

Janet paused with her fork of beef in midair and smiled. "He would be over the moon, just as I am."

"I thought so." Elise finished her meal. It was comforting to engage in conversation once again. She delayed rising from the table until after her mother was done eating.

Janet placed her plate in the dishwasher and turned toward her daughter. "It will be good to have a little one running around here, bringing joy and laughter to our home."

Elise nodded. For a split second, she viewed the future as something positive.

"Oh, I cleaned out your bedroom closet. The baby's room is empty too. So, whenever you would like to begin bringing your things over, let me know, and I can help you."

"I'm not certain what to do with most of my furniture." Elise rinsed her plate and placed it in the dishwasher.

Janet sighed, knowing her house would not be able to accommodate every piece her daughter owned. "Let's go and look at the rooms. Maybe you will be able to envision what you want to keep."

Elise would be sleeping in her childhood bedroom once again. It was large enough to accommodate her queen-size bed and her dresser. Her TV could go on the dresser or on a small stand across from the foot of her bed. The nursery was small, but a crib and Gabe's dresser would work well in the room.

"You have enough room to add a rocking chair, maybe even a changing table." Janet encouraged.

"I don't know. That seems like a lot to fit in here." Elise turned in a circle scanning the future nursery.

"Have you thought about a theme for the baby's room?"

"No. I need to find out if I'm having a boy or girl first." She sighed and looked at her mother. "I want you to be in the delivery room with me."

Janet smiled. "Absolutely. To think, I'll be the first one to see the baby."

"Good. I have a feeling I'll need you there."

"I'm sure you would do fine without me, but I'll be there to support you any way I can." Janet reached for her daughter's hand and gave it an affectionate squeeze.

~

Returning to her dark apartment, Elise turned on a lamp in the living room. She had taken the first step forward and was relieved to have made a few decisions.

Flipping through the channels on the TV, Elise discovered nothing of interest and shut it off. "Maybe," she said, remembering the bag of advance reader books Marge had packed. Curling up with a book sounded inviting. After taking a warm shower and dressing in her pajamas, she took the bag to the bedroom, crawled into bed, and began reading the synopsis and first chapter of each book until one caught her interest. When her eyelids became too heavy to keep open, Elise tossed the novel on the bed with the others, set her alarm, and turned off her lamp. She missed her goodnight kiss from Gabe, something they did every night before sleeping.

"Goodnight, Gabe." She whispered.

He smiled. "Goodnight, Elise." He leaned over and brushed his lips against hers.

~

Opening her eyes, Elise looked at her alarm clock. It had yet to sound. She slept better than she thought she would and seemed well-rested. "No sense in staying in bed." Rising, she pushed her legs through a pair of jeans. Scowling, she became astutely aware of the tightness in the waist as she tried to snap them shut. "I can't be showing already, can I?" She stood before the full-length mirror, scrutinizing her abdomen. "I don't see any difference. Maybe the dryer shrunk my pants." After donning a bulky sweater to match the rainy autumn day, she grabbed a muffin and a travel mug of coffee and drove to the bookstore.

"Good morning, Petey. Have you been a good watch cat? Any mice? Bats? Ghosts?"

The feline answered each of her questions with a deep meow.

"Good boy. Let's get you fed." Elise turned on her office lights and selected a can of cat food from the closet. She emptied the small can onto the shallow saucer, added dry cat food to Petey's bowl, and filled the water dish. After cleaning the cat box and washing her hands thoroughly, she sat at her desk and turned on her computer.

"Nice and peaceful." Elise sipped her coffee. She preferred a quiet start to her day. Some days, it was the only time to read emails and address other issues.

Satisfied with the completed task, she left her office, turned on the store lights, and straightened the books on the shelves. Where there was a vacant spot, Elise front faced a book knowing it would draw a customer's attention and encourage its purchase. She vacuumed the entry rugs, swept the hardwood floor, and dusted the front counter before turning on the 'open' sign and unlocking the front door.

It started off as a typical Monday. The mail lady delivered several bills and advertisements. As she was leaving, Ed held the door open for her to pass by him.

"Good morning, Elise."

Elise looked up from the stack of envelopes in her hand. "Hello, Ed. How are you today?"

"Fine. Just stopping by to see how you are doing." Ed leaned against the counter.

"I'm managing. I've no other choice. I'm going to be moving back in with my mom. I found out I'm expecting Gabe's baby too."

Ed grinned. "That's wonderful news. Congrats!"

"Thanks. I'm excited, a bit scared, but excited. How is your wife doing?"

"Jen, she's ready to deliver our little one any day now." A call came over his radio. "Well, duty calls. Take care."

By noon, only a few customers had visited and purchased very little. A delivery man dropped off three boxes of new books that needed to be added to the inventory and shelved. Marge had Mondays off, so Elise had the bookstore to herself for the day. She opened the boxes, placed the new books on the counter with the packing slip, and set the empty boxes by the back door to take home. It was quiet, too quiet. "Alexa, play 60s pop." Elise ignored the software's reply before the music began.

"60s pop? Really, Elise? A bit before your time." Gabe peeked over her shoulder at the computer screen. "Probably your dad's choice in music that you grew accustomed to over the years."

Petey came around the end of the counter, stopped abruptly, and arched his back. He hissed, causing Elise to look at him.

"What's up with you?" She ignored the feline, picked up the packing list, and began verifying which books were shipped or on backorder.

Gabe wondered if the cat could see him or detect he was there. "Petey, come here." He stepped forward, squatted, and reached for the cat, but Petey turned and scampered away. "Well, you may be the only one who knows I'm here."

Elise glanced over the checked items on the packing list. Two of the books were on backorder. "Never fails. There are always a few that are delayed in shipping." She began scanning the book's ISBNs and adding them to the inventory when the front door opened.

Elise glanced at the clock on the wall. "Good afternoon."

"Hello."

The gentleman's voice was unfamiliar to her. Assuming he was a first-time customer, she wanted to make him feel welcome. "Are you looking for anything in particular that I may help you find?"

"Do you have used books?"

Elise watched the elderly man as he approached the counter. His eyebrows resembled bushy caterpillars beneath the brim of his tweed ivy cap.

"I'm sorry. I only carry new books. What genre were you interested in?"

"It's an older book."

"I may have a new copy in stock. What's the title?" As he stated the familiar title, Elise typed it into the computer to see if it was in stock. "A classic." She scanned the screen. "Yes, I have a copy." She pulled two books from the classic section and returned to the counter where the gentleman waited. "Actually, I have two copies. This one is a paperback, and I have a nice edition that is leatherbound."

"How much are they?"

Elise read the prices from the back covers. Her customer seemed indecisive. "If this is a gift, many of my customers like to give the leatherbound. They make a nice keepsake."

The man looked from one book to the other. "I'll think about it. Thank you." He turned and left the bookstore.

"Probably going to buy it online," Elise grumbled as she returned the books to their proper places on the shelf.

The remainder of the day was busy. It was as if the bookstore had a revolving door. Customers came, purchased, and went as others entered. The phone rang so often that Elise eventually had to ignore the caller until she finished a sale. When she locked the door for the evening and turned off the 'open' sign, she looked at the stack of books she had yet to scan and add to the inventory.

Petey brushed against her leg. She picked up the cat and stroked his silky fur. "What a day, huh, Petey?" Her stomach grumbled. "I didn't even have time to eat lunch."

She set the cat on the counter, ran the daily sales report, and raised her eyebrows as the above-average total brought a grin to her face. She stroked Petey's silky fur as he tried to headbutt her face. "It's been a good day when I see totals such as these." Logging off and shutting down the computer, she turned off the lights. "You're staying here tonight." Elise gave Petey one last petting on his head and grabbed the empty boxes before exiting through the back door.

A quick stop at the store to purchase more page protectors and a drive-through for a crispy chicken dinner rounded out her ride home. Elise climbed the stairs to her apartment with the cardboard boxes, her meal, and office supplies in hand. She set the boxes next to Gabe's desk and tossed the page protectors on the kitchen table before turning on the TV. Plopping onto the couch, Elise took her fast food out of the bag and flipped the station to a sitcom.

Gabe sat in the overstuffed chair and placed his feet on the ottoman. "Oh, I love this show. We used to watch it together all the time."

Elise opened the side of mashed potatoes and gravy. "We used to watch this show all of the time."

Astonished by her nearly identical comment, Gabe looked at his wife as she spooned mashed potatoes into her mouth. "Yes, we used to laugh throughout the entire show. I gotta hand it to the writers. They're brilliant." It was like old times, just him and her.

Time passed as one episode ran into the next. When Elise finished her meal, she threw away the containers and stood by the kitchen table, staring at her project, her hands fisted on her hips. With

111

managing the bookstore, Elise needed to either pack more of her apartment or work on adding each letter to the keepsake. Too tired to sort through Gabe's clothes hanging in the closet, she sat and added the page protectors to the back of the binder. Elise decided to divide each year by a title page, which she would add later.

Determined to put the project behind her, she opened each letter and avoided reading them. Elise was tired of crying. Fully aware that she would have good and bad days, she decided to focus on what was right in her life instead of what was wrong. Touching her abdomen, Elise wondered how the loss of Gabe and her emotional turmoil would affect the baby. She wanted it to be born hugged in happiness, not sadness. Elise put the last letter into the keepsake before looking at the kitchen cupboard. "I wonder. Yes, it just might work."

Gabe's attention was drawn away from the sitcom. "What are you up to, Elise?"

Elise went to the kitchen and took two glass cylinder vases from the cupboard. "These were on our bridal party table. I believe they had floating candles in them. Strange, how I kept them." Going to Gabe's desk, she scanned the photos on her phone and selected her favorite one of Gabe and a photo of her father. "I think I saw a pack of vellum in this drawer." Sure enough, she found it and put several pieces in the printer. Sending the photos wirelessly, the printer quickly produced the copies.

Scowling, the photos were in the corner of each sheet of vellum. "Not exactly what I wanted. Elise sent the photos to the laptop via email. Taking a ruler from the top drawer, Elise measured the height of a container. She opened a formatting software, imported the photo into the correctly sized document, and printed it. Grinning, she smiled at her husband's face looking back at her from the vellum. "Perfect. Now, for Dad's picture."

When the second printout was finished, she trimmed each paper, wrapped it around the glass container, and held it in place with double-sided tape. "These will be nice in the baby's room. Wait until Mom sees them." Going to the kitchen, she took two votive candles from the cupboard. Taking the butane extended lighter from the drawer, she carefully dropped the candles into her remembrance creations and lit them. Her husband and father's faces were like angels peering down from Heaven. Her eyes welled with tears, and her heart ached. Her baby would never know their sense of humor, kindness, or love. She wiped the tears from her cheeks. "But the baby will come to know your faces as you watch over him or her in the nursery while it sleeps. I'll have to get a battery-operated candle or use a string of Christmas lights." She exhaled, pleased that her small project turned out well.

Gabe was distracted from the program as a glow caught his attention. "I remember that picture of me. It was from the first summer I returned home from college. I think you and I went to the beach for the day. Best day ever. That's when I knew in my heart that we were more than friends, but I was too afraid to tell you so." He smiled. "It's nice to know that our little one will know my face, and, in a way, I'll be watching over it during the darkness of night like a guardian angel."

Elise blew out the candles, turned off the TV, and headed toward the bathroom to shower. The remainder of the free publisher's books needed her consideration. She planned to scan through them tonight, return them to the bookstore tomorrow, and use them for a 'free promotion' for her customers.

Chapter 14

Elise opened her eyes as her cell phone rang. She glanced at her alarm clock. "Eight o'clock? Who in their right mind would call so early?" She reached for her phone and stared at the unknown local number, assuming it was a spam call. Against her better judgment, she answered. "Hello."

"Hello. May I speak to Elise Messenger?"

"Speaking."

"This is Doctor Martin's office. We have a request for an appointment for you from Doctor Griswold. Does this Thursday at 1:00 work for you?"

"Yes," Elise confirmed, knowing Marge would arrive at the bookstore by noon.

"Great. I'll text the address and confirmation. I assume I can send it to this number?"

"Yes, thank you."

"See you Thursday. Goodbye."

Sighing, Elise ended the call. She added the appointment to her phone calendar before getting out of bed and beginning her day. Flipping on the light in the bathroom, she sat on the toilet as an annoying buzz sounded from the bedroom.

"Dang it." After a quick flush, Elise shut off the alarm, dressed, and went to the kitchen in search of something to settle her queasy stomach. Opening the cupboard, she shifted several boxes to one side. "Where are the graham crackers?" Elise discovered a box containing an open sleeve. "Probably stale." Tossing it into the garbage, she settled for a cup of coffee and a piece of buttered toast.

Elise scanned the couch, ottoman, and desk as she stepped into the living room. "I hate to part with this furniture, but I know most of it won't fit in Mom's house." She sipped her coffee, contemplating the enormity of moving. Elise looked at the few cardboard boxes she had brought home. "I'm going to need more." She bit into the toast. "Gabe has so many clothes in the closet. The linen closet is overstuffed with towels, blankets, and extra pillows. Yep, lots of boxes."

After popping the last bite of toast into her mouth and draining her coffee cup dry, she bagged up the books she had reviewed, went to the bookstore, and mindlessly performed her morning routine before unlocking the front door.

Elise picked up the first book on the counter to add it to inventory as a customer entered the store. The woman was middle-aged, her brunette hair salted with gray, and chestnut eyes beamed with a look of determination.

Returning the book in her hand to the stack, Elise grinned. "Hello, can I help you?"

The woman tossed the book she carried on the counter. "I hope so. I want to return this book."

Elise looked at the title. "We don't normally have that book in stock. Did you purchase it here?"

"No, I received it as a gift. I believe my friend purchased it from Amazon."

Elise was tempted to look toward the ceiling but refrained. "I'm sorry, but if the gift was purchased online through a different retailer, it must be returned to that retailer for a refund."

The woman's mouth fell agape. "I don't understand. You're a bookstore, right?"

"Yes."

"So, I should be able to return the book here."

Elise took a deep breath and clenched her teeth. She could feel her heartbeat increase. "Let me try to explain. This book was never in my inventory. My policy is that I only allow a refund when a book has been purchased from my store, and the receipt must accompany the refund request."

"That doesn't make sense. This is a bookstore. I should be able to return it here." The woman persisted.

"I'm sorry." Elise pushed the unwanted book toward the woman, indicating she should take it and leave the store. "You may want to ask your friend where she purchased it and return it there. Thank you for stopping in."

The ignorant woman picked up the book. "Well, you're rude. I'm never coming into this store again." She marched out the door and slammed it shut.

Elise smirked and shook her head as she watched the woman through the display window storm down the sidewalk. "Lady, I'm sure you've never been in this bookstore before. Please let this be your first and last time you ever visit."

Gabe shook his head. "Elise, now I understand why you needed to vent after a challenging day of handling difficult customers."

Elise could have left the stack of books for Marge to check into inventory, but she disliked clutter. Instead, she picked up the book again, scanned it, and set it aside.

The door opened. Elise saw George close the door. He was a sweet elderly customer who lost his wife a year ago. "Good morning, George. I'm glad you came to see me today. How are you doing?" She scanned the next book.

"Still vertical and mobile." He joked, but he was thankful it was true.

Elise smiled. "Good. How can I help you today?"

The elderly man shuffled toward the counter. "I'm looking for a book."

Elise set the scanner down and gave her loyal customer her undivided attention. "Well, then you have come to the right place."

George chuckled. "I don't know the book's title, but its cover is blue."

Elise readied her fingers on the keyboard. "That doesn't give me much to go on, George. Do you remember the author?"

He tapped his fingertip on the counter and looked toward the ceiling. George shook his head. "No."

"Blue, well, that narrows it down to 2300 possibilities." Elise chuckled. "Do you know what it's about?"

While George tried to recall the storyline, Elise brought up his account to see what he had purchased in the past.

"Oh, my brain isn't working today. I guess I should have written it down." He confessed.

Elise tried to ease her customer's frustration. "That's OK. You can call the store when you remember, and I can set the book aside for you. Would you like me to recommend something else for you to read?"

George nodded. "I would appreciate it. You seem to be able to select a book that always holds my interest."

Elise explained some of the newly released books, focusing on genres George had previously read. She recommended several books, one of which he purchased. They chatted over the next half hour on various topics. George finally left the bookstore with a smile on his face. There was a smile on Elise's face too. He had brightened her day as much as she did his.

Before she could return to the counter, a woman dressed in clothing nearly three decades out of style entered.

"Hello, may I help you?" Elise grinned.

"Yes, can you tell me where the self-help section is?"

It was an inside joke between Marge and herself. Elise tried not to smile as she thought, 'why don't you try to find it yourself?' "Sure. This way." She politely escorted the woman to the section.

Returning to the stack of new books, she chose the top one, but a woman with three children entered before she could scan it. Elise wondered why the children weren't in school. Maybe it was a vacation day, or the children were homeschooled.

"Hello, can I help you?" Elise offered.

The woman did not reply.

Scanning the next book and setting it aside, Elise watched as the woman read the blurb on the back of a book and ignored her unruly children. The three brats ran around the store, chasing each other and pulling items from the shelves.

Curled up on the cozy cushion, Petey awoke with a start, became wide-eyed, and hid under his chair. He watched the children's antics hoping to remain unseen.

The little girl grabbed a plush pink cat from a shelf and asked her mother if she could have it. When the woman shook her head, the unruly child threw it down the aisle, where it landed on the floor.

Marge stepped through the back door as the stuffed animal landed at her feet. "What is the meaning of this?"

The children stopped running and looked at her.

Marge made eye contact with each child. "I'm sorry, but there is no running in the bookstore." She looked at the woman's scowling face, appalled that her children had been reprimanded. "Who threw this cute stuffed kitty?" Furthering her inquisition, Marge narrowed her eyes as she pointed to the stuffed animal lying on the floor.

The little girl lowered her chin to her chest and hid behind her mother's legs. Her brothers pointed at their cowering sister.

Marge glared at the guilty child before picking the plush cat up from the floor. "Stuffed animals do not belong on the floor." She put the pink animal in the basket with the other plush toys. The retired teacher pointed her finger at the children. "Do you know this bookstore is haunted? You better behave. The ghost doesn't like when children make a mess."

Gabe grinned. He chose a book on the shelf behind the children and sent it tumbling downward. It landed with a resounding smack on the hardwood.

The children screeched and turned around to see the book on the floor.

"See, the ghost isn't happy with you. I suggest you stand quietly by your mother while she shops, or the next book may fall on your head." Marge went to the fallen book, retrieved it, and placed it back on the shelf. She gave the children another stern look before joining Elise behind the counter. "My goodness."

"Thanks. I'm glad you arrived when you did. The entire morning has been hectic. First, a lady wanted me to accept a return that was purchased on Amazon, then George came in and needed help, and now these wildlings have been running amuck while their mother ignores them."

Marge glared at the children to ensure they remained next to their mother. "I can handle them. Nice timing by our resident ghost though." She looked at the clock. "It's noon. Why don't you go to your office, put up your feet, and eat lunch? I can take care of this customer." She looked at the stack of books on the counter. "I assume these need to be added to inventory."

"These two have been done and are ready to shelve." Elise realized she had forgotten to pack a lunch. "I'll have to go next door to the coffee shop and get something to eat. Do you want anything?"

"No, thank you." Marge glanced at the children before tilting her head to the side. "On second thought, I need a large mocha with coconut milk, no whip, please."

"You got it. In fact, that sounds so good. I think I'll get one for myself too."

"Let me give you some money." Marge offered.

"No need. You can buy the next time." Elise wrote the amount she was withdrawing from the register drawer on a scrap of paper. She exchanged the scribbled note for a twenty-dollar bill. She purchased the two coffees and a sandwich from the deli next door, delivered Marge's order, and retreated to her office to eat her lunch in peace and quiet.

Elise bit into the sandwich and closed her eyes. "BLT, my favorite." The warm coffee was soothing and encouraged her to relax and catch her breath. She brought up a spreadsheet on her computer, reviewed the daily sales for the month, and noted bills that were coming due. "Thank you, Dad, for teaching me how to balance the books and run the store."

"You're doing fine. I'm proud of you." Gabe chimed in. "I'm certain your dad is proud of you too."

With the holiday season approaching, Elise brainstormed ideas for decorating the display windows. She ordered books and other items to ensure she had enough in stock for the seasonal shoppers. "Always planning ahead."

Taking the calendar from the peg on the wall, Elise flipped through the months and wrote 'due date' on the 17th of April. She wondered how much time she would have to take off once the baby arrived. "How can I take any time off? Books need to be ordered, displays in the window changed, and regular bank deposits." She sighed. "Which I have neglected to do for several days." It made her uncomfortable to have the extra cash in the bookstore. Elise went to retrieve the bank bag from under the counter.

Marge was busy scanning the last few books in the stack.

"I have to leave on Thursday at 1:00 for a doctor's appointment," Elise informed her employee.

"Your first OBGYN visit?" Marge placed the last scanned book aside.

"Yes." She retrieved the bank bag and filled out a deposit slip. "I'm going to the bank. I'll be back soon." Elise glanced around the store. It was empty. "Our rambunctious visitors left?"

"Yes, thankfully." Marge picked up several books to shelve.

"Did she buy anything?"

"A book and the children stayed by her side the remainder of the time."

Elise chuckled. "Meanie."

Marge smiled. "You know it."

Chapter 15

When Elise returned from the bank, her employee had finished shelving the new books and tidied the bookstore. "The store looks great, Marge." She placed the empty bank bag beneath the counter.

"You know I like to keep the bookstore presentable. Oh, there are a lot of new releases for next week. I left them on the counter for you to scan through."

After returning to her office and finishing the bookkeeping, Elise familiarized herself with the new titles before placing them beneath the counter until their release date.

The door opened, and an unfamiliar customer entered. Marge greeted the stranger before reciting her spiel about the store being an independent bookstore and offered her assistance.

Elise checked the supply of gift cards. With the holiday season fast approaching, she made a note to order more. She recalled the bag of free publisher's books she had brought from home, retrieved it, and placed them on a shelf in the closet. They would be wrapped in brown paper and handed out to customers during the annual November promotion.

For a day that began poorly, the afternoon went smoothly. Elise and Marge discussed the holiday displays while they cashed out the register and printed the report of the day's sales. Sales were above average for the day, which pleased them both.

Over the next two days, Elise began to sort through Gabe's clothes in the closet.
She folded most of his garments reverently and placed them into a box to give away. However, she could not part with his favorite flannel shirt and imagined herself wearing it while walking through a wooded area on a crisp autumn day with their baby in a backpack or stroller.

On Thursday, Elise left the bookstore in the hands of her trusted employee and drove to her OBGYN appointment. The palms of her hands were clammy. She brushed them on her jeans as she exited her car. She wished Gabe was with her, or even her mother. She would have to get used to doing things by herself. Entering the lobby, she followed the arrows and room numbers posted on the walls to locate the correct office.

Elise exhaled to calm herself before pushing open the glass door and entering the small reception area. The perimeter of the room was outlined with chairs. Women, with their swollen bellies, waited for their names to be called. Elise went to the sliding glass window and signed in on a clipboard. The woman behind the glass watched as she finished writing, took the clipboard, and said, "Hello, Elise.

"Hi."

"I need your insurance card and driver's license to make a copy for our records. Fill out these forms." She handed Elise several papers attached to a clipboard and a pen.

Elise took her driver's license and insurance card from her wallet and gave them to the woman, found a vacant chair, and began filling out the forms. She wondered if her doctor had already forwarded her patient information and if filling out the forms was redundant.

After completing the information, Elise returned the forms, and the woman handed back her license and insurance card.

"You'll be called back soon."

Elise returned to the seat she had previously occupied. Glancing around the room, she noticed the woman who looked like she was about to give birth. The poor thing looked uncomfortable and often shifted on the cushioned seat. Across from her, a young woman looked as if she wasn't very far along in her pregnancy. On the other hand, maybe she was just having her annual physical. Another pregnant woman tried to control a toddler, a little boy, who was crying. Elise assumed he was missing his naptime. "Poor baby," she said under her breath.

She recalled the day a woman and her crying toddler, who needed a nap, came into the bookstore one early afternoon. The young mother had become frustrated with his bawling and spanked him. "Now, don't you cry," she scolded. Elise bit her tongue, but she thought, 'seriously, lady, your child is tired. You just spanked him. How else would he react? Take him home and put him to bed.'

"Elise," a woman standing in an open door called her name.

Elise rose, went through the doorway, and paused.

The woman motioned to a small room on the right. "We're just going to get your vitals in this room." Elise entered and stood, uncertain what she should do.

The nurse set the file on the counter. "Let's get your weight first."

Groaning inwardly, Elise swore a doctor's scale always read more than it should.

The woman recorded her weight. "Good. Please sit while I take your blood pressure, temp, and oxygen level."

The blood pressure cuff was put around Elise's arm, and the stethoscope's diaphragm was placed in the crease of her arm. She watched the needle on the circular gauge as the inflation bulb was squeezed and the pressure increased on her arm. When the valve was released, the arrow on the gage descended until it began to bob.

"Excellent." The woman opened the valve, fully releasing the remaining pressure, removed the cuff, and pinched an oximeter on Elise's index finger while inserting a thermometer under her tongue.

Within seconds, the thermometer beeped and was removed from her mouth. The woman took the device off Elise's finger and recorded the information onto her chart.

"This way, please."

Elise followed the woman to an examining room. She stepped up, turned, and sat on an examination table.

"The doctor will be with you soon."

"Thank you."

Elise was alone in the tiny room. She saw various items near the sink, charts on the wall, and a print of a mother and infant. Looking to her left, she saw a picture of a cross-section of a woman with an infant emerging through the birth canal. "Good lord, that looks painful."

The door opened, and a blond woman in a white coat entered the room carrying a file. Elise thought the doctor was in her late thirties, maybe early forties.

"Hello Elise, I'm Doctor Martin." She began. "Congratulations on your pregnancy."

"Thank you."

"It's nice to meet you. So, Doctor Griswold indicates you were about eight weeks along when you saw her. How are you feeling?"

"Nauseated most of the time, tired too."

"Your upset stomach should go away in the next few weeks. You're probably eating less, too. Fatigue can be expected. Since there are two of you now, rest when you can, even take a nap."

Elise nodded. "I own the bookstore in town, so my day can become hectic."

Gabe watched the exchange from the corner of the room.

"I usually order an ultrasound in the first trimester to ensure all is well. So, you'll have one during your next visit." Doctor Martin glanced at Elise's ring finger. "Your file indicates your blood type is Rh-negative."

"Yes, O negative."

"Does your husband have a positive Rh factor?"

Gabe looked from the doctor to his wife. "Yes, I do, or did. O positive."

Elise stared, a little stunned by her question. "I don't know."

"Do you think he knows?"

Elise looked away from the doctor. "He may have."

"May have?" The doctor scowled.

Elise took a deep breath before speaking. "He passed away in a motorcycle accident."

Doctor Martin was stunned into silence and took a moment before replying. "I'm sorry. Perhaps his doctor has his blood type on record. Would you like us to call his doctor and inquire?"

"Sure, he saw Doctor Williams."

"If it is not in your husband's file, then there is a high probability he was Rh-positive. When you are 26 to 28 weeks along, we will give you a RhoGAM shot. It will help you and the baby avoid any complications from Rh incompatibility. You'll receive another shot after your delivery."

Gabe nodded. "Good."

Elise's eyebrows drew together. "I don't understand."

The doctor did not want to cause her patient any unnecessary anxiety. "The injection will stop your body from building up antibodies against your child and any you wish to have in the future."

"I don't plan on having any more children," Elise stated adamantly as she lifted her chin.

Gabe stared at his wife. "Elise, you don't know that. You may meet someone someday and fall in love again. It would be nice if our baby had a brother or sister."

"Well, it would be precautionary. I wouldn't be a good doctor if I didn't insist you receive the injection." Doctor Martin smiled. "Do you have any pets?"

"Yes. Petey is our resident bookstore cat."

"It's recommended that you have someone other than yourself clean the litter box while you're pregnant."

Elise could have Marge do it, but she still had a litter box that Petey used in the apartment. Once she moved home with her mother, Petey would have to remain in the bookstore permanently.

"Coming in contact with the soiled litter may cause toxoplasmosis."

Elise nodded, unfamiliar with the disease. She would research it once she arrived at the bookstore. "What about wearing latex gloves and washing my hands thoroughly after cleaning the litter box?"

"Only if you have no other alternative. I'm going to prescribe prenatal vitamins for you. Do you have any issues swallowing pills?"

"No."

"Good. I'll give you a bottle to start and a prescription you can take to your pharmacy. I would like you to gain between 24 and 28 pounds. It's a

guideline. Some women gain less, others gain more."
She closed the file. "Do you have any questions?"

Elise had lots of questions. First, she needed
verification of her delivery date. Would the baby be
born in a delivery or birthing room? She needed
confirmation her mother could be with her during the
delivery too. No use in keeping her thoughts inside.

"Is my due date April 17th?"

Doctor Martin opened the file and scanned
the nurse's entry. "Yes, a spring baby. And since this
is your first, you may deliver before or after that date."

Gabe smiled.

"Will the baby be born in a birthing room?"
Elise had heard of the accommodation.

"Yes, the hospital has lovely birthing rooms
where you will deliver your baby. You and your little
one will remain in the room during your stay. Any
person of your choice may be present during the birth
and throughout that time. There are security
measures your guest will have to understand and
abide by."

Elise wished Gabe was still alive to
experience the birth of their child. She glanced at the
carpeted floor before looking at the doctor. "My mom
has agreed to be with me."

"That's good." She grinned. "I'll be there too to see you through the delivery and monitor your recovery." Doctor Martin could only imagine the array of emotions her patient was experiencing. "I'll see you in a month. Rest when you are tired, eat well, and if you have any questions, feel free to call the office."

"Thank you, Doctor Martin."

"You're welcome." She handed Elise the prescription and paperwork to check out. "Just follow the arrows on the hallway walls to find your way out. See you in a month."

The woman at the desk gave Elise a bottle of vitamins. Elise paid her co-pay and went to her car. Sitting behind the steering wheel, she stared at the bottle before dropping it on her lap. Willing herself not to cry, she longed for Gabe to be by her side, experience the birth of their child, and hold their baby when it took its first breath. But he was not there. She inhaled and exhaled a deep, cleansing breath to calm herself.

Gabe sat in the front seat next to his wife. He wished he could hold Elise, tell her that all would be well. Unable to resist touching her, he brushed his hand along the length of her arm.

Elise shuddered at the sudden chill. Even though she was alone, her instinct told her that everything would be alright. A part of Gabe would always be within her heart and their baby. She placed the palm of her hand on her belly and grinned. "We can do this."

Chapter 16

The next few weeks seemed to pass by rapidly. Elise could no longer fasten the waist of her jeans. Instead of purchasing maternity pants this early in her pregnancy, she bought a belly band to cover her expanding abdomen and wore hip-length bulky sweaters. As Doctor Martin had stated, her morning sickness eased, and her appetite resumed. She monitored her weight and made a weekly graph, hoping to stay within the doctor's guidelines. Unfortunately, her craving for lasagna had become nearly uncontrollable. As a result, Elise often ate the meal for lunch and dinner. A visit to the grocery store ended in embarrassment as she placed almost a dozen frozen lasagna dinners with other items on the checkout counter.

"Wow, having a party?" The young clerk, with her side ponytail and snapping her gum in her open mouth, scanned and pushed the items toward the bagger.

"No, just for me," Elise admitted.

The clerk shrugged her left shoulder before grabbing another item to scan as the bagger managed to pack all her groceries in three bags. "Would you like help with these out to your car?"

"No, thank you. I can manage." Elise watched as he loaded the last bag into her cart, pushed it to her car, and unloaded the heavy bags into the trunk. Once at the apartment, she was determined to carry all the groceries in one trip. With two grocery bags on one arm and one on the other, Elise paused in the lobby to collect her mail before climbing the stairs. Elise stepped onto the landing to take the second set of stairs when she felt a twinge in her abdomen, causing her to pause and look toward her belly.

Gabe stopped behind her. "It's too heavy, Elise."

Elise took a deep breath, climbed the remaining steps, and set the groceries on the floor outside the apartment door. Another twinge caused her to cringe. She unlocked the door, carried one bag at a time to the kitchen, and began putting the groceries away.

"Elise, call your mom. There's something wrong." Gabe urged as he paced.

"Am I getting cramps?" Elise went to the bathroom. When she wiped, she discovered a slightly bloody discharge.

"Oh, God, you're bleeding. Call the doctor. Go to the emergency room." Gabe encouraged.

Elise put a sanitary napkin in her underwear, flushed the toilet, and pulled her phone from her back pocket. "Mom, I have cramps, and I'm bleeding. What should I do? Should I call the doctor? Am I losing the baby?"

Janet knew her daughter was upset, pushed to the point of panic. She remained calm. "I can only tell you what I know. Many women bleed during their pregnancy. Some bleed when they would normally have their period. Others bleed throughout and until they deliver. I had a pink discharge for about three days when I was early in my pregnancy with you. Did you fall or do anything strenuous?"

"I carried the groceries from the car. They were kind of heavy."

"That will do it. No more lifting. Are you having any cramps?"

"A few twinges, not bad, though."

"Elevate your feet and rest. Do you need me to come over?"

Elise did not want to be needy, but she knew she would feel better if someone was with her. "Sure, if you don't mind."

"I'll pack a bag and spend the night. If you are still cramping in the morning, I think you should have Marge cover for you and call the doctor. I wouldn't be surprised if the doctor wants you off your feet until the bleeding stops."

Elise's bottom lip quivered. "I don't want to lose this baby. That's all I have left of Gabe."

Janet wanted to reassure her daughter that everything would be fine, but she had no guarantee that it would be. "I'll be there soon."

Elise propped the apartment door open with one of her shoes, laid on the couch, and placed her feet on a decorative pillow. Thankfully, her mother knew the code to enter the building, so she would not have to get up to let her inside. She turned on the TV and tried to distract her worried mind.

Gabe paced helplessly, glancing often at his wife.

"Hello," Janet greeted as she pushed open the door, removed the shoe, and locked it behind her.

"Janet, thank goodness you're here." Gabe stepped toward her.

"Hi, Mom."

"How are you doing?" Setting her overnight bag on the floor by the couch, Janet took off her coat and stood before her daughter.

"The cramping has eased, but that hasn't stopped me from worrying."

"Like I said, it's common. You may have experienced a Braxton Hicks contraction, but it's too early in your pregnancy. No more lifting or overdoing things." Janet scanned the furniture and bare walls. "Even though you have brought over some of your smaller items, I think we will hire a moving company to move the rest. It shouldn't cost very much." She looked at her daughter and crossed her arms over her chest. "How many groceries did you carry in?"

"Just three bags, but it was mostly frozen food, milk, and a little more than I usually buy."

"Did you eat dinner?"

"Not yet."

"Would you like me to go and get something for us to eat?"

Elise bit her bottom lip. "What I really would like is one of the lasagna frozen dinners."

"That sounds good. Do you have enough for the two of us?" Janet hung her coat in the entry closet.

Elise smiled. "More than enough."

Janet went to the kitchen, opened the freezer, and a package of lasagna fell out onto the floor. She laughed. "I guess you do. You have enough to feed a small army."

Chapter 17

Doctor Martin assured Elise there was no cause for alarm unless the cramping and bleeding increased. She instructed her patient to spend the next few days with her feet elevated.

Elise had Marge manage the store while she rested. By week's end, the moving men took the last of her remaining items from the apartment and relocated them to her mother's house. She watched helplessly as they assembled her bed and took her living room furniture to the basement for storage. Opening one of the boxes, she removed her favorite wedding photo of her and Gabe and placed it on her dresser.

As Janet escorted the moving men to the door, Elise sat in her father's reclining chair and elevated her feet.

Even though it was midafternoon, Elise closed her eyes and drifted off to sleep.

Gabe sat on the couch and stared at his wife. He was thankful she was resting.

Janet covered her daughter with a crocheted blanket and watched as Elise's eyes fluttered open momentarily. After finding room for Elise's groceries, she busied herself by making her daughter's bed and tidying the room. When she emerged from the bedroom, she found Elise standing before the open refrigerator looking for something to eat.

"Well, I was hoping you would take a long nap." Janet stood in the doorway with her fisted hands upon her hips.

"Just a cat nap, Mom."

"How are you feeling?"

"Better. I guess I was just pushing myself too hard." Elise admitted.

"I found room for your food in the pantry. The freezer is quite full now."

Elise chuckled. "I don't know why, but I can't seem to eat enough lasagna."

"Your body is craving what it needs. I can make a salad to go along with it, or maybe heat up a can of green beans with butter and almonds."

Gabe shook his head. "Ugh, lasagna again? Babe, you'll make me vomit, if that's even possible."

Elise glanced at the clock on the microwave. "Maybe later. It's too early for dinner. I'll just have a snack for now." She took a peach yogurt from the fridge and a spoon from the drawer. "What I need to do is go to the bookstore. I feel bad about dumping everything on Marge."

"She's a good employee. When I stopped by the other day, the Halloween decorations in the windows and throughout the bookstore looked good. She has the holiday books on the shelf too. So, I'm certain everything is fine."

"I'm going to go and help close the store tonight," Elise announced before spooning the yogurt into her mouth.

"I'll have dinner on the table when you return. No lifting." Janet warned.

"I know." Elise threw away her empty yogurt container, grabbed her purse and coat, and drove to the bookstore.

Marge heard the lock click and the back door open. Curious, she began walking toward the office.

Elise put her purse in her desk drawer, hung up her coat, and met her employee in the office doorway.

"Well, it's nice to see your smiling face again." Marge greeted. "Feeling better?"

"I feel fine. The doctor told me to take it easy. No lifting."

Marge shook her index finger toward her boss. "And you make sure you follow her orders."

"You don't have to tell me twice." Elise nodded, vowing to do absolutely nothing that would put the baby at risk. "So, how have sales been?"

"Steady. The Christmas book orders have started to arrive."

"Good. We will put the holiday books on display right after Halloween. People like to shop early." Elise glanced at the display window. "It looks as if the orange lights have managed to stay lit. I like the reading glasses on the skeleton's face. It gives the impression he is reading the book to the raven."

"Many have made comments about him too. He's an attention-getter."

A gentleman entered the store.

"Good." Elise walked up and down the aisles taking a silent inventory of what sold. She turned a few of the books to display their cover.

Marge offered to help the man find a needed book.

Satisfied with her completed tour, Elise went to her office to read through the accumulated emails over the past few days. She exhaled as she finished and looked at the framed photograph of Gabe and her. "We were so happy."

"Yes, we were quite a pair." He confirmed.

Opening the bookkeeping files on her computer, Elise updated the account books before shutting off her computer for the night as closing time neared. She gathered the deposits and put them in her purse before walking to the front of the store and turning off the neon open sign in the display window.

Gabe watched his wife. His heart swelled with pride yet ached with sorrow. He wanted her to know he was nearby, loved her, and always would. Glancing at the visionary genre books on the shelf, he recognized a title he had once read. He looked at Elise as she walked up the aisle. A devilish grin spread across his face. Gabe knocked the book off the shelf. It landed on its spine and opened to the chapter titled 'Conveying The Message.'

Elise looked at the opened book as she approached it. Nonchalantly returning the novel to its proper place, she stepped toward the counter.

Gabe knocked the book off the shelf a second time. It landed again with the same chapter open for her to see. "Read it, Elise."

She turned around to see the book on the floor. "Really?" She stooped over, picked up the book, and closed it, realizing it was the same book she had returned to the shelf.

Gabe sighed as he watched her turn away. He knocked the book off the shelf a third time.

Elise stopped, looked toward the ceiling, and exhaled. She went back to the book on the floor, picked it up, and read the title on the page, "Conveying The Message. OK, I got it. You are conveying a message. What do you want to say?"

Gabe grinned, pleased he had her attention.

Elise returned the book and stood next to the shelf. She pursed her lips and waited. "So, you have nothing to say now?"

"Oh, she's so cute when she gets agitated." Gabe chuckled.

Marge came around the endcap of the aisle. "Are you talking to me?"

"No, I'm talking to whoever is knocking this book off the shelf." Elise crossed her arms over her chest. "The same book has fallen to the floor three times."

Marge tilted her head to the left and shrugged her shoulders. "Apparently, the spirit wants to say something."

"Well, it's quiet now. Whatever the ghost wants to say must not be important." She continued to wait.

Marge locked the front door and began counting the money in the register.

Elise tapped her foot on the floor while looking up and down the aisle. She assumed the spirit had moved on and went to the counter.

Marge updated the sales report and handed Elise the bank envelope. "Are you going to make a deposit tomorrow?"

"Yes, thank you." Elise shut off the computer for the night. "I'll probably come in late tomorrow. It may be a good idea for me to ease back into work."

"I agree." Marge headed toward the back of the store to retrieve her jacket and purse from the office.

"See you tomorrow, and thanks for opening the store for me."

"Goodnight, Elise. Be careful driving home."

"You too." Elise waited until she heard the back door close before shutting off the lights, leaving one lit over the counter for security purposes. She put on her coat and purse and ensured she had the deposit for the next day when she heard a book fall to the floor.

"Really?" Elise was tempted to leave the book where it lay, knowing Marge would put it back on the shelf, but her curiosity got the better of her. "That better not be the same book." She marched to the aisle and could see an open book on the floor. Picking it up, she kept her thumb between the pages and looked at the cover. It was not the same book, but it was by the same author and the first book in the series. Elise read the chapter title, 'My Husband." She closed the book and froze, fully aware she was being watched by someone she could not see. Her hands trembled. "Gabe?"

Chapter 18

Elise returned the book to the shelf. The hair on her arms stood on end, prickling her skin. She stretched the palms of her hands out in front of her. The air was cold, almost frigid. "Gabe, are you here?" Her ears were met with silence.

"Oh, Babe, yes, I'm here." He reached for her dainty hands, but his hands passed through them.

"My heart wants to believe it's you, but I can't see you." She continued as she scanned the emptiness in front of her, wishing her beloved husband could manifest and magically appear.

He lowered his hands to his side, helplessly defeated. "I know."

Elise placed the palm of her hand on her abdomen and grinned. "I'm pregnant. I'm so happy to be carrying your child, our child. Even though my future looks bleak without you, I'm seeing it in a positive light for the first time." She wiped a tear away from her cheek. "I miss you."

"I miss you too, Babe."

"Gabe," she forced a single chuckle as it occurred to her that she may be speaking to a spirit other than her husband, "or whoever I'm talking to, you must think I'm silly."

Ever since Elise could remember, tales of restless spirits haunting the old bookstore building circulated within the community. She assumed the departed souls were trapped within the brick walls, uncertain of where to go or how to find their way to Heaven.

"If it's you, Gabe, I want you to know that I had to move out of our apartment. I couldn't afford it on my income alone. I'm living with Mom now." Elise exhaled, releasing her emotional stress. "Just believing you are here in the bookstore is reassuring. I'll assume every book falling from a shelf is a sign, a message from you." She paused. "I love you and always will."

"I love you too."

Elise scanned the area around her, wondering if her husband was still there. "Mom will be expecting me. Until tomorrow then, goodnight."

Gabe followed his wife out the back door. He smirked as he listened to Elise talk to herself during the drive home, rehearsing her experience to share with her mother.

Janet was setting the dinner on the table as her daughter arrived home.

Elise set her purse on a kitchen chair, removed her coat, and hung it in the closet. She explained what had happened at the bookstore while her mother tossed a salad of greens and vegetables and placed it on the table. "Do you think it could be Gabe?"

"Maybe." Janet wanted to believe it was possible, but her daughter's experience proved little evidence to make it plausible.

"It couldn't be a coincidence that a book would fall from a shelf three times," Elise emphasized. "The chapter headings seemed to mean something too."

"I guess you will have to see if it happens again." Janet thought her daughter was reading too much into the incident and assumed it was just another ghost story that would be passed down in the years to come. She removed a single serving of lasagna from the microwave.

Determined to convey every detail of her experience, Elise failed to realize the kitchen table was set with a bowl of fresh salad and a steaming bowl of green beans. She saw her mother place a single serving of lasagna on the table. "Are you having lasagna too?"

"No, just a salad for me. What would you like to drink?"

Feeling guilty for not helping with the meal, Elise insisted, "Sit, Mom, I can get it." She took two tall glasses from the cupboard and filled one with milk. "Do you want milk too?"

"No, thank you. I'll just have water." Janet set the lasagna container on a hot pad in front of Elise's plate. "I'm glad to have you back home. It's such a task to cook a meal for just one person and no fun to eat alone." She sat.

Elise placed their drinks on the table, sat, and removed her tasty meal from the container and onto her plate. She used the side of her fork to cut into her lasagna. "I agree, and to have an actual conversation with someone. Which reminds me, I want to know if you will be with me during my labor and birth of the baby? You can stay with me in the hospital afterward, too." She scooped the steaming bite onto her fork and blew on it.

Janet smiled. "I wouldn't miss it for the world. To think, I'll be the first to see this little one born. I'm excited to be a grandma."

As the evening ended, Elise showered and went to her room. She inhaled Gabe's aftershave and wondered if he could be nearby. Then she noticed a stack of boxes next to the wall and read the black marker on the side. "Gabe's clothes. Probably your lingering aftershave." The reality was disappointing. On a whim, she opened the top box, withdrew his flannel shirt, and placed the wrinkled garment on her pillow. Elise got into bed, shut off the lamp on the nightstand, and pulled the covers over her shoulder. Snuggling the shirt near her face, she inhaled the earthy fragrance. "Goodnight, Gabe. I love you."

"Goodnight, Elise. I love you too. Sleep well, Babe."

~

Elise entered the doctor's office for her next appointment. Her vitals were taken and recorded by a medical assistant, who escorted her to a dark room.

"This is Sarah, our ultrasound technician." The medical assistant informed as she motioned toward the middle-aged woman sitting on a stool.

Sarah rose. "Hello. I assume you're Elise?"

"Yes." Elise heard the door close behind her.

"Well, this is an exciting day. You'll get to see your baby."

Elise nodded, afraid her reply would reveal the emotion she was currently feeling. She bit her bottom lip to stop it from quivering.

"I just need you to lay on the table and pull your pants and underwear down to the top of your thighs."

Elise placed her coat and purse on the vacant chair near the door and lay on the examination table. She slid her garments down as Sarah put a paper sheet over her legs and tucked the top edge beneath her clothing.

"Have you ever had an ultrasound before?" Sarah began typing information into the keyboard of the machine.

Elise looked at the black screen as the letters appeared. "No."

"You're twelve weeks, correct?"

"Yes."

Sarah finished entering the information and picked up a plastic bottle the size of her palm. It resembled a ketchup or mustard plastic bottle at a hot dog stand. She held it over Elise's abdomen and squeezed the warm gel onto her patient's abdomen.

"This is a gel that helps the soundwaves work better." Sarah returned the gel to the warmer and picked up a device, placed it on the gel, and moved it about to spread it over Elise's abdomen.

Elise looked at the monitor and tried to interpret what was displayed. She watched and listened as Sarah moved the computer mouse and clicked it.

"I'm just taking a few measurements. I'll explain when I'm finished." The technician continued with her work.

"OK."

Elise stared at a dark spot on the screen. It seemed to be pulsing.

Sarah turned the screen toward her patient. "The dark area is amniotic fluid. And this is your baby's head." She pointed to it. "You can see its nose, eye sockets, mouth, and chin. Here is its tummy and the dark thing right here. That's its heart. See it beating?"

Elise nodded. "Yes."

Gabe stared at the screen. "Our baby. Elise, look what we did."

"You can see the arms, hands, legs, and feet." Sarah pushed a few buttons to take photographs.

"Can you tell if it's a boy or girl?" Elise thought she and her mother could begin decorating the baby's nursery if she knew.

"It's too early. Doctors usually order another ultrasound at twenty weeks. If your baby cooperates during the second ultrasound, you can find out then. If you would like to know sooner, there is a blood test, but you will have to ask your doctor for more detail." Sarah moved the transducer.

"So, the baby looks healthy?" Elise stared at the monitor, overwhelmed by what she saw.

"It looks perfect to me. There is plenty of amniotic fluid too."

Elise exhaled, not knowing she had been holding her breath.

The photographs were printed while Sarah used a paper towel to wipe the gel from her patient's abdomen. "Here is an extra one in case I missed anything." She handed Elise a paper towel.

"Thank you." Elise wiped off the remaining gel. She scooted from the table, pulled up her clothes, and adjusted the black elastic belly band.

Sarah took the photos from the printer and handed them to Elise. "Here you go. The first pictures of your baby. I've labeled the parts of the baby's body for you."

"Thank you." Elise stared at her little one captured in the black and white photos.

Gabe looked over his wife's shoulder, admiring the baby pictures.

"I guess I will have to start a baby book." She decided the first page would be a photo of her and Gabe, followed by the ultrasound photos of their baby on the second page.

Sarah opened the door. "If you follow me, I'll take you to your appointment with Doctor Martin."

Elise picked up her coat and purse and followed the technician to an examining room.

"Have a great day, and congrats," Sarah said before closing the examining room door.

"Thanks." She stared at the photos while she waited. "Hello, little one. I'm glad you're doing well. I already love you even though I don't know you. I can't wait to hold you in my arms." Elise touched the photo, tracing the tip of her finger along the baby's chin. "Oh, Gabe, you have given me the greatest gift I could ever ask for."

Gabe smiled as he looked at the photo.

Doctor Martin entered, carrying a folder. "Hello, Elise."

"Hi."

The doctor flipped through the paperwork and read the technician's report. "It looks as if you have a healthy baby. No more bleeding?"

"No, I only bled for a day, and it wasn't very much."

"Good. Are you resting? Taking your vitamins? Eating well?"

"Yes, as best as I can."

"Well, no lifting over ten pounds."

Elise thought of the boxes of books arriving several times a week. The delivery men and women always asked where she preferred them to be placed. She could easily unpack the boxes without moving them and only carry a few books at a time.

Doctor Martin raised her eyebrows and waited for a reply. "Elise, nothing over ten pounds."

"OK. The technician said it was too early to tell if I was carrying a boy or girl. It would be nice to know so I can decorate the nursery."

"There is a blood test, but most health insurance plans won't cover it unless we suspect a chromosomal abnormality. I can have the receptionist contact your insurance and see if they will cover it. Otherwise, you should be able to find out the gender of your baby at twenty weeks when you have your second ultrasound."

Wanting to keep her medical expenses to a minimum, Elise said, "That's all right. I can wait another eight weeks."

The doctor looked at the file. "The baby's heart looks good. Let's see if we can hear its heartbeat."

Elise was instructed to lay on the examination table and pull down her belly band.

Doctor Martin used gel and an instrument to locate the heartbeat. A squishing, pulsing sound emanated from the device.

Looking at the doctor, Elise smiled. "That's my baby's heartbeat?"

"Yes. It's strong. About 140. Isn't that the most beautiful sound you've ever heard?"

Elise nodded.

Gabe smiled. "Yes."

Doctor Martin wiped up the gel from Elise's abdomen. "Do you have any questions?"

Elise returned her belly band to its proper place. "When should I start showing?"

"Everyone is different. Some show right away, while others don't appear pregnant until much later."

"Really?"

Doctor Martin smiled and nodded her head. "Yes, but that doesn't happen very often. You should begin to show within the next few weeks. At that time, your uterus will rise above your pelvic bone."

"Ok."

"If you have any questions, write them down, and I can answer them during your next visit. See you in a month."

"Thank you."

Elise went to the bookstore to share her photos with Marge.

"It's amazing they can let you see what your baby looks like." Marge stared at each photo, four in all, before handing them to her boss.

"I want to begin a baby scrapbook. I should be able to order one through the store account." Elise set the photographs on her desk.

"Can I host a baby shower for you?" Marge handed the photographs back to Elise, who set them near the keyboard of her office computer.

Taken back by the offer, Elise stared at her employee. "That would be lovely, but I don't know who you would invite. I haven't been in contact with many of my high school friends since graduation. It may be strange to have Gabe's side of the family there."

"I'm certain they would want to be invited." Marge insisted.

"I don't know about that. Gabe's mom never liked me much." Elise admitted. "But not inviting them would only cause more trouble." She smiled. "Thank you, Marge. I'm sure Mom will want to help too."

Gabe hovered in the corner of the room. "That's very nice of you, Marge. My mother will be there for certain, at least I hope she will. Maybe my grandmother too."

The bell on the front door rang as a customer entered the store.

"Duty calls." Marge left the office and stepped behind the counter. "Hello, may I help you find something?"

Elise listened to the rehearsed greeting of her employee before leaving her office. She glanced at the elderly woman who had entered the store and retrieved a few books from the stack of new releases to be shelved. Elise walked toward the genre and put the books in their proper place.

"I'm just browsing. Thank you." The customer replied.

Gabe could hardly contain his happiness any longer. Scanning the books, he tossed one from the shelf.

Elise looked in the direction of the noise before staring into the startled customer's eyes.

"I didn't touch it. It just fell." The woman defended as she turned toward the fallen book.

"I know. I'll get it." Elise approached the open book on the floor and kept her voice calm. "This is something that often happens in the bookstore." She picked up the book and stared at the chapter heading, 'A Dream Come True.' Elise turned away from the customer and went to her office. She closed the door behind her and picked up the baby's ultrasound photos. "Gabe? I can only assume the baby is a dream come true for you." She sighed as she smiled. "It's a dream come true for me too."

Chapter 19

When Elise arrived home, her mother had dinner on the table. She secretly placed the ultrasound photos in her lap as she sat and looked at the meal before her.

"Mom, you are going to spoil me." She cut a one-inch square of her lasagna and shoved it into her mouth.

Gabe cringed. "I swear, Elise, you'll never eat another bite of that stuff without gagging once the baby is born."

"I assumed you would be hungry once you arrived home." Janet grinned as her daughter closed her eyes, savoring the bite in her mouth. "Besides, it's nice for you to sit for a moment and tell me how your day was."

Elise took the photos from her lap and slid them across the table to her mother. "These were taken today of your grandchild."

Janet stared at the black and white photos.

"The technician labeled the body parts," Elise explained. "There isn't much to look at yet, but these are the first photos of your grandson or granddaughter." She watched her mother's face for her reaction while she put the next bite of lasagna on her fork.

Janet picked up the photos and examined each one. "Oh, there's the baby's head. I see its arms and legs. It's little tummy and the dark spot labeled heart." She looked at her daughter. "Did you find out if it is a boy or girl?"

"The technician said the baby is too tiny for her to tell. The doctor said I could find out the baby's sex through a blood test, but my insurance may not cover the expense. So, I've decided to wait until twenty weeks when the next ultrasound is done. The technician would be able to tell then."

"That's exciting. Are you hoping for a boy or girl?"

Gabe smiled. "I'm hoping for a little girl. I always dreamed of escorting my daughter down the aisle on her wedding day." He sighed. "Too bad I won't be there physically to do so."

"I'm hoping for a healthy baby. It doesn't matter if it's a boy or girl." Elise ate another bite of lasagna. "It would be nice to have a boy to carry on Gabe's last name, though. But a little girl would fit in nicely with the two of us."

~

The crisp autumn air and colorful leaves falling to the ground like nature's confetti foretold a change of the season.

Elise sat on a chair near the front door of the bookstore. A large bowl of candy was on her lap. The children entered dressed in their Halloween costumes and shouted, "trick or treat!" Her mother sat next to her, smiling at the parade of young visitors.

"To think that this time next year, you'll be taking the baby out to get candy." Janet dropped candy into one of the children's bags.

"I'm looking forward to it." Elise paused with her hand in the candy bowl. "The baby will only be six months old. Dressing the baby in a costume and visiting a few houses will be fun."

The bookstore's Halloween decorations were taken down the next day and replaced with a Christmas tree, lights, and various books. An uptick in sales indicated holiday shopping had started.

Thanksgiving dinner was quiet, just Elise and her mom. Their anticipation of a third member joining their household in four and a half months brightened the overcast shadow of Gabe's absence from the holiday meal.

With her prominent belly bump growing daily, Elise purchased several maternity pants. She was not particularly fond of the stretchy panel over her belly, but it was comfortable.

Excited about her twenty-week ultrasound, Elise secured the first appointment, so she could open the bookstore on time.

"It's nice to see you again, Elise." Sarah greeted. "Let's see how your baby is doing."

Familiar with the scan, Elise lay on the examination table and readied herself for the technician to begin.

"Ah, your baby is cooperating. Do you want to know the gender?" Sarah pressed the photo key while she waited for a reply.

"Can you write it on a piece of paper? It would be nice for my mom and me to find out at the same time."

"Sure. I'll put it in an envelope for you to open together."

Gabe was eager to know the gender of the baby but resisted the temptation to look over the technician's shoulder. He preferred to share the reveal with his wife and mother-in-law.

After her monthly prenatal appointment, Elise had enough time to stop by the bakery at the grocery store. "Hello, I need three cupcakes made for a baby reveal."

"Only three?" The baker raised her eyebrows in question.

"Yes." Elise needed a cupcake for herself, her mother, and one for Marge. She handed the woman the envelope. "By this evening, if that's possible."

"Sure. Would you like white, yellow, or chocolate cupcakes?"

"Yellow with either blue or pink filling."

"They will be ready by 4:00." The baker opened the envelope to see which filling color was needed.

"Great. Thanks." Checking her phone for the time, Elise hurried to her car. While waiting for the red traffic light to exit the parking lot, her cellphone rang. "Hi, Mom."

"Did you find out?"

Elise grinned, hearing the excitement in her mother's voice. "Yes."

The light turned green.

"Well?"

"I'll tell you when I get home." Elise's heart thumped in her chest, excited to know if she was carrying a boy or girl.

"You're going to make me wait?"

Elise smiled. "Yes, and we can find out together."

Janet was silent for a moment. "You don't know either?"

"Like I said, we'll find out together. I'll be stopping by the grocery store after work, so I'll be a few minutes late."

"OK."

"Would you like me to pick up something for us to eat for dinner?" Elise chuckled. "Other than lasagna."

"Does a rotisserie chicken from the deli sound good?" Janet suggested.

"Sure, I'll get a few side dishes too." Elise pulled into her parking place behind the bookstore. "I'm at the bookstore. I'll see you tonight."

~

The steady flow of customers throughout the day gave Elise little time to read her emails. She was tempted to call Marge and have her work in the afternoon, but she was already working an extra day a week to help meet the holiday demand.

The bell to the front door rang.

"Hello, can I help you . . ." Elise recognized her high school classmate. "Jen." Smiling, she noticed a baby carrier on Jen's arm. "And you brought the baby."

"I thought you would like to meet Cynthia Anne." Jen pulled back the protective cover of the carrier.

"Aw, she is precious."

"Ed said you are expecting a baby."

"Yes, in April."

"Do you know if you are having a boy or girl?"

"My mom and I are going to find out tonight."

"We'll have to set up playdates for the babies." Jen glanced at the clock on the wall. "I gotta run. Dinner time. It's good to see you again."

Tired yet excited, she ensured Petey had plenty of food and water before closing for the night. "Goodnight, Gabe. I'll let you know if we're having a boy or girl tomorrow." Elise made a quick stop at the grocery store and headed home. She carried their meal into the house and placed it on the kitchen table.

Anticipating her daughter's arrival, Janet had set the table, including their drinks. She looked eagerly at her daughter. "Well?"

Elise removed the food from the grocery bag. "I asked the bakery to make us some special cupcakes." She held the trio of desserts for her mother to examine.

Janet looked at the decorative frosting of pink and blue with a plastic question mark in the center. "So, I have to eat a cupcake to find out if you are expecting a boy or girl?"

Elise grinned and nodded. "Yes. If the filling is blue, then it's a boy. If it's pink, then I'm having a girl."

"Why are there three?"

"One is for Marge. Since she was kind enough to host a baby shower with you, she should be one of the first to know."

"Aw, that's nice." Janet sat at the table. "And very thoughtful."

Elise and Janet conversed little throughout the meal, anticipating dessert. They placed their silverware on their plates and set them aside when their appetites were satisfied. Elise opened the container of cupcakes and grinned. "Well, are you ready to find out if you will have a grandson or granddaughter to cuddle?"

"Yes." Janet waited for Elise to place a cupcake before her.

""Take off the liner, and we will bite into the cupcakes at the same time." Elise removed the waxy paper as she watched her mother do the same. "Ready?"

Janet nodded.

Gabe peeked over his wife's shoulder.

"One, two, three."

They bit into the cupcakes to reveal the icing inside. It was pink.

Chapter 20

Petey greeted Elise the following day as she entered the back door.

"Hello, Petey." She petted his silky ebony fur before turning on the light. The hungry feline followed her to her office.

She looked at her husband's photo on her desk and turned on her computer. "Good morning, Gabe. We're having a little girl."

"Yes, and I'm over the moon. To think, a daughter, a little girl." He watched as Elise fed Petey, tidied the shelves, and turned on the counter computer before clicking on the neon open sign. Unlocking the door, she walked to the counter.

Unable to contain his happiness, Gabe knocked a book to the floor.

Elise looked toward the sound and scowled. "The children's section?" As she came around the endcap, she spotted a book on the floor, picked it up, and looked at the cover. "Guess How Much I Love You. Aw, this is one of my favorite books."

A book fell behind Elise, startling her. She turned, stared at the illustrated little girl on the book's cover, and picked it up.

Gabe looked for the next book. He had a particular one in mind. "Where is it? Where is it?"

"Aw, for our baby girl. Good idea, Gabe. I'll have to get a bookshelf for her room."

She went to the computer to zero out the books from the inventory when another book fell. Elise chuckled. "I can't afford to take every book home." She picked up the book. "Oh, this one is nice too."

Elise deleted the books from inventory, reordered them, and placed them in her office. She heard the front door open as she exited and greeted a group of women. Two of the younger women were twins, maybe in their late twenties. "Hello."

"Hi." The eldest woman replied.

"Is there anything I can help you find?"

"No, thank you. We're just browsing until our reservation next door at the restaurant is available. We're having a grandmother-mother-daughter day out."

Elise looked at the cheery faces of the four blonde women. "Sounds like fun."

A knock sounded on the back door. Elise opened it, allowing the delivery man inside.

He wheeled in several boxes on a dolly. "Good morning. Where would you like these?"

"Right here, behind the counter, please." Elise watched as the dolly was raised vertically and the boxes set in place. "Thank you."

"Have a good day."

"You too." Retrieving the utility knife, she cut the tape on the first box and opened the flaps.

"Can I set these here while I continue shopping?"

Elise turned to see one of the twins holding three books. "Sure."

The woman leaned forward as she set the books on the counter and lowered her voice to a whisper. "Can I ask you something?"

Elise nodded.

"Is this place haunted?"

Tales of the building's spirits were well known in the small city. Its strange happenings and mysterious fragrances were acclaimed by many who visited. However, Elise assumed Gabe was responsible for the latest occurrences. "Yes. How did you know?"

"My twin sister is a medium. She gets a headache when there is a spirit nearby."

"That's interesting." Elise watched as the woman's sister approached the counter.

"Yes, my headache came on when I entered the store." She explained. "The spirit is a man about our age."

Elise's eyes began to well with tears. "My husband died in a motorcycle accident several months ago." She took a facial tissue from the box on the counter and dabbed the corner of each eye.

The medium went on. "I can feel his presence is stronger over here. He's by your side as if he is watching over you. Maybe he has unfinished business."

Elise tilted her head to one side. "Unfinished?" She grinned, wondering if he remained nearby until the baby was born. "I thought he was near me. It's nice of you to confirm my suspicion."

"I can't see him. I just feel his energy." The woman reached for Elise's arm and placed her palm upon it. "I didn't mean to upset you. I just thought you would like to know."

"Thanks. Do you detect any other spirits in the store?"

"I did detect a father figure, but I think it is more of a residual energy."

"My dad used to own the bookstore. It was passed down to me when he died about eight years ago."

"That makes sense." The medium confirmed.

Elise glanced at the books they placed on the counter. "Have you finished shopping?"

"Yes, we're all set."

"I think you'll enjoy reading these." Elise scanned and inserted each purchase into a shopping bag. She looked at the medium. "Thank you for your spiritual insight."

"You're more than welcome."

The women left the store eager to experience the acclaimed restaurant food next door.

Taking a deep breath, Elise exhaled. "Well, that was an emotional experience, yet comforting." She removed the books from the boxes, added them to the inventory, and shelved them in their proper place. A rotation of stock was needed. Elise pulled books that had remained on the shelf too long, put them on sale, and set them on a cart near the back of the store.

Marge greeted her when she arrived at noon and looked at the empty boxes. "I see we received books today."

"Yes. It's been slow. I managed to get the books checked into inventory and shelved."

"I'll break down the boxes and take them out back." Marge picked up the utility knife, cut the tape, and collapsed the cardboard.

"I pulled old stock and put the books on sale. I would rather sell them at a discount than return them." Elise explained. "If they don't sell, we can include them with the returns next month."

Gabe had to tell someone. "Marge, we're having a girl!"

Marge walked to the back door with the collapsed boxes in her hands.

He turned to his wife. "We're having a girl!" He was practically dancing.

Elise failed to acknowledge him as well.

"I wish someone could hear me. It doesn't matter. I'm still excited. Who am I kidding? I'm beyond excited!" He reached his arms toward the ceiling, shouting the good news to Heaven.

Elise turned toward her office and walked through her husband's spirit. She stopped abruptly and began brushing invisible cobwebs away from her face and arms.

Returning from the errand, Marge stared at her boss. "What's wrong?"

"I swear I just walked through a giant cobweb." She looked toward the ceiling. "But I don't see any."

Marge scanned the ceiling. "I'll get the broom and go around the store to ensure we don't have any dangling webs. We don't want our customers to think this place is dirty." She turned to go to the utility room.

Elise followed her employee. "You had your lunch, right?"

Marge looked over her shoulder. "I always eat it before coming to work."

"Good, because I have something for you." Elise went into her office while Marge retrieved the broom.

They met in the hallway. Marge, with a broom in her hand, and Elise presenting a cupcake.

"What's this?" Marge stepped closer to view the details of the frosting.

"My baby reveal. I thought you would like to know if I'm having a boy or girl." Elise smiled.

Marge's mouth dropped open, and her eyes widened. "Oh, I would love to know."

"Here, I'll hold the broom while you take a bite of the cupcake. The frosting inside reveals the baby's gender." Elise instructed.

Marge handed over the broom, accepted the cupcake with a devilish grin on her face, and peeled back the liner. She removed the plastic question mark. "Oh, this is exciting." She bit into the cupcake and saw the pink icing. Her eyes became as big as saucers, and she squealed with excitement.

Elise laughed. "Don't choke."

Gabe laughed too.

Marge hurried to swallow the cupcake and hugged Elise. "Congratulations. A little girl, aw, so sweet." She reached for the broom as she took another bite. "This is delicious."

"Thank you." Elise's stomach grumbled. She looked down at her abdomen and placed her hand on it. "I guess it's time for me to eat lunch." Taking a can of soup from the closet in her office, she dumped it into a paper bowl and heated her meal in the microwave.

The small break gave her time to sort through emails and catch up on the list of best-selling books to stock in the store. An email from the city reminded her of the holiday parade on Saturday. "I'll have to stock up on hot chocolate. Maybe Mom can make some cookies too."

At the end of the day, Elise bid Marge farewell, closed the store, and headed home with the three books in her hand.

Janet heard the backdoor open and close as she withdrew a tuna noodle casserole from the oven, paused, and looked at the books Elise placed on the table. "New books?"

"No, they have been in stock for a while. Apparently, Gabe thought the books would be nice for the baby to have. So he knocked all three from a shelf, one right after the other." Elise inhaled the aroma of the steaming casserole. "Smells delicious."

Janet set the hot dish on the table, set the hot pads aside, and picked up the small stack of books. She shuffled them as she read the titles. "Aw, he chose wisely. Such nice books. I can't wait to read them to the baby."

"We need to get a bookcase for her room. She can have her own library then." Elise decided.

"Maybe we can purchase one this weekend." Janet thought for a moment. "What if we have the baby shower guests give a book for her library instead of wrapping their gift?"

"That's a wonderful idea. Wrapping paper is wasteful, and gift bags are expensive."

"I'll have to remember to suggest it to Marge." Janet made a mental note to do so. "Have you thought of a theme for the nursery?" She retrieved two glasses from the cupboard.

Elise brought up the favored theme on her phone. "I searched the other day for nursery theme options and decided on unicorns, fairies, and woodland animals. What do you think?" She handed her phone to her mother.

"It's lovely."

"I'm glad you like it." Elise accepted her phone and pointed to each photo as she explained her plan. "Three walls will be painted an antique pink with the fourth wall in a light sky blue. The curtains can be simple, maybe in off-white. I'll order wall appliques in a forest theme; a large tree, a glow-in-the-dark moon and stars to put on the wall above the crib, a mystical unicorn, and several fairies dressed in various colors."

"That sounds lovely. Marge and I can begin looking for shower invitations and decorations. We need to choose a date for the shower too."

"Oh, and I need to register for shower gifts." Elise sat as her mother placed the drinks on the table.

"Yes, hopefully, you'll receive many of the necessities then. I'll buy the crib and mattress." Janet insisted as she sat.

"Thanks, Mom. I guess we'll have to pick a day to go shopping." Elise scooped a steaming spoonful of casserole onto her plate.

"We'll make a day of it. It'll be fun to pick out the items for your registry. We can even purchase the paint for the nursery too."

Chapter 21

The next afternoon, the door of the bookstore opened. Elise and Marge instinctively looked at the customer who entered. Her designer clothes, shoes, and purse were embellished by her pristine makeup, red lipstick, and fake eyelashes. The woman's brunette hair was perfect, not a single hair out of place.

Elise smiled. "Hello, can we help you find something?"

"Yes." The woman took a piece of paper from her coat pocket and handed it to Elise. "Do you have this book?"

Elise read the scribbled notation. "The title is unfamiliar to me. Let me check to see if it is available." She went to the counter and brought up several warehouse websites that indicated the book was unavailable. "I'm sorry. The book is out of print, and the warehouses do not have a copy in stock."

The woman glared at Elise. "The book is a Christmas gift, and I need it by tomorrow."

Elise tried to explain a second time. "I have no way of getting the book for you, let alone be able to get it by tomorrow."

"But I need it by then."

Elise handed the paper back to the woman. "You may want to ask for the title at a used bookstore or even at one that carries antique books."

"Can you call them for me and find it?"

Elise glanced at Marge, who stood behind the customer displaying her angry face and shaking her head. "I'm sorry, but we don't provide that service. I wish you luck. It's going to be a difficult book to find."

The woman huffed before turning and leaving the store.

Marge perched her fisted hands on her hips and watched through the display window as the woman marched down the sidewalk. "There must be a full moon tonight." She looked at Elise. "Who does she think we are? Her personal shopping service."

"She probably waited too long to try to find the book." Elise chuckled. "Sorry, but I don't do miracles."

A knock sounded on the back door. Marge opened it, allowing the delivery woman to wheel in a dolly filled with boxes. "Good afternoon. Where would you like these?"

"Over here, please." Elise pointed to a spot on the floor behind the counter. She watched as the boxes were put in the designated place. "Thank you."

"Have a good day."

Elise read the packing slip on the outside of the box. "This one has books." She examined the next box. "Oh, our paper shopping bags have arrived. I can't believe how expensive they've gotten. I wish customers would bring reusable cloth book bags for their purchases."

Marge began pulling books from the box to scan to inventory. "As Ben Franklin said, "Take care of the pennies, and the dollars will take care of themselves.""

"It isn't easy. The books are already priced when we receive them. Thank goodness we have side items to help us stay in business."

The bell rang as the front door opened. Scurrying footsteps of little feet entered.

"Now, remember you can only select one book each, so choose wisely." The elderly voice echoed throughout the store as the door closed.

Elise came from behind the counter and saw an older woman with three young children. "Hello. Can I help you find something?"

The grandmotherly woman grinned. "Yes, where are the children's books?"

Elise looked at the youthful faces staring up at her. She estimated their age. "Right this way." She led them to the children's section and pointed as she explained the locations. "This section is for the younger readers, this one middle, and this one advance."

"Thank you."

"If you need any assistance, let me know." Elise returned to the counter, picked up the packing slip, and checked off the books as Marge continued to remove them from the box. "Looks like only one is on backorder."

"That's good." Marge began scanning the books into inventory.

"I think we are ready." The grandmother herded her three grandchildren to the counter.

Elise smiled. "So, have each of you chosen a special book?"

The children nodded and placed their books on the counter.

Elise scanned each book and announced the total. The woman took out her credit card and waited as Elise put the books in a paper bag.

"Oh, could you please put each book in a separate bag? The kids would like to each carry their own book."

Elise forced a smile on her face as she accepted the woman's credit card. "Sure." She withdrew two of the books and put them each in a bag before running the credit card in the machine to complete the sale. "Here's your credit card and receipt." She returned the card to the woman and picked up the three bags. "And here are your books. Thank you for stopping in. Please, come again." She watched the children peek inside the bags to ensure they had their correct books.

"Thank you. Let's go, kids." The woman led the way out of the bookstore with the children following. One spotted Petey sleeping on his chair and wandered toward him. She gently stroked his fur without him waking.

"Leave the cat alone. We have to go." The grandmother commanded before stepping onto the sidewalk. The little girl left the store and shut the door behind her.

Elise sighed. "Didn't I just say how expensive bags have become?"

"Ironic, isn't it." Marge continued to scan.

"I think our customers need an incentive."

"What do you have in mind?" Marge placed a scanned book on the growing stack to be shelved.

Elise thought for a moment. "What if we encourage customers to bring in a reusable book bag for their purchase? If they do, then we can enter their name into a monthly drawing for a gift card."

"Brilliant, Elise. Good idea." Gabe proudly stated.

Marge tilted her head to the side as she nodded. "It may work, but we will have to post it on our website and social media. A sign in the display window would be a good idea too."

"With so many shopping for Christmas gifts, it may help us save on bag usage."

Marge shelved the new arrivals and stored the books that would be released early next week.

Elise added the promotion to the bookstore website, made a sign for the window, and posted it on social media. She took the clear glass fishbowl from the closet, printed a second sign, and taped it to the bowl. "We have pre-made slips for drawings, don't we, Marge?" She brought up the documents on the computer.

"I think they are under 'Gift Basket Drawing Slip.'"

Elise scanned the list of documents. "Here it is." She printed off several sheets and cut the blank entry slips apart. "The holiday parade is Saturday. I need to pick up some hot chocolate to ensure we have enough. I'm certain many will be stopping into the store to warm up."

"Let's hope they do some holiday shopping too." Marge smiled.

Chapter 22

The following day, winter blew in with a vengeance. It was eager to make its presence known after slumbering for three seasons.

Elise delayed leaving for the bookstore, allotting time for the road crews to clear the streets. She backed her car out of the garage and admired the picturesque whiteness covering the trees like sprinkled powdered sugar. Driving in the blustery weather was an undaunting challenge for her. The only element she feared was ice, both while driving and walking. She guarded her steps as she went to the bookstore's back door, unlocked it, and entered.

~

Boxes with the perfect off-white crib, nightstand, and low dresser, which would also be used as a changing table, littered the living room. With Elise at work, Janet painted the empty nursery. She stepped back to admire the colorful walls. "Looks good. Now for the curtains."

Janet retrieved the sewing machine from the hallway closet and the few yards of off-white fabric they had purchased for the curtain. She managed to finish the window covering as her daughter arrived home from the bookstore.

Eager to see the nursery in its entirety, they ate a simple dinner of sandwiches and chips. They assembled the furniture and set it in place. Janet hung the curtains while Elise applied the appliques to the walls. They stood near the doorway and admired their accomplishment.

"It's perfect." Janet put her arm around her daughter's waist and squeezed.

"Lovely, for our little princess." Gabe smiled.

"I like it. We just need a rocking chair and maybe a throw rug by the crib to complete it." Elise thought out loud. "Oh, I made something for the nursery." She went to her bedroom, took the vellum-covered containers from a box, and set them on the nightstand. "I made these. The baby will know what her daddy and grandpa's faces looked like. I thought they would make nice nightlights." She paused as she stepped back and looked at the photos. "Gabe and Dad can watch over the baby while she sleeps."

"They're lovely," Janet added. "Maybe we can put them on a shelf or on top of the bookcase once we get it. She should be able to see them easily then."

"Good idea." Elise agreed.

"Well, we'll have to set a date for the baby shower."

"Isn't it too soon?"

"No. We may have to rent a hall, and you know how quickly they can be booked." Janet cautioned.

"True. I was thinking sometime at the end of February or early March. Obviously, on a Sunday. Maybe a brunch or early afternoon luncheon. What do you think?"

"I guess it will depend on the venue and what is available."

"Some of the restaurants have banquet rooms. So that may be an option too." Elise added.

"I guess we will have to inquire and see which option is best. Marge and I will call and inquire."

Janet looked at the room once again. "Absolutely beautiful."

Gabe stood with his arms crossed over his chest as he leaned against the doorframe. "It's lovely, as she will be."

~

The morning of the holiday parade brought additional foot traffic into the bookstore. It continued throughout the day. Marge tried to mop the slushy snow tracked inside, hoping to avoid anyone slipping and falling. Having done her best, she returned the mop to the utility room. On her way to the counter, she saw a misplaced book on a shelf, picked it up, and passed Elise standing behind the counter.

With the bookstore hours extended for additional holiday shopping, Elise warned Marge. "It's going to be a long weekend."

As a group of customers entered, they assisted those seeking certain books, ordered books, and were pleased to see newly stocked books selling quickly.

"It's nice to have customers who support a small independent bookstore," Marge added as she finished a sale. "It looks like your promotion to have customers bring in their own shopping bags is working." She pointed to the fishbowl that was half-full of entries.

"We'll have to remember to draw a winner at the end of the month."

People gathered along the street as the start of the Christmas parade neared. It was usually time for the bookstore to close, but tonight many of the people attending the festivities would flood into the store to warm up and shop afterward. Elise watched from the display window as the parade began.

A man rushed into the bookstore and went to the counter.

Marge looked up from the computer screen. "May I help you?"

"Can I have a bag?"

In question, Marge's eyebrows raised. "For?"

"My daughter needs one to collect the candy they throw during the parade."

Taken back by the rude request, Marge did not want to hand out an expensive bag the store used for paying customers. Instead, she looked under the cupboard and found a plastic shopping bag they used to line the garbage can and gave it to the man.

"Thanks." He hurried out the door to join his family.

"Some people." Marge simply shook her head and joined her boss at the window to watch the parade with its high school band leading the way.

Janet entered through the front door. "Sorry, I'm late. I couldn't find a parking spot."

Elise watched her mother take off her coat and toss it over a stool behind the counter. "I was wondering where you were."

"Glad you could make it," Marge added as Janet joined them at the window.

"Oh, look how the horses are lit with lights." Elise smiled.

"They're beautiful." Janet touched her daughter's arm. "Did you want to come and watch the tree lighting ceremony with me?" She assumed Marge could watch the store.

Elise shook her head. "We've been extremely busy. I'm sure we'll be swamped with customers until we close at nine o'clock."

"Well, I promised some friends from church I would have a late dessert with them. I'll meet you back home," Janet explained.

Elise nodded as she watched a colorfully lit float with a holiday theme pass by the window.

~

When Elise arrived home at ten o'clock, her mother's car was absent from the garage. She entered the dark house and flipped on the kitchen light. It had been a long day. She wanted nothing more than to take a shower and crawl into bed. She turned on the living room lamp on her way to the bathroom. Elise smiled as she saw the decorated artificial Christmas tree her mother put up during the day. Plugging in the lights, she took a step backward to view it in its entirety. Elise recognized several ornaments from her childhood, some handmade during her elementary years. As was her family's tradition, an angel atop with its arms open looked down upon her.

She thought of Gabe. Tears crept into her eyes as she stared at the gifts beneath the tree, knowing his name was absent from the tags. However, in his place were plenty of presents with 'baby' on them. Pleased her mother had taken the initiative, Elise was eager to wrap the little dresses in various colors, tights, tiny shoes, and the one-piece sleeper pajamas she had in her bedroom closet and place them beneath the tree.

The back door opened and closed. "Hello." Janet's voice rang out as she hung up her coat.

Elise wiped her eyes and forced a smile on her face. "Did you have fun with your friends?"

"Yes, it's always a good time when we get together. So how were sales today?"

"Whenever the city hosts an event, sales are always good. I believe we even outsold what we did last year."

"Good." Janet joined her daughter before the Christmas tree. "I think it looks nice this year."

"It's lovely, Mom."

"Did you notice the gifts for the baby?"

Elise smiled. "Yes, I'm eager to see what you got for her."

Janet looked at her daughter's face. "You look tired."

"I am. It's been a long day. I think I'll take a shower and go to bed. I have to work tomorrow."

"On Sunday?"

"Yes, extended holiday hours, and Marge has tomorrow off. Goodnight."

~

Elise spent the next few weeks baking cookies with her mother, wrapping presents, and putting in extra hours at the bookstore. She planned to lock the front door on Christmas Eve at three o'clock. Anticipating a last-minute rush, Marge insisted on coming in to help. At noon, Elise gave her loyal employee a gift card to an upscale restaurant, a box of chocolates, and a bottle of wine and insisted she leave at noon to prepare for the holiday with her large family.

Locking the front door at closing time, Elise waited for the last customer to make his purchase.

"I'm sorry to keep you so late." He apologized as Elise handed him the paper bag containing his purchase.

"Quite all right. Merry Christmas." Elise walked to the front door, unlocked it, and opened it for the customer.

"Merry Christmas," he said as he left the store.

Alone, Elise flipped each light off, systematically casting the store into darkness before going to the check-out counter. Illuminated by the single overhead light, she began her closing routine. Elise updated the website and printed a new sign for the front door to announce the change in store hours. "It will be nice to have Sunday to myself again." Satisfied with the profitable holiday sales, she looked around the store and sighed. "Dad, I think I've done you proud."

Gabe smiled. He went to a bookshelf and knocked a novel onto the floor.

Elise smiled, knowing her husband was the reason the book fell. She went to the aisle, picked up the book, and tilted it to illuminate the chapter title. "Determined To Succeed." She sighed. "Yes, Gabe. I'm determined to succeed in the bookstore and," she placed her hand on her growing belly, "determined to be the best mom I can be to our child. I just wish you were here to help me do so."

"I am." He conveyed.

She placed the book on the shelf and left the bookstore. "Now to go to church and then a day off to celebrate Christmas.

As was their tradition, Janet and Elise attended midnight Mass. The church's lights were dim as they entered a pew. Elise knelt, bowed her head, and prayed for the safe delivery of her child, for Gabe's guidance, and for God's grace in her endeavors throughout the remainder of her life. Even though Gabe was not physically by her side, she was comforted to know he was nearby. She looked at the altar, beautifully decorated with pine trees illuminated with white lights and pots of poinsettias. A manger with its symbolic statues was to the left of the altar. Music echoed throughout the vaulted nave as the choir sang from the balcony. It was a calm and peaceful way to end the day. She sat in the pew and listened to the choir's rendition of Oh, Come All Ye Faithful.

The baby's hand, or perhaps her foot, traced the inside of her belly. It was a feathery touch, a gentle reminder that she continued to grow safely within her. At twenty-four weeks, it was finally obvious she was expecting a baby instead of some people assuming she was gaining weight. She placed her hand on her abdomen, looked down, and smiled.

Janet's attention was drawn to her daughter. "Is she moving?"

Elise nodded, took her mother's hand, and placed it beneath her palm, where she felt the baby's tickling touch. An icy coolness settled on the back of her hand. She assumed the cold draft was from someone entering the church. As if right on cue, the baby kicked, causing both women to smile and look at each other.

"Merry Christmas, Elise."

"Merry Christmas, Mom."

"Merry Christmas to you both." Gabe leaned toward his wife's bulbous belly. "And Merry Christmas to you too, little one." The baby kicked again.

~

Janet and Elise slept until mid-morning. They began their day with a big breakfast of eggs, bacon, and French toast. They took their time opening gifts while Christmas music played in the background.

"Here, Mom, you open this one for the baby." Elise insisted as she handed her mother a present she had purchased and wrapped.

Janet smiled, curious to see what was inside. She removed the decorative Christmas paper and opened the box to reveal a frilly little dress. "Oh, it's precious. Can't you just imagine her in it?"

"I thought it was cute," Elise admitted.

"Now, you open one for the baby." Janet urged as she pointed to the intended gift.

Elise untied the rattle from the ribbon and set it aside. She tore off the wrapping paper and opened the box to reveal a framed mat with photos of her, Gabe, and an empty oval spot for the baby's picture. She was silent as she stared at the thoughtful gift.

"Now, I didn't want to make you cry, but I thought this would look nice on the baby's nursery wall," Janet explained.

Elise touched the glass where her husband's smiling face stared back at her. She had forgotten his smile, the features of his face, as if they were slowly fading from her memory. "Thank you, Mom. It's perfect."

"Open another." Janet encouraged.

A large box topped with a bow puzzled Elise. She pulled it toward her and unwrapped it to reveal two blankets made from Gabe's tee shirts, one for her and a small one for the baby. "Mom, they're perfect."

They remained in their pajamas for the entire day, read the books they gave each other, and enjoyed a lovely ham dinner. The evening concluded with a movie and a big bowl of buttered popcorn.

As Elise went to bed that evening, she reflected on a year ago when she and Gabe celebrated their first Christmas together as husband and wife. Little did she know that it would be their last. "Goodnight, Gabe. Merry Christmas." She whispered.

"Goodnight, Elise. Merry Christmas to you too."

Chapter 23

Elise rose the next morning feeling rested. It was Sunday, which meant the bookstore was closed. "Two days off work in a row? I almost don't know what to do with myself."

She washed the baby's new clothes and added them to the nursery closet and drawers. Elise hung the gift from her mother on the wall, eager to add the baby's photo. Removing the last of her presents from beneath the Christmas tree, she stood for a moment. It looked bare. After putting her gifts away, Elise munched on Christmas cookies while reading the book she began the previous day. In the evening, she helped her mother with a jigsaw puzzle.

"I think I'll display the bookstore Christmas decorations until January 6th." Elise placed another piece in the puzzle.

"Ah, the Epiphany and the twelfth day of Christmas." Janet reasoned as she scrutinized the pieces for a possible fit.

"Meanwhile, I can put some of the Christmas books on sale and pack away the rest for next year, pull items to return for credit, and think about starting inventory." Elise thought out loud as she placed a piece into the puzzle.

Janet sighed. "Running a bookstore never stops, does it?"

"Nope. I always have to think ahead."

"Would you like me to come in and help with inventory again this year?" Janet tried to put a piece of the puzzle in place, but it did not fit.

"Yes, it will get done quicker with the three of us working at it." Elise tapped a piece into place. "I'll have to put up Valentine decorations soon too. Maybe a display of romance books as well."

~

On a frigid Sunday in mid-January, Elise, Janet, and Marge tackled the enormous task of taking inventory of the entire bookstore. Thankfully,

Elise and Marge had pulled and sent books back to the publisher, thus giving them less to count.

The trio took a break when pizza, salad, and breadsticks were delivered for lunch.

"Ah, it feels good to sit down for a minute," Elise admitted as she sat in a folding chair and bit into a slice of pizza. Petey circled around her legs, often looking toward her with a silent plea for a taste of her food.

"Your growing baby bump is pulling on your back muscles." Marge stabbed her salad with a plastic fork. "I hate to say it, but it's only going to worsen until you deliver."

"You may want to reduce your work hours too," Janet suggested.

"My customers expect the bookstore to be open during its normal times." Elise insisted.

"True," Marge began, "but, when I'm here, you can open in the morning, go home and rest during lunch, and then return to close, or take a day off now and then."

Elise considered their suggestions while she ate another bite of pizza and politely swallowed before replying. "As I get closer to my delivery date, I'll see how I feel. On days when I'm tired, I'll put in fewer hours. On the other hand, I may be able to work right up until I deliver. I mean, other women do it." She handed Petey a tiny bite of sausage. He sniffed it and gently took it from her hand.

Janet nodded. "Marge, I think your ideas are good, and it's nice to know Elise can rely on you if the need should arise."

"With my children on their own, working at the bookstore helps fill my time. It keeps me busy and my mind sharp." Marge bit into a warm, doughy breadstick.

With their appetites appeased, the women returned to work for a few more hours until Elise was ready to quit working.

"We still have non-fiction and puzzles to do. I can do that tomorrow." Elise sighed as she ran the palm of her hand over her bulbous abdomen. "I think it's time we all went home."

"Sounds good to me," Janet added.

Marge scanned the bookstore. Many of the shelves were disheveled and needed fluffing to make them presentable. "We definitely accomplished a lot."

Unbeknownst to the women, the cold winter day had turned to a blustery blizzard. They brushed off their cars as their engines warmed in the darkness of night and carefully drove home.

Janet looked through the falling snow at the covered road. "It looks pretty thick. Do you want me to drive?"

Elise gripped the steering wheel. She was sure her knuckles were turning white inside her gloves. "No, I got it. We'll just go slowly."

Even though they didn't have far to go, the drive took twice as long for Elise and Janet to arrive home. They spotted several cars in ditches and even a rollover accident. The emergency vehicles, with their flashing lights, surrounded the scene.

The car fishtailed as Elise drove up the driveway. She pulled into the garage and exhaled with relief as she put the car in park and shut off the engine.

"Well, that was a fun ride," Janet commented, heavy with sarcasm.

"At least we arrived unscathed." Elise entered the house carrying a bag of books to review. "Since publishers have reduced the number of books they send us lately, I need to review these and get them wrapped so we have enough for next month. We will allow our customers one 'blind date with a book' with every purchase."

"Would you like some help? We can turn on an old movie while you review it and I wrap them. Maybe have a cup of hot chocolate too?"

"Sounds great, Mom."

~

The bookstore was decorated for Valentine's the next day. A display of adult romance novels and themed books for children were featured. Elise glanced at both display windows, pleased with their presentation. Between herself, Marge, and her mom, they had wrapped every free book in brown paper and wrote three clues about their subject matter.

As the month on the calendar changed, Elise filled a basket with the blind dates and allowed customers to choose one after paying for their purchase.

She joined Marge behind the counter. "I must say, romance novels can be a letdown to reality."

Marge looked away from the computer to her boss. "How so?"

"They always have a happy ending. Not exactly reality, is it?"

Assuming Elise reflected on the tragedy in her life, Marge added her perspective. "I think life likes to test us, some more than others. I agree, there isn't always a happy ending, but I think what is more important is to treasure the happy moments."

Gabe nodded. "Well said, Marge."

Marge ventured a suggestion. "You never know, Prince Charming may walk through the door one day and sweep you off your feet."

Elise scowled as she busied herself posting the blind date promotion on the website. "I'm not interested in any Prince Charming."

The customers were pleased with the promotion. However, with many blind dates to choose from, some had difficulty selecting only one book.

Elise looked at a woman who stood before the basket and labored over her choice of a blind date. She held a book in each hand and one in the crook of her arm. "Have you chosen your blind date with a book?"

"No," the woman replied as she shuffled the books while looking at the clues written on the brown paper wrappings.

"Well, it's a tough decision, but you'll have to choose only one," Elise emphasized.

The woman stared at Elise as if she had spoken to her in a foreign tongue. "But they all look interesting. How am I going to choose just one?"

Elise smiled. "Of the three, which is the least interesting to you?"

The woman shuffled the books, singled out one, and handed it to Elise. "This one."

Elise took the book and placed it back in the basket. "Now, let me have the remaining two."

The woman reluctantly handed the books to Elise, who put them behind her back and shuffled them back and forth between her hands. "There, now pick one of my arms."

The woman looked from one arm to the other and then pointed to Elise's left arm.

"Here is your blind date with a book. But just like an actual blind date, some are good, and some are bad. Let's hope you selected a good one." Elise presented the book.

The woman smiled. "That was fun, and you made my choice an easy one. Thank you, and thanks for the book."

"You're welcome. Come back again." Elise returned the unchosen book to the display.

"Well done, Elise." Marge complimented.

Chapter 24

Elise's belly had grown substantially, and her 'pregnancy waddle' developed over the next month. She treasured every day of her pregnancy, knowing she would only experience the miraculous event once in her life.

"I wish the weeks of March would go by quicker than they do," Elise admitted to her mother as she drove to the baby shower. "It's such a dirty month. The snow is no longer white, and puddles of water are everywhere."

"It's Mother Nature's way of announcing the rebirth of a season. Trees will be budding soon.

Some of the spring flowers have already pushed through the remaining snow."

The car jarred suddenly. "And it is pothole season once again." Elise joked as she turned her car into the restaurant parking lot.

Janet met Marge earlier that morning and decorated the banquet room in pink and off-white with unicorns, fairies, and plenty of balloons. The women thought it would be nice and less messy to serve cupcakes for dessert. The menu consisted of chicken salad, fruit salad, broccoli salad, warm rolls with butter, and various beverages.

After parking the car, Elise entered the banquet room before her mother.

Marge stood to one side of the gift table with her phone poised as the guest of honor entered.

Elise took one step into the room and paused as she looked about the room. "Oh, it's lovely."

The cupcakes were topped with pink icing and candied unicorns and fairies. Bouquets of balloons were placed around the room. The tables were cloaked in pink linen. In the center of each table was a lovely potted plant and mints scattered at its base.

Elise looked at her mother and employee, who was a dear friend. "Thank you. This is more than I imagined."

"Come," Janet urged, "we need to take your picture before the guests arrive. Stand in front of the serving table."

Elise smiled as she posed, and her mother and Marge snapped several pictures.

"Turn sideways, so we can get a photo of your baby bump," Janet instructed. Her daughter happily complied.

Within minutes, guests passed through the doorway. Elise recognized most of the women. Those she did not know, she assumed, were guests of Gabe's family. Her heart seemed to skip a beat when Gabe's mother and grandmother entered the room. She leaned toward her mother and whispered. "Wish me luck."

Marge greeted the guests, accepted their gifts, and placed them on a table with the others.

Elise knew she had never earned her mother-in-law's approval. She assumed it was because Gabe was Barbara's only son, and she wanted him to marry Samantha, a wealthy young lady, and her preferred choice for his wife. Even though Gabe insisted he and Samantha were only friends, his mother insinuated the two were destined to wed.

Elise and Barbara had not spoken since she informed her of her pregnancy. She recalled how her mother-in-law had ignored her at Gabe's funeral and assumed Barbara blamed her for his death. Taking a deep breath, Elise approached the two women.

Barbara scowled and stared at her protruding belly.

"Hello, Barbara, Grandma Helen. It's good of you to come." Elise greeted.

"Yes, well, you're carrying my grandchild. I'm obligated." Barbara looked past Elise as if inspecting the room. "I assume the baby is a girl."

Grandma Helen stepped forward and embraced Elise. "You look lovely, my dear. Pregnancy obviously agrees with you."

Elise was at ease in the woman's arms. She took a step back. "Thank you." Sighing, she searched for a topic of conversation. "I think Mom and Marge did a wonderful job decorating. It's the baby's nursery theme. Do you like it?"

Barbara looked to the ceiling. "Unicorns and fairies are old clichés. Everyone seems to be using that theme."

"Now, Barbara." Helen scolded. "I think the theme is lovely. Very princess-like and a fantasy theme that will spark your daughter's imagination."

"Thank you, Grandma Helen."

Janet recognized the tension in her daughter's face and went to her side. "We're glad you could come to the shower." She looked at Gabe's mother. "It's nice to see you again, Barbara."

The shrewd woman simply nodded with a smirk on her face.

Janet turned to Helen. "And you look wonderful, Helen."

"Thank you." Helen extended her arms and embraced the hostess of the gathering. "I wouldn't have missed this for the world. I've several grandchildren, but this will be my first great-grandchild."

"It's exciting, isn't it? Well, we are about to begin. Would you like something to drink?" Janet led the women to a table and retrieved their requested beverages.

Elise's false smile faded from her face. She was troubled by the women's attendance and thought it may have been better if they had just sent a gift.

Marge stepped beside Elise and crossed her arms over her chest. "This ought to make the shower interesting." She stared at Gabe's relatives.

Elise watched as the women sat at a table, and her mother went to retrieve their drinks. "She's never liked me. I can't for the life of me understand why. I've been kind, courteous, and polite, often going out of my way to please her."

"From her perspective, you took her little boy away from her. She tried to control him and set him up with a woman of her choice. One thing a parent cannot do is control their child's heart. Gabe chose you. He was a wonderful husband who loved you dearly. I think she couldn't accept that he went against her wishes. She's a bitter woman."

Gabe nodded. "Marge is right. Mom was controlling."

"So, you're saying Gabe was a mama's boy?"

Marge smiled and nodded. "In Barbara's eyes, yes." She watched as Janet took her place before the serving table, looked at her, and nodded. "I think that's my signal that we are to begin. Time to take your seat, Elise."

As Marge joined Janet at the front of the room, Elise sat in the decorated chair designated for the mother-to-be.

"Hello, everyone. Thank you for coming to Elise's baby shower. We have a few fun games for you to play while eating. The first is to write the vocabulary word for a baby animal. For example, a baby swan is a cygnet."

Elise glanced at her mother-in-law, who sighed and looked to the ceiling in disgust.

"The second game," Janet continued, "is to guess the number of candies in the baby bottle that will be passed around the room. We have one other game, which we will explain later. I'll pass out the pens and game cards while you help yourself to lunch. Marge will let you know when your table can go through the buffet line."

Marge stood next to Elise. "Since you are the guest of honor, you are first to go through the buffet."

With her bulbous belly leading the way, Elise selected a plate and filled it with a sampling from each dish. She was soon joined by the women at her table. Some she knew from church, Jen from high school, and a few dear customers from the bookstore. The conversation was kept light with the usual questions of 'How are you feeling?', 'Is the nursery ready?', 'Have you chosen a name?', and 'When are you due?'. While waiting for their table to be dismissed, the guests focused on the games, trying to guess the number of candies as the baby bottle came to their table. Others discussed the correct vocabulary words for baby animals.

Even though Elise tried to avoid eye contact, she glanced at Barbara, who ate a bite of chicken salad and sternly looked at her. Their eyes locked like two alley cats about to fight. Elise grinned, causing Barbara to look away.

Aileen, the bookstore's frequent customer, noticed the silent exchange. She leaned toward Elise, who sat next to her and placed her hand on her arm. "Don't let her get to you. We all know she's a bitch."

Elise chuckled as she looked into the elderly woman's kind blue eyes. "Thanks. I needed to hear that." She sighed as she looked back at Barbara. "How can one person be so wicked?"

"I think the word is jealous, maybe even spiteful." Aileen stared at the shrewd woman.

Elise looked at her dear customer. "Because I married Gabe?"

"Yes, you took her baby boy away from her." The elderly customer patted Elise's hand reassuringly.

It eased Elise's mind to hear Aileen reiterate Marge's opinion.

Jen leaned toward Elise. "Try to ignore her. This is your day, remember." She finished giving Cynthis a bottle and managed to burp her before the woman next to her insisted on holding the baby.

Gabe toured the room. He was ashamed of how his mother was treating his wife and considered tipping her glass of punch onto her lap so she would leave the party early. He sighed, knowing the baby was her granddaughter, and even though she was obstinate, he wanted her to be a part of the celebration.

Janet and Marge sat to eat their lunch. When the waitresses came to clear the dishes, guests helped themselves to the cupcakes and mints. The answers to the games were revealed, and prizes were awarded.

"Since many of you don't like to play shower games, the last game is quite simple." Janet began. "Under one chair at each table is a pink bow. The person who has the bow under their seat may take home the potted plant on your table."

The women looked under their chairs until someone at each table discovered a bow. As luck would have it, Barbara sat in a winning seat. She took the plant as it was placed before her and pushed it toward her mother as if it were poisonous. "I don't want that thing. It's probably infested with bugs."

"Now, Barbara." Helen scolded. "It's a lovely plant. I'll take it home and set it on my windowsill."

"Elise," Janet began as she placed a chair before the gift table, "it's time for you to open your gifts."

Elise stared at the many presents before taking her place. "My goodness. You have all been very generous."

Gift after gift was placed before her. Elise read the card and passed it to Marge. She held up each book and announced the accompanied present while Marge recorded the gift on the back of each card.

"This is the last one." Janet placed the final gift before her daughter.

Elise read the card. It was from her mother. Inside the package, she discovered a beautiful baby quilt made in the nursery's colors. The edge was trimmed in three-inch eyelet lace. It was perfect in every way, made with love by her baby's grandmother. Tears pricked Elise's eyes as she looked at her mother. "Thank you, it's lovely."

Janet smiled, holding back her tears as well. She turned to the guests. "We have the room for another twenty minutes. If you haven't helped yourself to dessert, feel free to do so. You're welcome to stay and visit until they kick us out." Several women chuckled. "Thank you all for coming and helping Elise celebrate her baby."

Elise ensured she thanked each guest for attending as they said their farewells and left.

Barbara and Grandma Helen waited for their moment with Elise.

"What a lovely baby shower, Elise." Helen began. "The food was wonderful, and your gifts are lovely." She winked. "I really like my plant too."

"I'm glad you do. It was good to see you again. Thank you for coming." Elise wrapped her arms around Gabe's grandmother and kissed her cheek. She turned to Barbara.

"Thank you for the gift and for attending." Elise forced herself to grin.

Barbara's face was unsmiling. "You're welcome. I assume you will call when the baby arrives."

"Yes."

Without another word, Barbara turned away and left the room.

Grandma Helen smiled apologetically. "I hope you have an easy delivery. Call or stop by for a visit anytime. Goodbye, dear."

"I will. Goodbye."

As the last guest left the room, Elise looked at the table of gifts and the stack of books for the baby's library. "I don't know if all of this will fit in my car."

Marge paused in gathering the uneaten mints from the table. "I'll put some of them in my car and follow you home."

Janet stood with two bouquets of balloons. "I hate to pop these. Should we take them home and let them float on the nursery ceiling until they lose their helium?"

Elise smiled. "I think that's a lovely idea. We'll have to take a picture of it for the baby book."

With both cars filled with gifts, Janet tried to keep the balloons out of her daughter's line of vision as they drove home.

"Marge, do you want to see the baby's room before I release the balloons?" Janet offered as she carried the last gift from the car.

"Absolutely, Elise has told me about the details, but it would be nice to see the finished product."

Janet, the proud grandma-to-be, led the way, opened the door, and turned on the light.

Marge inhaled. "Oh, it's lovely. I love the tree and the stars and moon on the wall above the crib. It's perfect."

"We just need to add the items Elise received as gifts today, and the nursery will be ready for the baby to arrive."

Elise stood in the doorway, secretly wishing the baby would arrive now, but she had four weeks until her due date. Looking down at her feet, they were swollen. Her back ached too.

"Well, I shouldn't keep you." Marge stepped toward the doorway.

"Thank you, Marge, for helping with the shower. I truly appreciate all you have done." Elise hugged her employee and friend.

"You are more than welcome. I'm glad I was a part of it."

Janet added. "Yes, thank you."

They escorted Marge to the door and said their farewells.

Janet turned to her daughter, who looked tired. She glanced down at Elise's swollen feet bulging from her ballerina flats. "Why don't you sit in Dad's chair and put your feet up. Maybe you would like to begin writing the thank you cards."

With a sigh, Elise gladly accepted the suggestion.

Chapter 25

Spring announced its presence with budding trees, blooming flowers, and rain. Lots of rain. Even though her back ached, Elise insisted on working until she delivered the baby. She loosened the laces on her tennis shoes to accommodate her swollen feet.

Marge shook her head as she watched her boss waddle to the front door and lock it, closing the bookstore for the evening. "When is that daughter of yours arriving?"

"The doctor said any day now." Elise placed the palms of her hands on the small of her back and arched backward. "My due date is Sunday."

"On Easter?" Marge returned a wayward pen to the pencil holder.

Elise smiled. "Hopefully, my little Easter egg will hatch early." Even though she was uncomfortable, she cherished each roll of the baby, kick, and delicate touch. In a way, she did not want her pregnancy to end, yet she was eager to hold her daughter in her arms and experience motherhood.

"Well, she looks as if she is ready to greet the world." Marge stared at the baby bump that had shifted downward.

"Yes, her head is grinding on my pelvis. I assume she will push her way out soon."

"With any luck, I'll receive a call from you to cover the store tomorrow. Goodnight." Marge headed for the back door.

"Let's hope so. Goodnight, Marge."

Alone in the store, Elise sighed as she began her register closing routine. Her abdomen tensed, causing her to freeze for a moment and breathe deeply. "Goodness, another Braxton Hicks. I sure have had a lot of these for the past three months."

Gabe stared at his wife. "That one seemed pretty strong. Are you sure nothing is wrong?"

Elise swept the floor before turning off the lights. Dumping the contents of the dustpan into the wastepaper basket, she paused to catch her breath as another contraction sent a shockwave through her body. Returning the dustpan and boom to the utility room, she ran her hands over her abdomen. "Time to go home and put my feet up." Liquid trickled down her legs. "Seriously, I'm peeing myself?"

Gabe paced. "There is something wrong, isn't there?"

Elise waddled to the bathroom, pulled down her dampened clothes, and sat on the toilet. After relieving herself, she went to stand but sat back down again as liquid continued to trickle from her. "My goodness. I still have to pee?" She tried to stand again. A contraction forced her to sit. More liquid dribbled out of her. "Am I in labor?"

"Labor? Oh, God, Elise, go to the hospital." Gabe urged.

Reaching inside her pants pocket, she retrieved her phone and called her mom.

"Hello, Elise."

"Mom, what does it feel like when your water breaks?"

The tone in her daughter's voice caused Janet's heart to beat a little faster. "I don't know. The doctor had to break my water. Why do you ask?"

"I'm sitting on the toilet because I thought I had to pee, but every time I try to get up, I just keep peeing."

"Any contractions?"

"Yes, they started after lunch, but I thought they were just Braxton Hicks."

"Have you started timing them?"

Elise shook her head. "No, I was trying to ignore them to get a few more things done before coming home."

"Time them and call me back. If the contractions are five minutes apart, drive to the hospital, and I'll meet you there. Otherwise, come home. We'll wait until they are within five minutes and go to the hospital together.

"Ok." Elise put the stopwatch app on her phone and waited for the next contraction. She pressed start. When the second contraction began, she pressed 'stop' and looked at the elapsed time. "Eight minutes."

Frantically pulling on the roll of toilet paper, Elise wadded it around the palm of her hand, put it in the crotch of her underwear, and pulled up her clothes. After flushing the toilet, she held her hand beneath her swollen abdomen for support as she finished closing the bookstore and drove home.

Janet turned toward the back door as she heard it open and watched Elise step into the kitchen. "I thought you were going to call me?"

"Sorry, but I'm preoccupied at the moment." Elise went to her bedroom, grabbed a change of clothing, and entered the bathroom.

Janet paced outside the bathroom door. "How far apart are your contractions?"

"When I left the bookstore, they were eight minutes apart." Grabbing a sanitary napkin, she adhered it to a clean pair of underwear and finished dressing.

Gabe exhaled, relieved Elise had made it home safely, and someone was nearby to help her. He paced in the hallway.

Elise opened the door and tossed her soiled clothing into the hamper in her bedroom. She looked at her mother's worried expression. "Well, it feels good to have dry clothes on again. I'll call the doctor and tell her my water broke and how far apart my contractions are."

"Good idea." Gabe nodded.

"Since your water broke, she may want you to go to the hospital right away." Janet assumed.

Elise waved her hand toward her mother, signaling her to remain quiet as the phone rang and the service answered.

"Hello, Doctor Martin's Office."

"Hello, this is Elise Messenger. Doctor Martin told me to call her if my water broke. It broke about a half-hour ago."

"How far apart are your contractions?"

"About eight minutes, maybe less."

"When is your due date?"

"Tomorrow."

"Is this your first child?"

"Yes."

"When your contractions are five minutes apart, go to the hospital and be admitted. I'll let Doctor Martin know of your current labor condition."

"OK."

"Call if you have any other questions."

"Ok. Bye." Elise looked at her mom. "We have to wait until my contractions are five minutes apart."

Elise arched her back again. The pressure on her spine was increasing. She grabbed the kitchen chair and squatted, hoping to alleviate the pain.

"Let me know when you are having a contraction." Janet brought up the stopwatch on her cell phone and waited.

"Now." Elise rubbed her abdomen. She could feel it tighten beneath the palm of her hand. Exhaling, she stood. Her back pain increased. "This is really starting to hurt."

"Breathe through it." Her mother encouraged her. "The baby is probably dropping lower."

Gabe walked beside his wife as she began to pace. She stopped as another contraction started.

"Now," Elise told her mother.

Janet pressed stop. "Six minutes. I'll get your bag and put it in the car."

Elise nodded. "It's in my closet." She continued to pace.

Janet retrieved the bag and placed it in the car. She turned to see Elise at the back door. The strained look of labor masked her daughter's face. "We better go to the hospital now. Let me grab my purse while you buckle yourself in."

Elise felt another gush of amniotic fluid as she sat in the front seat of her mother's car.

Gabe slid in behind his wife. "You'll be fine, Elise. Just breathe."

Janet tossed her purse into the back seat, causing Gabe to instinctively duck as it passed through him.

Elise fisted her hands with each contraction, tried to breathe, and prayed they would arrive at the hospital in time.

Within minutes, Janet parked the car near the hospital entrance, retrieved a wheelchair, and pushed Elise to the registration desk. "I'll be right back." She reassured her daughter as she left to park the car in the lot. As Janet entered the hospital with her purse and daughter's bag in hand, she saw Elise being wheeled down the hall by a gentleman and hurried after her.

"Mam," the man behind the counter addressed Janet, bringing her to a halt, "you must have a band on your wrist before entering."

"A what?" Janet went to the reception desk.

"A band around your wrist. Your daughter has one, and so will the baby. It's for security." The gentleman held a strip of white plastic before her.

Janet held her hand out and watched as her daughter disappeared through the double doors.

The receptionist announced with a snap and a cut to trim the bracelet. "You're all set."

Janet looked at her wrist and then at the receptionist. "Thank you." She hurried to catch up with her daughter.

Elise was wheeled into a private room. "Oh, this is nice."

"You're welcome to make yourself at home. Your nurse should be with . . .," the young man turned to see a woman dressed in scrubs entering the room, "and here she is."

"Hello, I'm Tara. I'm your assigned nurse for your delivery." She scurried around the room and selected a gown from a cupboard. "After you change into this, I'll take your vitals. The intern will come in to assess how far your labor has progressed soon."

"Progressed?" Elise accepted the gown as she stood up from the wheelchair. Her escort pushed it from the room as he left.

"Dilated and effaced." Tara began raising the head of the bed with the power button.

Elise watched her mother enter the room and sit in the cushy chair. She appeared out of breath.

With the hospital gown in hand, Elise dressed in the private bathroom. Another nurse was wheeling in a small, elevated platform with a warmer above it when she emerged. She assumed it was for the baby.

"Elise, I need you to sit on the edge of the bed for a moment while I get your vitals," Tara instructed.

Sitting on the mattress, Elise watched as the blood pressure cuff was wrapped around her arm, the pulse oximeter clasped onto her finger, and a digital thermometer paused before her open mouth and was placed beneath her tongue. The nurse took her blood pressure, read the oxygen readout and her temperature, and recorded the information on her chart.

"Looks good." Tara smiled. "You are free to walk around the room or rest in bed. The intern will be in soon."

With another trickle of amniotic fluid signaling the start of a contraction, Elise opted to lay in bed instead of having the liquid run down her legs. She held her breath, stiffened her legs, and balled her hands into fists in response to the pain.

Tara raised the bed rails, securing her patient safely.

Janet went to her daughter's side. "Try to relax, breathe through it. It goes easier when you do."

As the contraction eased, Elise took a deep breath and looked at her mother. "I vowed to do this without medication. But I'm beginning to regret my choice."

"I'm right here." Janet brushed a wayward strand of her daughter's hair away from her eye.

"Me too," Gabe added.

"Focus on something else," Janet suggested.

"Like what?"

"Being at the beach, walking in the sand, finding seashells, and lying in the sun."

Elise closed her eyes. "Sounds heavenly. It's been a long time since I've had a vacation."

"Maybe we can pick a warm and sandy place that you've always wanted to see, and the three of us can go for a week and relax."

Elise groaned as another contraction began. She grabbed the bed rails and moved her legs as if trying to push the pain away.

"Relax, breathe through it." Janet reminded her daughter.

A young intern walked into the room. He spoke to Tara before turning toward his patient. "Hello, Elise. I'm going to check to see how far along you are dilated." He placed his hands on Elise's abdomen. "Head down. Good." He pulled two latex gloves from the box on the wall and performed a quick pelvic exam. "About three centimeters."

"Three?" Elise looked at him as if he were crazy. "I'm only a three?" She knew she had to be dilated to ten centimeters for the baby to be born.

Elise stared at her mother. "This is going to get much worse, isn't it?"

Janet nodded and leaned close to her daughter's ear. "I think they can give you a muscle relaxer if you want one, or even an epidural for the pain."

Elise shuddered as she pictured someone inserting a needle into her spine. She hoped to deliver the baby naturally and avoid her childhood aversion to needles.

A male nurse, carrying a tote with supplies, entered the room. He placed the tote on an elevated table and turned her wrist to read her wristband. "Hello, Elise. I'm going to insert your IV."

"An IV?" Elise cringed. "Why do I need an IV?"

He began selecting items from the tote. "If you need any medication, they can administer it easily through the IV." The nurse perceived his patient's apprehension. "It's to keep you hydrated too."

Elise looked away as the needle was inserted into the top of her hand. The mere experience caused the blood to drain from her face. Thankful to be lying down, she blinked her eyes, trying to remove the black spots that appeared in her line of vision. Her head seemed disconnected from her body.

"All done." He gathered any wayward items to be discarded and picked up his supplies.

"Thanks." Elise looked at her mom and lowered the volume of her voice as the nurse left the room. "I think."

"You're doing fine, Elise." Tara encouraged. "Would you like some water or ice chips?"

"No, thank you."

Janet spotted the TV on the wall. She found the remote in the nightstand drawer and turned it on. "Maybe there is something you would like to watch to help pass the time." She pulled her chair next to the bed and patted her daughter's hand. They decided on a sitcom.

Elise tried to breathe through the contractions. Her stomach became queasy. "I think I'm going to get sick."

Gabe looked at his wife's face as it drained of color. "Sick? You mean like throw up?"

Tara retrieved a kidney-shaped vessel from a cupboard and held it before her patient's mouth, whose projectile vomit overshot the bowl.

"Is this normal?" Elise wiped her mouth with the gown sleeve as her nurse disposed of the bowl, retrieved a clean gown, and dampened a paper towel.

"Yes, it's a sign that you're dilating." Tara helped Elise remove the soiled gown, washed her body, and dressed her patient in a clean garment. The nurse clasped Elise's wrist and took her pulse. "Are the contractions getting stronger?"

Elise nodded as another one began. Janet clasped her daughter's hand and traced her fingertips up and down Elise's arm to help her relax.

"You're doing fine," Tara reassured. "If you want something for the pain, let me know. Doctor Martin will arrive once you are dilated to a five."

The hours ticked by, and the strength of the contractions increased. Monitors were attached to Elise's abdomen, and the intern checked her hourly. Her progress was slow. After midnight, she finally dilated to a five and asked for pain medication. Once Doctor Martin arrived, she ordered a muscle relaxer to make her patient more comfortable.

As the medication was injected into her IV, Elise could feel her body relax, and her head seemed to sink into the pillow. She closed her eyes and managed to drift off to sleep. Janet, constantly vigilant, dozed in the chair only to have her eyes blink open at the tiniest, unfamiliar sound.

When Elise woke, Doctor Martin was standing before the monitors assessing the information they displayed. "How are you feeling, Elise?"

"I've been better."

The doctor smiled. "Well, you have been able to rest for a little while. You and the baby are both doing fine. It shouldn't be long now."

Elise exhaled, closed her eyes, and nodded as a contraction began. Her eyelids were too heavy to keep open. She listened as the staff prepared for the birth. Her legs were lifted and placed into the holders.

The end of the bed was lowered, additional lights wheeled in, and the infant warmer turned on.

"I feel like I have to push." The urge was strong, and Elise began to bear down.

Doctor Martin sat on a stool at the end of the bed. "I need you to stop pushing, Elise. I need to verify that you're fully dilated." After a quick pelvic check, she instructed. "Ok, with the next contraction, go ahead and push."

Elise took a deep breath and pushed as the contraction began.

Janet, standing by the side of the bed, placed the palm of her hand over her daughter's clenched fist gripping the railing. She rubbed her upper arm soothingly and encouraged her daughter to bear down.

What began as one push turned into many. Over the next hour, Elise pushed without success. With little strength left in her body, she let the next contraction come and go without pushing.

Gabe paced the room. "Push, Elise."

Doctor Martin sensed her patient's fatigue. "I know you're tired, Elise, but you have to push."

The sensation of her baby entering the birth canal caused Elise to open her eyes.

Tara used a handheld fetal monitor and moved it on her patient's abdomen in several locations. She masked her face with calmness when she could not detect the baby's heartbeat.

Gabe stared at the monitor as its silence caused his heart to skip a beat. "Come on, Elise. Push."

"Gather your strength. Your baby is almost here." Janet squeezed her daughter's hand.

The absence of a swooshing sound caused Elise to push with a sudden urgency as she sensed her baby was in danger.

As the head crowned, a nurse on each side of Elise held back her legs, and Doctor Martin announced, "Here she comes. Elise, I need you to take a few deep breaths to give your skin time to stretch."

The urge to push was overwhelming, but Elise complied.

"Take another deep breath."

"I want to push."

"In a minute, deep breath."

"And then I'm pushing." Elise was determined to get the baby out of her. She took a deep breath. When the next contraction started, she curled her upper body forward as if trying to do a sit-up and pushed. The baby's head squeezed through the opening.

"Hang on, I have to turn the baby's head." Doctor Martin instructed.

Elise took a deep breath and lay back on the bed.

Tara handed the doctor a bulb aspirator to remove any mucus or fluid from the baby's nose and mouth.

"Now, let me ease the shoulders out, push Elise." Doctor Martin guided the baby out of the birth canal. The infant began to cry.

Gabe stared in awe, frozen by the sight of his infant daughter emerging from his wife.

Janet breathed a sigh of relief. Her eyes welled with happy tears as she stared at her newborn granddaughter.

Elise exhaled, relieved. Her baby was placed on her chest. The nurse used the aspirator while another covered the baby with a warm cloth and wiped away a waxy coating.

"What's all over her? It looks like butter." Elise watched as the nurse continued to wipe the goo away.

"It's a protective coating called vernix," Tara explained as she wiped.

"Congratulations, Elise." Doctor Martin placed her fingers around the umbilical cord. "We'll leave your little one there until the umbilical cord quits pulsing." The baby continued to cry. The doctor smiled, pleased by another successful delivery. "Isn't that the most beautiful sound in the world?"

Elise admired her daughter's face, her dainty features. Holding her baby within her arms erased the pain she endured. The delivery seemed like nothing more than a bad dream.

Gabe stood at the head of the bed, staring at his daughter. "Elise, look what you did. She's beautiful."

Tears trickled down Janet's cheeks. "She's beautiful." Blessed to have witnessed the birth of her granddaughter, spellbound, she watched in awe at the baby's first moments of life. Then she thought of Gabe's absence and looked from her granddaughter to her daughter.

Elise was overcome with emotion. She covered her eyes with her free hand, and she cried as the responsibility of motherhood settled upon her shoulders.

The infant's father was usually given the honor of cutting the umbilical cord. Doctor Martin thought the new grandmother would be a suitable substitute. "Janet, would you like to cut the umbilical cord?" She presented her with the scissors handle first.

Janet looked at the medical scissors. "Sure."

Gabe placed his hand upon Janet's as she accepted the instrument.

The baby was rolled onto her side and clips placed on the umbilical cord. "Cut between the clips," Tara instructed the new grandmother.

The back of Janet's hand felt cold. She looked at the ceiling for a vent, but there was none. Cutting the cord, she was puzzled by its strange texture. "It feels like I'm cutting a thick rubber band."

When the baby was detached, Tara took the infant to the warmed elevated bed to be weighed, measured, and vitals were taken.

Gabe smiled as he peeked over the nurse's shoulder. He watched the woman bathe and dress his daughter. He looked at his hand as he rotated it in the dim light. "I'm still here. Apparently, witnessing the birth of my daughter wasn't the unfinished business that would break the bonds that keep me here. What other reason can there be?" He looked at his wife. "Is it you, Babe?"

Doctor Martin pressed on Elise's abdomen and coaxed the placenta out of her patient's body. "When you feel up to it, you can take a shower, or Tara can bathe you while you rest. The pediatrician on staff should be in soon to examine the baby."

"Thank you, Doctor."

Doctor Martin looked at Janet. "Congratulations, Grandma."

Janet dried the tears from the corners of her eyes. "Thank you."

As the doctor turned to leave the room, she stopped in the doorway and looked back at her patient. "Oh, what are you naming your daughter?"

Elise had kept the secret, never uttering it to anyone. "Melanie Marie Messenger."

Chapter 26

Over the next two days, Elise remained in the hospital with Melanie nearby. She tried to rest as much as possible, but unfamiliar noises and interruptions by the nursing staff made it difficult to sleep. Her call to Gabe's parents resulted in their uncomfortable visit to see their granddaughter.

Janet hovered over her daughter and granddaughter, eager to hold Melanie whenever Elise needed rest. She managed to return home for a short time to shower and bring snacks for Elise, whose appetite had increased exceedingly. When mother and baby were released from the hospital, Janet pulled the car near the entrance. The nurse pushed the wheelchair to the open car door to shorten the distance for her patient.

Elise managed to put tiny Melanie into her car seat. She sat in the back seat next to her as the trio left the hospital.

Janet looked at her daughter's reflection in the rearview mirror while waiting for traffic to clear at an intersection. She grinned with pride as she listened to Elise explain to Melanie where grandma was taking them. Once the car was pulled into the garage, the new mother cradled her bundled newborn in her arms while Janet snapped a photo.

The baby swing received as a shower gift was immediately put to good use. At night, Melanie slept in a bassinet next to Elise's bed. The nightlight with Gabe's photograph was moved from the nursery and placed on her nightstand near the bassinet. Elise often watched Melanie sleep during the day. When it was difficult to see her chest rise and fall, she would place her finger beneath the baby's tiny nose to ensure she was still breathing.

"Thank goodness this thing has wheels." Elise rolled the bassinet from the kitchen into the living room after lunch. She ensured sleeping Melanie was covered with a blanket before sitting in her father's chair and putting her feet up. Sighing, Elise looked at her mom, who was tidying the kitchen. "How did you do it, Mom?" She was beyond tired and nightly breastfeeding deprived Elise of her usual sleep.

"The best advice I can give you is to sleep when the baby is sleeping. Hopefully, she will be sleeping through the night in three to six months."

Elise cringed. "Three to six months? How am I ever going to run the bookstore and take care of her too?"

"You aren't the first woman, and you won't be the last to juggle the responsibilities of a child and a job. We women are resilient and manage multi-tasking quite well." Janet smiled. "Besides, you have me to help you."

After a few recovery days, Elise took her newborn daughter to the bookstore and worked with Melanie, wrapped close to her chest with a long binding. Janet watched her granddaughter several days a week when Elise was required to work more hours. An opening at the church daycare helped bridge any gaps in their schedule.

Elise was pleased when her daughter began sleeping through the night at three months old.

~

When Melanie outgrew the bassinet at six months, she began taking afternoon naps and sleeping at night in her crib. One night as Elise read a book in her bedroom, she paused to listen to her daughter cooing in the nursery. "It's as if Mel is talking to someone." She assumed her daughter was staring at the stars and moon on the wall or Gabe's illuminated photo and resumed reading.

Gabe lay in the crib beside Melanie. He admired her deep blue eyes with their long dark lashes, cute little nose, and the blonde wisps of hair on her scalp. "You're such a pretty little girl, just like your mama." He watched her eyes focus on his face, and she tried to talk, but only cooing emanated from her mouth as she reached her hand toward him. "I think you can actually see me, can't you?" He kissed her hand and used the tip of his finger to trace the outline of her soft cheek. "My pretty little girl. I love you so very much, but you need to go night-night." He hummed a tune hoping to lull her to sleep.

Elise looked up from her book, tilted her head to the side, and listened. "Did Mom leave the TV on?" She got out of bed and went to the living room, but everything was turned off. She turned and paused before the nursery doorway. The soft lighting of the illuminated nightlights allowed her to see Melanie's arms moving. She looked above the crib at the glowing stars and crescent moon. Was her daughter reaching for them? Sighing, she entered. "Mel, are you still awake?" She located the absent pacifier from her daughter's mouth and inserted it. "Goodnight, sweetheart."

Gabe smiled as he watched Elise leave the room. "You have the best mommy in the whole wide world." He kissed his daughter on the forehead. "Goodnight, Mel." Staring at the delicate features of her face, he watched her heavy eyelids close. It comforted his restless soul to know his daughter was able to see him.

In his spiritual, entrapped existence, Gabe celebrated Melanie's first birthday, her first steps, and first words. Always the silent observer, he watched Elise struggle with parenting Melanie through the terrible twos, thrilling threes, and fearsome fours. There were days he chuckled at his daughter's misbehavior yet admired Melanie's determination for independence.

As the years passed, he noticed the open window to Melanie's perception seemed to close. Upon celebrating her seventh birthday, she no longer acknowledged his spiritual existence.

Now nine years old and a fourth-grader, Melanie's nightly acknowledgment helped to make his solitude bearable. "Goodnight, Daddy." She stared at his illuminated face until her eyelids became too heavy to keep open.

Gabe listened for his daughter's rhythmic breathing. "Goodnight, Mel." He kissed her forehead, sat on the end of her single bed, and watched her sleep.

As the lamp clicked off in Elise's bedroom, Gabe rose and went to his wife's side. He was proud of her and the way she handled her single parenthood. He leaned forward and kissed her forehead before lying next to her in bed.

As the sun rose, announcing the start of a new spring day, Gabe watched the small family's morning routine. He stared out the living room window as Melanie walked to the end of the driveway to catch the school bus. He continued to shadow his wife throughout her day and anticipated his daughter entering the bookstore after school.

In the afternoon, the bookstore door opened. Gabe turned and smiled as Melanie stepped inside with her heavy book bag on her back.

"Hi, Mom."

Elise looked up from the computer screen to see her daughter's smiling face. "Hi, Mel. How was your day?"

"Fine." Melanie went to the office, placed her backpack on the floor, and grabbed a snack before joining her mother.

Elise swiveled the barstool's seat to give her daughter her undivided attention. "Just fine."

Melanie sighed. "I think my teacher hates me."

Scowling, Elise was curious. "Mrs. Morton? Why would you say that?"

"Because she is always picking on me. Cynthia and I were talking, and she told me to be quiet. Why didn't she tell Cynthia to be quiet too?"

"Maybe you shouldn't be talking at all." Elise was aware of parents who thought their children could do no wrong and the fault was always with the teacher. She would hear both sides of the story before drawing a conclusion. "You've had this teacher all year. Did you do something to make her dislike you?"

"No, I just think she doesn't like me."

"Spring parent/teacher conferences are next week. I'll ask and see if your teacher has an explanation for only scolding you."

Melanie became saucer-eyed as she momentarily held her breath. "Mom, don't."

Elise sighed. "I'm not promising anything."

Gabe's anger reached its boiling point. "How can a teacher single out one student when two are involved?"

The following week after closing the bookstore, Elise walked into the classroom at her appointed time for the conference. Melanie had been praised by her former teachers, many conveying that she was a pleasant student and a joy in class. Keeping an open mind, Elise entered the fourth-grade classroom. Its walls were decorated with posters, the seats in neat rows, and a teacher's desk at the front near the whiteboard. Elise sat in the chair at the semicircle table across from the teacher.

"Hello, I'm Melanie's mom."

Mrs. Morton remained unsmiling as she peered over her reading glasses. The stocky woman, who looked close to retirement, sighed. "Your daughter has an attitude."

Elise was taken aback by the brazen comment. "An attitude? This is the first I'm hearing of it."

"Yes, well, she rolls her eyes and turns up her nose disrespectfully. I'm at a loss as to what to do with her."

"I'm surprised the old bat doesn't know how to handle the situation. I don't like this teacher, Elise." Gabe was tempted to toss a book at the mean woman.

Elise recalled the comments of Melanie's previous teachers during conferences. One indicated her daughter was her favorite student, another wished she had more children because Melanie was well behaved, and another said she made her laugh every day. It was evident to Elise that the problem was not with her daughter. It was with Mrs. Morton. A personality conflict, perhaps? Instead of getting into an argument, she decided to appease the woman. "I'll speak with her. How is she doing academically? I mean, isn't that what we are supposed to be discussing?"

"She's doing well. However, her attitude is most prevalent when the class reads together."

Elise smiled, fully aware of the assigned reading book. Melanie had little interest in the subject matter, especially since she could select any book in the bookstore at her convenience. Aware of her daughter's exceptional reading ability, Elise took a deep breath and exhaled. "Melanie doesn't like the book she is being forced to read. I assume the only reason it is part of your lesson plan is that you have used the book for many years. The assignments associated with that book, such as worksheets, quizzes, and tests, are simply being copied and handed out to the students, making your job quite easy."

Mrs. Morton sat stunned.

"That's telling her." Gabe crossed his arms over his chest and nodded.

"Since I own the bookstore in town, I'm fully aware of the available books for students to read. Perhaps a little more creativity in your lesson plan is needed. Would it be too much to allow the students to select a book of their choosing?"

"They can do that for silent reading."

"Then I suggest you adjust your curriculum or break up the students into groups and allow each group to choose a book. Reading should be fun, not a begrudging task. Now, I believe my five minutes are up. Is there anything else you wish to discuss?"

"No."

Elise rose and stormed out of the classroom.

~

The following week began without incident. Melanie reported Mrs. Morton was absent on Monday, and she had an excellent substitute teacher. Unfortunately, upon her teacher's return the next day, the wrath of Mrs. Morton came down upon the class.

Melanie entered the bookstore after school. Her eyes were puffy and reddened. It was apparent to Elise that her daughter had been crying.

"What's wrong?" She watched as Melanie burst into tears and ran to the office. Elise glanced at Marge.

"If that woman doesn't like teaching, why doesn't she quit?" Marge spoke as if reading Elise's mind.

Sobs echoed from her office as Elise went to the back of the store and stepped inside.

"Mel?" Her daughter was sitting at her desk. "What happened?"

"My teacher is mean."

"What did she do now?"

"We had a sub yesterday, and he told us to make a poster for health. So, I drew a picture of a man smoking a cigarette and a red circle around it with a line through it."

"I get it. Don't smoke. Sounds like a good design." Elise elaborated.

"Right. When Mrs. Morton came into class today, she read the sub's note he left on her desk and was upset. It said our class was bad. She went through the posters, picked mine out, and held it up in front of the class. She said it was terrible and threw it at me, telling me to redo it. Then she turned away, and I heard her call me, I know I'm not supposed to say this, but she called me a 'little shit.' Mom, she has the entire class hating me. No one wants to sit with me at lunch or be my friend."

Gabe paced. "Elise, you have to do something."

"I'll set up an afterschool appointment and go talk with her. This has got to stop."

"No, Mom." Melanie wiped the tears from her cheeks.

"Yes, Mel. Enough is enough." Elise was uncertain how to handle the precarious situation. If she confronted the teacher, would it make matters worse? Should she involve the principal?

Elise lay in bed that night with tears trickling from her eyes. How would she handle the conflict calmly? She prayed the good Lord would give her the strength to say what she must to protect her daughter without bawling like a baby. Elise wondered how many other children throughout Mrs. Morton's teaching career had their self-confidence and self-esteem shredded. "For all the emotional pain Melanie and other children have suffered, may it come back on Mrs. Morton tenfold."

Two days later, Marge was in charge of the store while Elise went to the elementary school at dismissal time. She instructed Melanie to wait in the car before walking into the classroom, where Mrs. Morton waited at her desk.

"Hello, Mrs. Messenger." She set aside a stack of papers and dropped her red pen on top.

"Hi, thank you for meeting with me." Elise wanted to begin the meeting on a pleasant note. She was sure it was not going to end that way.

"You requested a meeting."

"Mel came home in tears the other day. She said you humiliated her in front of her classmates, that you have turned the entire class against her, and no one wants to be her friend."

"Again, it's her attitude." Mrs. Morton defended.

Elise shook her head. "She has had two preschool teachers and four teachers before you. None of them complained about her having an attitude."

"Maybe they just didn't see what I see."

"Apparently, you received a note from a substitute indicating the children in your class had not behaved appropriately during your absence."

"Yes, the entire class's behavior was disappointing. Unfortunately, the student's completed health assignments were equally as disappointing." She picked up the poster Melanie had been made to redo. "This is your daughter's second attempt at the assignment. As you can see, there is a misspelled word."

Elise looked at the poster. It was as Melanie described. "Was it misspelled on her first attempt?"

Mrs. Morton stared blankly. "I don't know."

"So, you had my daughter redo an assignment when you don't know if there was anything wrong with the first one?"

"The entire class did a poor job on the assignment."

"The entire class? Then why was my daughter the only one who had to redo the assignment? Why didn't the entire class have to redo it?"

Mrs. Morton did not reply. Instead, she shifted in her chair as if suddenly uncomfortable.

"Let's face the truth, shall we. There's nothing wrong with my daughter's attitude. The attitude problem is with you. You have a personality conflict with her, and this will stop now."

Again, silence from Mrs. Moton.

"If you are incapable of treating every student in your classroom equally, then I suggest you retire from teaching. You are an embarrassment to the occupation." Elise rose, marched out of the building, and plopped into the driver's seat as she joined her daughter. She took a deep, cleansing breath.

Melanie stared at her mother. "What did she say, Mom?"

Elise looked at her daughter's askance face. "It's what she didn't say that makes me angry."

"Really?"

"Yes, I think she knew I was right." Elise went straight to her office and sent a scathing email to Mrs. Morton's principal.

The following week, Elise met with the principal. They discussed switching Melanie to another class, but they were at capacity. The principal said she had already talked with Melanie, who confirmed the teacher's conduct, as stated in Elise's email. The principal assured Elise the issue would be addressed.

By the week's end, Melanie skipped into the bookstore after school. "Guess what, Mom? We have a substitute teacher for the rest of the school year. She said Mrs. Morton was placed on administrative leave."

Elise nodded with a grin on her face. "That's good news."

"Well done, Elise. I'm proud of you." Gabe knocked a book from the shelf.

Melanie went to the aisle, picked it up, and read the first word of the title. "Trudging? What does that mean?" She handed the open book to her mother.

Elise read the title. "Trudging On. Trudging means having a heavy foot as you walk. In this case, I believe it means to continue moving forward no matter how difficult life can become and solving the problems we encounter as we go along."

"Like Mrs. Morton?"

"Exactly, like Mrs. Morton."

Chapter 27

Carson glanced at his watch to ensure he was on time for his appointment. He turned his car into the winding driveway lined with budding trees. "The lampposts along the driveway add a nice touch." As the custom-built home came into view, the experienced and successful realtor was eager to list the lakefront house. Carson noted the three-car garage, the excellent construction, and the beautiful landscaping. "Very nice." He parked his car, shut off the engine, and reached for his leather binder on the passenger seat. Walking up to the front door entrance, he rang the doorbell and waited.

The elegant door with its oval beveled stained-glass window opened. "Hello, Mr. Hunter, I assume." The owner greeted.

"Hello." Carson extended his hand toward the gentleman, estimating his age to be in the mid to late sixties. "It's nice to meet you. Please call me Carson."

"Come on in, Carson. We can talk in the living room."

"Sounds good." Carson took in the detailed crown molding, inlaid wood flooring, and size of the entry. "You have a lovely home."

"Thank you. Are you from around here?"

"Close by, but I've sold houses in this area for many years. I've always admired the historic city, though."

"Perhaps a tour would be a smart way to begin." The owner suggested.

"Sure." Carson opened his binder to take notes. "Why do you want to sell?"

"My wife and I built the house five years ago. I'm in construction, and this is our dream home. However, we've decided the dream comes with more responsibility than we want at our age. We plan to buy a motorhome and travel. So, everything you see, except for our personal items, will be sold with the house."

"Only the two of you live here?"

"Yes, our kids are grown and gone. No grandkids yet, so now is a good time for us to travel." He proudly led Carson through the large house, pointing out many custom details. There were five bedrooms, one being an en suite master, an elegant formal dining room, living room, and library. As they entered the breathtaking kitchen, Carson especially admired the vaulted beamed ceiling, the tall cabinets, granite-topped island, and a cozy fireplace at the end of the room with a pair of wingback chairs before it.

They toured the backyard and walked along the edge of the lake.

"Are you planning to sell the dock and boat as well?" Carson noticed the groomed sandy beach as he readied his pen to scribble the owner's reply.

"Yes, it goes with the house."

The realtor nodded as he looked at the patio and decking on the backside of the house.

Knowing the price would be out of reach for many buyers, the owner inquired. "Do you think it will be a tough sell?"

"Not at all. In fact, it's already sold."

"Really? To whom?"

"To me. We just have to agree on the terms."

~

"Another school year begins. Back to reality." Elise poured herself a coffee as her bagel popped up from the toaster.

"Summer sure seems to fly by quickly. It's hard to believe Mel is a fifth grader." Janet agreed.

Elise stared at her ten-year-old daughter as she stood in the kitchen doorway, ready for a new school year. "Wow, you look nice. Your last year of elementary school."

"Melanie, you look beautiful." Janet complimented her granddaughter's choice of clothing and her neatly combed hair. "I need to get a picture. You know I always take one of your first and last days of school."

Melanie sighed, looked toward the ceiling, and complied. She stood before the fireplace with her backpack and smiled like a fashion model, secretly enjoying the attention.

"Now, I need one with both of you. Elise, get in there." Janet encouraged.

Elise cherished their yearly photos and liked to compare them from year to year. Her daughter's childhood features were yielding to the beautiful young lady she was becoming. Melanie had her father's hazel eyes with their sparkling flecks of gold.

Elise stood next to Melanie, tall for her age, and smiled as Janet took the photo.

"Perfect. What time does your bus come?" Janet inquired.

"I'm not taking the bus on the first day of school. Mom is dropping me off before she goes to the bookstore."

Janet glanced at Elise before redirecting her attention to her granddaughter. "Are you going to walk to the bookstore after school, take the bus home, or do you want me to pick you up?"

Elise looked at her daughter as she picked up a bag of books she had reviewed and slipped her purse over her shoulder. "Mel, what did you decide?"

"I'll walk to the bookstore. I'll do my homework in the office."

During the summer, Elise added another cell phone to her policy and monitored Melanie's usage closely. She trusted her daughter's judgment, but with numerous scammers and countless spam messages lately, Elise wanted to ensure her daughter did not become a victim. "If you change your mind, call Grandma or me to let us know."

Janet smiled at her granddaughter before Melanie disappeared from her sight. The closing of the bathroom door echoed from the hallway. Janet looked at Elise. "First day of school jitters?"

"More like she wants to make sure her hair is perfect. She's at that age." Elise set the heavy bag on the floor and waited. "Hurry up, Mel, you're going to be late." She looked at her mother. Frustration masked her face. "She has little sense of urgency. I feel like I'm the bad guy, always raising my voice."

"Wait until she becomes a teenager. It gets worse." Janet smirked, knowing she was no replacement for a second parent. If nothing else, she was a buffer, someone neutral between her daughter and granddaughter. Even though Janet seldom pushed the issue, she wanted Elise to be happy, find a husband, and share her life with someone. "You know if you had someone. . ."

Elise held up her palm toward her mother. "I know what you will say, and I don't want to hear it, Mom."

"I know, but it would make me feel better saying it."

Elise anticipated the comment, looked heavenward, and picked up the bag of books as Melanie came out of the bathroom.

"Gabe has been gone for a while now." Janet persisted.

"I'm not interested, Mom."

"I'm just saying, you never know when a man will walk into your life."

Elise stepped toward the door. "Come on, Mel. Let's go."

Janet sighed. "All I'm saying is keep an open mind and heart. It's no fun growing old by yourself."

"Like you." Elise glared at her mother. "Then why haven't you found someone to share your life with?"

"Oh, I've been approached a few times. It just never worked out." Janet smiled. "Trust me, I'm keeping my options open." She winked.

Elise looked at the ceiling again before following Melanie into the garage.

~

The novelty of a new school year had worn off by the following week.

"Mel, time to get up." Elise shook her slumbering daughter's shoulder for the third time.

Melanie growled as she threw back the covers. "I'm up."

"Oh, you're just a ray of sunshine this morning." Elise shook her head. To say her daughter was not a morning person was an understatement.

Melanie glared at her mother, whose sarcastic comment only enraged her more.

Elise mumbled to herself as she went to the kitchen to begin breakfast. "I pity your husband."

Within a few minutes, Melanie shouted. "I can't find anything to wear."

Elise marched into her daughter's room. "How can you not find anything to wear? You have an entire closet full of clothes." She reached into the closet and pulled out a pair of jeans and a sweater. "Here."

"I don't want to wear that."

Honing her parenting skills under the guidance of her mother, Elise knew she needed to empower her daughter. "OK, I'm going to pick two outfits, and you choose one of them." She returned the sweater, chose another, and selected a second outfit she was sure her daughter would refuse to wear. "So, which outfit do you want to wear?"

Melanie stood in her underpants and training bra with her arms crossed over her chest. She scowled at the choice of clothing and finally pointed. "That one."

"Good choice, now hurry, or you'll be late for school." Elise returned the unchosen outfit to the closet, went to the kitchen, and picked up a cereal box to pour into her daughter's bowl. Considering Melanie's current mood, she set the box on the table and took a second one from the cupboard. While Elise retrieved the gallon of milk from the refrigerator, Melanie plopped her bottom on the chair. She had yet to comb her hair.

Elise placed the milk on the table. "Which cereal would you like?" At this point, she could only humor her daughter.

Melanie simply nodded in the direction of one of the boxes as she wiped the sleep from her eyes. Elise poured a half bowl and added milk. "Eat up. The bus will be here soon."

Janet watched the exchange between the two from the corner of her eye as she sipped her coffee and ate her toast topped with homemade strawberry jam. She chuckled inside, knowing her curse had worked, a curse most mothers bestow upon their children – 'I hope you have a child just like you someday.' She smiled as she watched Elise demand her daughter brush her hair before leaving the house.

With Melanie on the bus, Elise dressed and went to work an hour before opening. Alone in the bookstore, she reviewed emails, deleted most of them, ordered books, and analyzed daily sales. Her mother's prodding echoed within her mind. She looked at the framed photograph of Gabe and herself on their wedding day. The intense passion in his eyes while staring at her was evident. She thought over time, her love for him would wane. It may have dimmed, but a crescent of it remained within her heart.

Gabe stood beside her chair. He leaned forward to view the photo. "That was the best day of my life. The day you finally became my wife." He looked at Elise, who seemed melancholy. "Babe, you deserve to be happy. Janet is right. Find someone to share your life with." He left her office, went to a shelf, pulled a book, and let it fall to the floor. It landed with a resounding bang.

Elise looked toward the open office door. "Gabe, how did you know I was thinking about us?" She rose from her chair and scanned each aisle until she saw the open book on the floor. "Is this what you want me to know, Gabe?" She picked up the book and read the chapter heading. "Moving Forward." Elise sighed. "You want me to move forward? Find a guy to share my life with? It's not easy for me to do so, Gabe." She closed the book, put it back on the shelf, and turned away as another book fell behind her.

Elise turned around and read the title. "A New Chapter." She picked up the book. "I'm not certain if I want to begin a new chapter in my life. The old one is quite comfortable." Replacing it on the shelf, she crossed her arms over her chest. "Now, if you don't mind, I need to get back to work." She glanced at the clock on the wall. "I only have fifteen minutes until I have to open."

"It's time for you to move on with your life, Elise. Time to find happiness once again." Gabe vowed he would do what he must to see that she did.

Chapter 28

Carson moved into his new home by summer's end. He had driven through the quaint town numerous times for work, too busy to browse through the mom-and-pop shops. Encouraged by his clients, he managed to stop a few times in the acclaimed quaint restaurant to grab a mouth-watering sandwich and drink for lunch.

He looked at his watch and had a few minutes before he had to meet with a client for a late evening appointment. With his father's birthday a week away, Carson wanted to purchase the book his dad had mentioned. By happenchance, he noticed the small bookstore on his route through town, parked his car along the street, and hoped it had the book in stock.

The heavy rain, which began shortly after lunch, had trailed off to a light shower. Carson crossed the street to the sidewalk and lifted his sodden dress shoe from the puddle that was deeper than he anticipated. "Damn it!" He shook his foot before pulling his suit coat over his head as the rain intensified.

Elise looked up from the computer screen as the bell to the front door rang. "Hello, is there something I can help you find?" It was close to closing time. She knew Melanie was eager to go home. She hoped the customer would find what they wanted to purchase quickly.

Carson shook his suitcoat, freeing it of dampness, and approached the counter. "Yes, do you have this in stock?" He brought up the book cover on his phone and showed Elise the screen.

"Let me check." Elise quickly searched the bookstore inventory and discovered it was not in stock. "I don't seem to have that one on the shelf. I can order it for you, though."

Carson sighed as he returned his cell phone to the inside pocket of his suitcoat. "When will it be in?"

276

Elise looked at the gentleman's unsmiling face. He seemed impatient. "If I order it today, it should be here by Tuesday."

Melanie emerged from the office and glanced at the man standing before the counter. "Mom, do you want me to shut off the open sign."

"Yes, Mel. Thank you." Elise looked at the customer, awaiting his reply.

"Should be?" Carson questioned. "You mean you don't know if you'll have it by then?"

Elise rolled her lips inward and bit down before she replied. She was tired of dealing with rude customers who lacked the knowledge of how an independent bookstore operated. "Yes, but some things are beyond my control, such as our mail system. According to my wholesale sources, the warehouse has several copies, and it should be here by Tuesday."

"Fine. I'll come back then." Carson turned to leave.

"Sorry, but I need your contact information."

"For what?"

"To notify you when it arrives."

"You just said it will be here by Tuesday." Carson glanced at his watch.

"It's a courtesy to notify our customers when their book arrives. So, if it's delayed, you won't be wasting a trip."

"But you just told me it would be here by Tuesday."

Elise glared at the man. "Do you want me to order the book or not?"

"I just said that I did."

"Then I need your information so we may contact you when it arrives. Name?"

"Carson Hunter."

Gabe stared at the man. He seemed vaguely familiar. "Carson Hunter, not a name I recognize."

Elise paused her fingers on the keyboard. "I need your phone number and email address."

Carson complied as he retrieved his wallet while his information was added to his customer file and his order processed.

Elise watched as he withdrew a fifty-dollar bill. "You don't pay until you pick up the book."

"Really?"

"Really." Elise struggled to keep the sarcasm from her reply.

"Thank you . . ." Carson waited for her reply.

Elise stared at him, puzzled by what he wanted next.

"Your name?" He insisted.

"Why do you want to know my name?"

"Because I want to know who I'm speaking to when you call to tell me my book is in."

"My name is Elise, but my employee, Marge, will probably be the one calling you." Carson glanced at his watch again. "Thanks, Elise."

As the customer left the bookstore, Melanie locked the front door, patted the elderly feline on his head, and began turning off the lights. "I thought he would never leave."

"It's been a long day," Elise admitted. Her daughter had a half-day of school because of the teacher's professional development day. "I appreciate your help around the store today. We got a lot done. I think this is a great pizza night. Call Grandma and tell her we are picking up pizza for dinner." Elise cashed out the drawer, readied the bank deposit, and shut off the computer while Melanie made the call and walked around the store, shutting off the remaining lights.

"Tuna noodle casserole?" Melanie looked at her mother and pretended to gag.

Elise chuckled. "Tell her we will be home soon."

Melanie put her hand over her phone. "But Mom," she mouthed silently.

Tilting her head to the side, Elise's eyes widened, signaling her daughter to do as she was told.

After Melanie ended the call, she complained. "You know I don't like tuna noodle casserole."

"I know. That's why we are picking up a pizza on the way home." Elise placed her arm around her daughter's shoulders as they went to the office, put on their raincoats, and left the bookstore.

~

Marge entered the bookstore shortly after it opened the following day.

Elise looked up from the box she was cutting open. "Hello, Marge. You're in early."

"Yes, I have a dentist appointment, remember."

Elise nodded. "Ah, yes."

Marge stopped before a shelf. "I see we've had a disgruntled customer again."

"Oh, really." Elise took out the invoice and placed it on the counter.

Marge pulled the book that had been inserted backward between books. "Yes, apparently they don't like this book in our inventory." She placed it correctly on the shelf.

"Well, you know how I feel about that. I think everyone should read banned books, and no one, not even an independent bookstore owner, should censor a book from their stock just because they have an opinion against the subject matter."

"I agree, Elise. Freedom of speech." Gabe went to the display window. He liked to watch the world go by, a world he was no longer a part of. It had become a pastime of his.

Marge joined her boss behind the counter. They checked in new books, added them to inventory, and called the customers who had special orders.

Sales were good for a Tuesday, with many customers picking up their special orders.

Gabe uncrossed his arms from his chest as a beautiful, quite expensive car parked in front of the bookstore. He watched Carson Hunter emerge dressed in a custom-tailored suit. He carried two coffees in a carrier and a small brown bag. "Ah, Carson Hunter, yes, the book you ordered arrived on time." Gabe watched as he entered the bookstore. He followed the gentleman, wondering his intent. "Apparently, you are after something else too."

Marge placed a book on a shelf and noticed the customer. "Hello, is there something I can help you with?"

"Hello, you must be Marge. I'm here to see Elise." Carson smiled, displaying his straight white teeth. A dimple donned each cheek.

Hearing her name, Elise looked up from the computer screen.

Marge noticed the nicely tailored suit. She looked up into the man's chestnut eyes and grinned. She had to admit he was handsome, tall, and well built. His hair was short on the sides and curly on the top. "Elise is at the counter."

"Thank you, Marge." Carson turned away, went to the counter, and placed the food down before Elise. "Hello, Elise. Marge called and said my book is in."

"It is." She turned and retrieved it from the shelf behind the counter and rang up the sale. Elise announced the total.

"I want to say I'm sorry for how I behaved the last time I was here. I had a terrible day, but that is no excuse for taking it out on you. I was rude." He handed her his credit card.

Elise was in no mood to deny the truth. "Yes, you were." She ran the card, handed it back to him, and placed his book in a bag. Throwing the receipt inside, she folded the top shut and extended her hand for him to take his purchase.

He grinned as he accepted his purchase. "I brought a peace offering." He motioned toward the food. "It's lunchtime. I was hoping we could have lunch together."

Marge joined her boss behind the counter and pretended to look up something in inventory.

"Lunch?" Elise looked at the clock. It was twelve-thirty. She had been so focused on her work that she missed her usual lunchtime an hour ago.

"Yes, lunch. I stopped and picked up a sandwich and two coffees. I was told you like a mocha, with coconut milk, no whip."

Elise slowly turned her head toward Marge, who shrugged her left shoulder shyly.

Gabe watched the exchange between Carson and Elise. "I think she has met her match." He looked at his wife. "Still beautiful." He looked at Carson. "She could do worse."   "I'm not hungry at the moment." Her stomach betrayed her as it grumbled.

Carson glanced at her abdomen. "Your stomach indicates otherwise." He smirked.

"Then . . . I don't have lunch with my customers."

"Then I can return this book and no longer be your customer."

Elise tilted her head to one side, tired of bantering. "I don't accept returns on special orders." It was a half-lie.

"Then I'll stay in the bookstore until you accept my invitation."

"No loitering."

"Then I'll purchase every book in the store."

Elise looked at his expensive clothes, glanced out the display window, and wondered if the luxury car was his. Then, looking back at him, she rebutted, "Then I'll have no inventory and will have to shut down for several days until more books arrive."

"And your loyal employee, Marge, would be out of a job. So, I say we're at an impasse." Carson once again displayed his pearly white teeth complimented by his dimples.

Elise placed her arms over her chest and crossed them.

Carson continued. "I refuse to take 'no' for an answer."

Gabe knew his wife had dug in her heels. "So stubborn. Come on, Elise, at least hear him out." He went to a bookshelf and pushed not only one but two books to the floor.

Elise heard the books hit the floor. "If you'll excuse me." She marched from behind the counter and went to the fallen books. "Making Introductions," she read aloud, and "A Leap Of Faith." She looked up to the ceiling and whispered. "Gabe, you really want me to have lunch with this guy?" She returned the books to the shelf. Elise turned and nearly bumped into Carson, who stood behind her with their lunch and his purchased book in his hands.

"Sorry," she apologized as she took a step backward.

"Do you always talk to yourself?" He looked down into her sapphire eyes.

"Yes, it's a bad habit of mine," Elise admitted.

He leaned toward her slightly and whispered, "Marge said she could cover the store while we eat. It's a nice sunny day. There's a bench in front of the bookstore where we can share what I brought for us to eat as friends. What do you say?"

"First, I'm not your friend."

Carson cringed. "Oh, that's harsh. Let's just reclassify it as 'yet.'"

Elise sighed. "Fine, no more than ten minutes."

"Marge," Carson announced like a proud rooster, "Elise and I will be on the bench outside."

"Enjoy your lunch." Marge grinned and watched the couple exit the front door.

Elise plopped down on the bench. Carson set the food between them as he sat. Gabe stood nearby, crossed his arms over his chest, and waited.

"I have a large mocha coffee for each of us and a turkey sandwich. I thought we could split the sandwich since it's quite large. I hope you like turkey." He looked at her unsmiling face.

"Yes, thank you." Elise was guarded against the stranger's true intention, unable to relax.

Carson unwrapped the sandwich and motioned for her to select one of the triangle halves, which she did. "I think we started off on the wrong foot. Totally my fault." He sat up straight and held out his hand. "Hello, I'm Carson Hunter."

Elise stared at his extended hand. This 'new friend' of hers was doing his best to apologize. She appeased his attempt, released one side of the sandwich before she was able to take a bite, and shook his hand. "Elise Messenger." She bit into the sandwich.

Carson took the remaining sandwich from the wrapper and bit into the stacked turkey on wheat. Even though he found her attractive in a sassy way, he noticed the diamond on her finger. "I assume you're married?" He motioned toward her ring finger.

Elise's jaw stilled. She stared at him as if he had mentioned a sacred topic she did not want to discuss. She became instinctively defensive, picked up the cup of coffee, and took a sip to delay her reply. "Widowed."

It was Carson's turn to pause as the reality of her reply was emotionless and cold. "I'm sorry for your loss." It was a topic he would not bring up again.

"Thank you."

"So, how long have you owned the bookstore?"

"My dad owned it before me. When he passed away, it became mine. So, it has been in the family for some time now."

Carson looked over his shoulder through the display window. "There aren't too many of them around anymore. I read that many of the big bookstores are struggling." He took a sip of coffee.

"A lot of the independent bookstores are doing well. Even though some people use electronic devices to read books, many people prefer to hold a book and turn its pages to help them escape reality for a while."

"That's a good way to describe the experience. An escape from reality." Carson nodded.

"I have a lot of loyal customers who visit frequently and prefer to purchase their books from me. A lot of people like to eat at the restaurant next door. Sometimes while they wait for their reservation to be called, they shop in my bookstore."

Gabe watched the exchange between them and was pleased to see his wife lower her guard.

Through their conversation, Elise learned Carson was in real estate. If his car was any indication, he was doing quite well in his career. She finished her sandwich and looked at her phone for the time. "Well, I need to get back to work." She stood with her unfinished coffee in her hand and watched as Carson threw away the carrier and sandwich wrapper in the city garbage container. "Thank you for lunch."

He stood before her. "So, am I back in your good graces? Apology accepted?" Carson smiled.

His expression was infectious. Elise mirrored his smile briefly. "Yes."

"Good. The next time I stop by the bookstore, I'll get a book for myself." He picked up his package from the bench. "Have a good day. Thank you for having lunch with me."

"You're welcome. Bye." Elise entered the bookstore and joined Marge at the counter.

"Well, he's a cutie. Quite handsome if you ask me." Marge insinuated.

"It was just lunch. I doubt I'll ever see him again."

"Ah, you never know. I recognized that look in his eye. He's interested in becoming more than just a friend." Marge grinned as she winked.

"Well, I'm not, and that's what's important." Elise went to her office to avoid her employee's inquisitive stare.

Gabe looked at Marge before staring at his wife's retreating figure. "I'm with Marge. Carson seems sincere. His gesture was thoughtful. Their conversation seemed effortless. It's time to move on, Elise. I may need to give you a little nudge."

Chapter 29

With school in session for the third week, Elise went to the bookstore and began removing the back-to-school items from the display window. She paused to notice several trees along the street and sidewalks were donning their autumnal color. It was nature's way of announcing the change in season. She finished emptying the display windows and pulled the Halloween decorations from storage. She and Marge should have the store decorated by the end of the day.

"They look great." Elise complimented as she changed the lighting on a spooky tree to orange.

"I've always liked the witch. She looks scary." Marge straightened the black dress of the ominous figure.

"I could use a coffee. Do you want one? My treat." Elise offered as she went to the counter to retrieve the money.

"Sounds amazing." Marge pulled a ceramic pumpkin from a tote and dusted it off.

"The usual?"

"You know it." Marge placed the pumpkin in the window next to the witch as her boss left the store.

Elise entered the quaint restaurant and got in line behind a man dressed in a nice suit. Scanning through the news app on her phone, she assumed the man in front of her had finished with his order when she stepped forward and nearly bumped into him.

"Hello, Elise."

She looked up and into Carson's chestnut eyes. "Hello, Mr. Hunter."

"Carson." He insisted.

"Excuse me." She scooted past him, ignoring his plea, and ordered the coffees. Elise realized Carson was waiting at the end of the counter for his order. She reluctantly joined him.

"How's the book business lately?" He kindly inquired.

"Good. Marge and I changed the displays today. Getting ready for Halloween sales."

"Yes, it seems as if that holiday is almost as popular as Christmas."

"Carson!" The clerk called.

Carson stepped forward and picked up his order. He turned toward Elise. "It's good seeing you again, Elise."

"You too." It was a white lie, but she was compelled to just say it to be polite.

"Take care." Carson went to exit the restaurant.

"Elise!" The clerk called.

"Elise grabbed the two coffees, promising to keep her encounter with Carson a secret from Marge.

~

Carson entered the bookstore the following week. He went to the counter, anticipating Elise would be there but discovered Marge instead.

"Hello, Marge." He greeted her with a smile and then turned away, scanning the store for Elise.

Marge grinned, recalling his last name. She displayed his customer file on the computer. "Hello,

Mr. Hunter." She waited as he continued to look about the store. "Is there something I can help you with?"

He looked at her and grinned. "I was hoping Elise could recommend a book for me to read."

Marge scanned his account for the book's genre he had purchased and was aware of several others she could recommend. She smiled at Carson, knowing the true intention of his visit. "Elise researches each book before ordering them. She's in her office. I'll let her know you are here."

"I don't want to bother her if she is busy."

"It's no bother. Elise needs to take a break anyway." Marge walked to the office door and stepped inside. "There is a gentleman who needs your assistance."

Elise looked away from her computer screen. "They asked specifically for me? Who?"

"Mr. Hunter." Marge left before her boss could refuse the request.

Elise groaned as she left her office and looked toward the counter where Marge stood. Her employee pointed to the aisle where Carson selected a book from the non-fiction shelf. Grimacing, Elise plastered a slight smile on her face and went to his side. "Mr. Hunter, how can I help you?"

"Carson."

"What?"

"My first name is Carson. Mr. Hunter sounds too formal."

Elise inhaled as she glanced to the floor before complying. "Very well, Carson, how may I help you?"

"My father thoroughly enjoyed the last book I purchased."

"Good."

"Well, I like to read similar books. Is there another you can recommend?"

"I assume non-fiction, possibly current events?"

"Yes." Carson put the book back on the shelf and gave her his undivided attention.

"Come with me." She led him to the bestseller shelf. "Many of these are popular now. There are several that cover current events. This one," she picked up the book from the shelf and handed it to him, "may be of interest to you. If you like fiction," she chose a second, "this is an excellent thriller."

Carson read the blurb on the back covers while Elise scanned the remaining books on the shelf, hoping to find a third recommendation.

"I'll take both." He followed her back to the counter where he purchased the books. "Do you have time to go and get a coffee with me?"

Elise glanced at his expensive suit. "Don't you have to work?"

Carson looked at his watch. "My next appointment is at three o'clock."

"It's a slow day, Elise. I can cover for you." Marge insisted.

Clenching her teeth, Elise realized she was outnumbered. "Let me get my sweater." She retrieved the garment and her wallet, hoping he would allow her to pay for her own coffee. As she went back to the counter, she looked at Marge. "Do you want me to get a coffee for you?"

"No, thank you. Take your time." Marge gave an all-knowing grin.

They exited the store and entered the crowded coffee shop. Carson ordered their coffees. He turned to Elise. "Would you like anything else?"

"No, thank you." She opened her wallet to pay for her coffee, but he insisted.

"My treat."

With a freshly made drink in their hands, they went outside and sat at a table for two to enjoy the autumn afternoon.

"So," Elise began, "you like to read?" It was the only topic that came to her mind.

"It occupies my time when I'm not working."

"In real estate." She stated the fact.

"Yes." He watched as she refused to make eye contact. Did she wish to be far away from him? "You seem uncomfortable. Is it me?"

Elise looked at him, raising one eyebrow. "I don't really know much about you."

"Well, there is only one way to find out. Ask?" Carson sipped his coffee, sensing she had become defensive.

"Ask? What if I don't want to know." She knew Marge would pressure her to relay any information she discovered about him. Elise was determined to find a flaw in him and end her employee's matchmaking.

"Honestly, Elise. I would think a bookstore owner would know to never judge a book by its cover. There is more to me than what you see." Carson knew his comment had hit true.

Elise took a sip of her coffee, giving herself a moment to think. "I don't see a wedding ring. So I assume you're not married."

"Correct."

"How old are you?"

"Forty-two."

"Have you ever been married?"

"No." Carson sipped his coffee.

Elise perceived he was successful. After all, his suits were of the finest quality. She had to admit, he was handsome and in good physical shape. She assumed he must have had plenty of women he pursued over the years. A player? Perhaps. "Any children?"

Carson nearly choked on his mouthful of coffee. "No."

"You have a girlfriend, or you're gay?"

Carson laughed. "No to both."

"Then why have you never married?"

"For two reasons. I've made my career a priority, and I have yet to meet the right woman."

Elise nodded before taking a sip of her coffee.

"But now," he explained, "I'm where I want to be, financially, and I'm tired of living alone. I'm ready to share my life with someone. Someone to talk to in the evenings instead of filling them with watching TV and reading books." He tapped the bag on the table containing the two books he had purchased.

Elise thought of her evenings with Gabe. She missed his perspective, conversation, and laughter.

Recalling Carson's first purchase, she ventured. "And your father?"

"He insists on living alone. Mom passed away several years ago from cancer."

"Sorry."

"Thanks. I call Dad every day, and we go out to dinner once a week."

"Any brothers or sisters?"

"Yes, a sister and a brother. They're married and live out of state."

Elise finished her coffee and looked at her watch. "I need to get back to work."

"Me too." Carson drank the last of his coffee, took both cups, and threw them away in the trash can. "Thank you for taking the time to have coffee with me. I hope we can do this again soon." He walked Elise back to the bookstore. "Marge, thank you for allowing your boss to escape for a while."

"Hi, Mom." Melanie entered the bookstore.

Elise turned toward her daughter. "Hi, Mel. How was your day?"

Carson looked from the lovely girl to Elise. He estimated the child to be ten years old. "You have a daughter?"

Elise nodded. "Yes, this is Melanie." She turned to her daughter. "Mel, this is Mr. Hunter."

Carson presented his hand. "Hello, Melanie."

Melanie shook his extended hand. "Hello. It's nice to meet you." She turned to Elise. "I have a ton of homework to do over the weekend."

"Well, start it now."

"I will. I may need help with Math." Melanie went to the office in search of an afterschool snack.

"Do you want my help?" Elise called.

"No, Mom. All you do is frustrate me or teach me the wrong way." Melanie yelled over her shoulder.

"She's lovely." He stared at Melanie's retreating figure.

Assuming Carson drew the wrong conclusion, she was compelled to explain. "I discovered I was pregnant a month after my husband died."

He looked at Elise. "I wasn't judging." He began, lost in thought. "I can only imagine."

"Imagine what?" Elise crossed her arms over her chest.

"I can only imagine the difficulty of raising your daughter without your husband by your side."

"But I did it with the help of my mother."

"Your daughter is very polite. A reflection of your parenting." He watched Melanie disappear into the office. "Well, I must go. Thanks again for having coffee with me."

"You're welcome." Elise walked past Marge's inquiring stare and went to her office. Melanie sat at her desk with a stack of sandwich cookies and a full glass of milk.

"Who was that guy?" Melanie dunked a cookie into her glass and took a dripping bite.

"Carson?" Elise corrected herself. "Mr. Hunter. We had coffee together."

"He's pretty hot for an old guy."

Elise's eyebrows raised. "Old guy? He's only a few years older than I am."

~

Halloween came and went, and the holiday season began. The bookstore extended its hours to accommodate shoppers.

The city was a buzz on the morning of the Christmas parade. Elise ensured there was plenty of hot chocolate and cookies throughout the day, and sales were at an all-time high. Even Melanie aided customers in locating a book or two.

As the day's events neared and darkness blanketed the city, the main street was blocked off. Runners decorated in Santa costumes and lights began the 5K race. The hum of chainsaws echoed from the park as blocks of ice were turned into works of art. A band sheltered beneath a tent played Christmas carols.

Carson came into the bookstore as the parade was about to begin. He was dressed casually in a heavy, bulky sweater, jacket, and jeans.

Elise finished ringing up a sale and spied Carson approaching the counter. "Are you here to shop or take in the festivities?"

"The festivities. It's impressive. The streets and sidewalks are crowded with people." Carson rubbed his gloved hands together. The end of his nose was rosy, pink.

"A little cold out there?" Elise grinned.

"A little." He watched as Melanie joined her mother behind the counter. "Since this is my first time attending the parade and such, would you like to accompany me?"

"Yes!" Melanie answered for her mother. "Let's go, Mom. Come on." Melanie went to the office to retrieve their coats.

Elise tilted her head to one side and grimaced. "I guess that means yes." She accepted her coat as Melanie nearly threw it at her. "Let me talk to Marge before we leave."

Carson followed Elise and waited for her to speak to her employee. Eager to join the crowd lining the street for the parade, Melanie raced out the door.

"Marge, I'm going to give Carson a tour of the happenings in town. I won't be very long." Elise explained.

"Take your time. Most people have shopped, and they'll just be coming into the store to warm up."

Carson opened the door for Janet to enter.

"Thank you." She looked at Elise. "Hi, busy day?"

Elise turned toward the sound of her mother's voice. "Hi, Mom. I'm leaving for a little while to give Carson a tour."

Janet turned to look at the handsome gentleman who had held the door open for her.

"Mom, this is Carson Hunter. Carson, this is my mom, Janet."

"It's nice to meet you, Janet."

"Same here." Janet smiled. "I can help Marge while you're gone."

Marge interjected. "And I told her to take her time." She winked at Janet, who nodded once.

"Absolutely, I can watch the parade from here and help Marge if she becomes overwhelmed."

Elise displayed a sarcastic scowl and tilted her head to one side, knowing her mother knew very little about running the bookstore.

"Well, I can at least put purchases in the bags for Marge." Janet defended. "Go, have fun." She waved toward the doorway, encouraging her daughter to leave.

Carson opened the door and ushered Elise onto the busy sidewalk.

Melanie stopped short before her mother. "Mom, can I walk around with Cynthia?"

Elise watched as her daughter's friend stepped beside Mel. "Fine, but make sure you come back after the fireworks."

The girls squealed with delight as they wandered down the sidewalk.

"Well, they seem excited." Carson buttoned the top button of his jacket, shielding his body against the chilly evening.

"It's a big event. People come from surrounding cities for the parade, eat dinner, and watch the fireworks. And don't forget the visit with Santa." She smiled. "Let's go to the park and see the ice sculptures."

The sculptures, sponsored by local businesses, were illuminated with colorful lights.

"Here's the bookstore's sculpture." Elise circled it, taking in the detail of the open book with its many pages. "Nice." She rubbed her hands together, realizing they were cold. Patting her coat pockets, her gloves were missing. Cupping her hands, she brought them to her mouth to warm them. "I guess Mel dropped my gloves in the office."

Carson removed his leather gloves lined with thick fleece. "Here, take mine."

"No, that's fine. I'll be fine."

"I insist." Carson held open one of the gloves for her to insert her hand.

"Thanks." She rubbed her gloved hands together as they began to warm.

Elise and Carson found a vacant spot along the street and watched the parade. A chuckle escaped from Carson as he watched the nearby children scamper for the pieces of candy thrown from the floats. A candy bar landed at his feet. He picked it up and handed it to a little boy.

At the end of the parade, they went to the community center, sang Christmas carols, and watched the lighting of the tree, followed by fireworks.

Elise and Carson walked back to the bookstore. They had to wait for a family of five to exit before entering.

"Thank you for letting me borrow your gloves. Would you like some hot chocolate? We also have chocolate chip cookies." Elise offered.

"Sounds great." Carson tucked his gloves in his pocket and followed Elise to the snacks. He helped himself to a cookie while she poured a cup of hot chocolate and handed him the cup.

"Homemade?" He examined the tasty treat.

"Yes, by my mom."

"Very good." He looked about the store. "There are lots of people in here still."

"Most of them are just getting warm." She glanced at the clock on the wall. "We close in fifteen minutes."

"Well, you have things to do before then. So, thank you for accompanying me this evening. I've really enjoyed spending time with you." Carson ate the last bite of his cookie. He raised his cup of hot chocolate in a silent toast of gratitude.

"You're welcome. Goodnight."

"Goodnight." Before leaving the bookstore, Carson tossed the empty cup in the trash can and nodded to Marge, who was staring at him.

~

Elise began to feel the pressure from customers the following week. Many placed special orders and expected them to arrive in time for Christmas. Between Marge and herself, they made every attempt to ensure every customer was satisfied and pleased with their purchase.

Her phone dinged, indicating she had received a personal email. She opened it and read it. "Oh, no."

Marge looked up from the computer screen. "What's wrong?"

"Mel's teacher says she is failing Math."

"She needs a tutor." Marge heard the bell ring, looked toward the door, and grinned as she watched Carson approach the counter. "Hello, Mr. Hunter."

"Hello, Marge." Carson read Elise's thoughts. He placed his hand on the counter and leaned forward. "You look troubled."

Elise looked up from her phone. "Hi, Carson. I am. Mel is failing Math. Marge says I should hire a tutor."

"No need. I can tutor your daughter."

Elise raised her eyebrows, questioning his offer. "Really? Aren't you too busy?"

"I'll make time."

"How much do you charge?"

Carson shook his head. "Nothing." He looked at the ceiling for a moment. "On second thought, a nominal fee."

"Which is?"

"I need you to go with me to a movie tonight?"

Elise glared at him.

He outstretched the palms of his hands like fans as he read her mind. "My treat."

"That doesn't make any sense. You're going to tutor Mel, and your fee is to treat me to a movie with you?"

"It's a deal you can't turn down." He smiled, displaying his dimpled cheeks.

Elise tried to recall the last movie she watched in a theater that had not been rated for children. "What's the movie?"

He pulled out his phone and brought up the app that displayed what was playing at the local theater. "I have it narrowed down to this one," he turned the screen toward Elise, "or," turning his phone back toward himself, he paged down to the other selection, "this one." Carson turned his phone toward her and waited. "Your choice."

"I believe the first one is based on a novel I read."

"Then let's see that one. You can tell me how it differs from the book. What time would you like to go?" He read off the start times and waited for her reply.

Since it was Thursday, Elise would have to take Melanie home after closing. Even though Janet had only received a quick introduction to Carson, Elise was sure Marge had shared her opinion of him with her mother. So, she devised a plan to go home, grab a bite to eat, and meet Carson at the theater to avoid her mother's inquisition. "I close at six. We could make the seven o'clock movie in time. I could meet you there?" She suggested.

"No sense in both of us driving. I'll pick you up at your house." They exchanged phone numbers. "Text me your address. I'll be there at six-forty-five."

"OK." Elise conceded.

Gabe still thought of Elise as his wife. Since he could not be with her other than in his spiritual form, he could do nothing more than observe her interaction with Carson. Gabe had to admit he liked Carson, who was respectful, not too pushy, and a gentleman. Gabe was aware of Elise's stubborn streak. He was pleased Carson had also recognized it. If she could open her heart to him, he would be suitable for her, and maybe Melanie too.

Chapter 30

Melanie entered the kitchen with a smirk on her face. "Mom has a date tonight." She leaned against the counter and nodded toward the doorway as her mother entered the room.

Janet finished rinsing a pan and set it in the sink to dry. She turned and looked at her daughter. "A date?" She noticed that Elise had changed her clothes, refreshed her makeup, and neatly brushed her hair.

"It's not a date." Elise insisted. "I'm going to a movie with a friend."

"With handsome Mr. Hunter." Mel teased. She took a dishtowel from the rack beneath the sink, dried the washed pan, and placed it in the drawer beneath the cooktop.

Janet looked from her granddaughter to her daughter. "Sounds like a date to me."

Elise scowled. "We're just going to a movie as friends. That's all."

A knock sounded on the front door. Elise glared at her daughter and mother, silently warning them as she held up her index finger. "Remember, he is just a friend. Oh, and Mel, he has offered to tutor you in Math."

"Tutor? Math?" Melanie looked heavenward. "Augh."

Janet elbowed her granddaughter. They grinned at each other while Elise turned away to answer the door. "Hi, come in while I get my coat." She turned to see her mother and daughter standing in the kitchen doorway, expecting an introduction.

"Hi, Carson." Melanie greeted.

"Hi, Melanie." He nodded and grinned politely. "I understand we are going to be doing Math together."

"Yeah, great." Melanie sighed.

Carson nodded toward Janet. "It's nice to see you again, Janet."

"Same here." Janet looked up at the tall gentleman, impressed by his confidence. She had to agree with her granddaughter. He was handsome.

Elise pushed her arms through the sleeves of her coat and dropped her cell phone and wallet into the pocket. "Ready," she announced as Carson motioned for her to proceed out the door before him. He looked at the inquisitive pair. "Goodnight, ladies." He followed Elise out the front door, closing it tightly behind him. He paused and tilted his head toward the door. Did he hear giggling?

Carson stepped past Elise and opened the car door for her to enter.

"Thanks, sorry about that." She slid into the front seat as he closed the door.

Joining her, he inserted the key in the ignition and started the car. "Sorry about what?"

"My mom and daughter are so nosy. Before you arrived, they were teasing me about this being a date."

"Teasing? I thought they were polite." He glanced at her profile as he backed out of the driveway. Was she blushing?

As far as he was concerned, Carson thought of their outing as a date, but her demeanor conveyed otherwise. He was tired of eating and spending evenings alone. Elise filled his daily thoughts. He looked forward to each visit to the bookstore, engaging in interesting conversation and sharing a coffee or sandwich with her. Astutely aware Elise was not ready to move forward in a relationship, Carson wondered if she still mourned the loss of her husband. It had been over a decade, but who was he to judge? For now, he would settle for her friendship but dared to pose what his heart questioned. "If this was a date, would it be such a bad thing?"

Elise refused to entertain the thought. Instead, she looked at his profile. "I told them we are just friends."

Her comment warned him not to cross the line she had drawn in the sand. However, Carson dared to reveal a sliver of his heart. He grinned as he glanced at her. "Good friends."

Elise stared at the cheeky grin on his profile as he drove, uncertain if she classified him as such. Did she enjoy his company? Yes. She had to admit, he was handsome and possessed a likable personality, yet she remained guarded. Had her mother and daughter's teasing put her on edge?

Pulling into the movie theater, Carson parked the car. Elise did not wait for him to open the passenger door. He presented his bent arm as he joined Elise and waited for her to thread her arm within his.

She looked up at his askance expression and hesitantly complied.

Sensing her uneasiness, Carson redirected their topic of conversation to something mundane. "I'm in the mood for a big bucket of popcorn with lots of butter and salt. How about you?"

"Oh, yes. Lots of butter." She smiled. "What is it about going to a movie theater that gives us the impulse to sit, watch a movie, and shove an insane amount of buttery popcorn into our mouths?"

Carson shook his head and laughed. "I don't know, but we do it." He unthreaded her arm from his, opened the door, and placed his palm on the small of her back as she entered the lobby before him. He ordered a pair of tickets, a large bucket of popcorn with real butter, and two bottles of water. Elise grabbed several napkins and doused the popcorn with salt as he held it before her. They entered the darkened theater and agreed on a pair of seats.

"Not too crowded, thank goodness." Carson steadied the popcorn on the armrest between them. As ads and previews played on the screen, a couple sat next to Elise. The man carried a drink, hot dog, and chips. The woman had a tray of nacho chips with cheese. Elise looked at Carson and wrinkled her nose.

"What's wrong?" He peeked into the bucket of popcorn, assuming she had eaten a popped kernel that was too salty.

"The smell of his overcooked hotdog is awful." She tilted her head toward the man sitting next to her. "And I've got a feeling she'll be munching on her nacho chips throughout the movie. Do you think we can move?"

Carson leaned forward to view the offenders. He scanned the nearby seats and spied a vacant pair near the end of their row. "Let's move down." He motioned with a nod of his head, and they relocated.

"Much better. Thank you." Elise reached into the popcorn as Carson did the same. As their fingers entwined, he smiled at her. She grinned, shook her head, and looked away as the movie began.

After the movie, the couple recapped the storyline, questioning what made little sense. Elise shared the details from the book that were omitted as they walked to the car arm in arm.

Carson politely opened the passenger door for Elise to sit. As he got into the driver's seat, he paused before starting the engine. "This was fun. I'm glad you came to the movie with me. And you know what?"

"What?"

"I really like spending time with you." He confessed and started the engine without waiting for her reply.

Elise looked down at her hands in her lap and grinned. Did she enjoy spending time with him? Of course, yes, but somehow the admission to herself did not feel right.

Concerned by her silence, his strong hands reached for hers and clasped them. "Are you OK?"

She glanced at him before nodding.

"You're suddenly quiet. Is it something I said?" He caressed her dainty fingers with his thumb before returning his hand to the steering wheel.

"No, well, yes, in a way." Staring at her hands as she gathered her courage, she looked at his profile as he drove. "Is this a date?

He raised his eyebrows, taken back by her blunt question. "Do you want it to be?"

"Do you consider this a date?" She persisted.

He assumed Elise was struggling with her emotions, conflicted in some way. Uncertain of what she may be thinking, any bold declaration on his part may frighten and push her away. "I consider it a date between two friends. Would I like us to be more than friends? Yes, but I also believe you aren't ready for a relationship, at least not yet. I'm a patient person, Elise. The day I walked into the bookstore in my sour mood, I looked into your eyes, and my heart skipped a beat. My fondness for you has grown and continues to increase every day. I enjoy being in your company, and when I'm not with you, I think about you. I've never met another woman who has affected me so. I can't understand why, but I know you're someone I want to spend time with, perhaps the rest of my life. Am I in love with you? I ask myself that same question. I get it. This is scary, a risk, a leap of faith, but the future is what we make it."

His words stung. They struck true, piercing Elise's heart. Her eyes filled with tears. Future? She once faced a rosy future with Gabe, but it dissipated into thin air the day he died. She brushed a tear from her cheek and looked out the passenger window.

Gabe listened from the back seat of the car. "He's right, Elise."

Realizing he had upset her, Carson pulled into a restaurant parking lot. "Hey, I'm sorry if I've said something wrong."

"No, you said something right. The only person I've ever loved was Gabe. We were high school friends. He went away to college, and I had to run the bookstore after my dad died. We dated long-distance, married after he graduated, and a day after our first anniversary, he was killed in a traffic accident. You said the future is what we make it. The day Gabe died, my future with him ended. It was taken away. I guess I've been stuck there ever since, never looking forward."

"I'm sorry for your loss, truly." Carson was determined to turn the topic of conversation from something sullen to something positive. He placed his hand on the back of her seat and leaned forward. "But hey, you have Mr. Prince Charming right here, offering his heart to you."

Elise grinned.

Carson continued. "You may not love me now, but I tend to get under people's skin; kind of like a bad rash."

Elise chuckled.

"Seriously though, we can take this slow. OK?"

She nodded her head. "I think this is something I need to come to terms with. It may take a while. Thanks for the therapy session, Doctor Hunter."

He smirked, pleased that her sense of humor had returned. "Wait until you get my bill."

"Elise, he's your guy." Gabe sat back in the seat, crossed his arms over his chest, and enjoyed the remainder of the ride home.

As they pulled into the driveway, Carson shut off the engine. He wished the evening would go on but feared he would be asking for too much. "I'll walk you to the door."

Elise noticed her mother had left the outdoor light on.

"Such a gentleman." Gabe passed through the car and turned to see Carson open the door for Elise. "Yup, a gentleman." He passed through the front door and waited on the other side.

Carson placed his hand on the small of Elise's back as they climbed the steps to the front door. "Despite making you cry, I think our first date went pretty well."

Elise tried to grin as she clasped her hands before her. She looked up into his chestnut eyes. "I agree. Sorry I got so emotional."

"No need to apologize. I think you've kept it bottled up inside you for a long time. I'm glad I was the one to coax it out of you." He hooked his index finger within the palms of her hands.

"Yes, thank you, Doctor Hunter." She genuinely grinned.

"Doctor Hunter, that reminds me . . ." He became sarcastically serious.

Her grin faded. "Of what?"

Carson looked skyward as he thought for a moment. "Payment for my services," he said slyly.

Elise smirked as she looked up at the stars in the cloudless indigo sky. "I can only imagine. Dare I ask? What is your fee?"

Carson stared into her sapphire orbs before looking lower to her lips. "A single kiss." Brushing his knuckles along the edge of her chin, he threaded his fingers over her ear and into her soft blonde locks. He lowered his head, pausing to ensure she was willing. She offered no resistance or objection. Carson touched his lips to hers and pulled her hands toward his chest.

Instinct told Elise to push him away. She forced herself to relax, and she placed her palms on his muscular body.

Carson put his arm around her waist, drawing her closer.

Elise raised onto her toes as her hands had a mind of their own and wrapped around his neck. It had been a long time since she experienced a warm embrace and kiss from a gentleman.

He often imagined her complacency in his arms, holding Elise as if she were fragile and might break. Carson reluctantly pulled his lips from hers and kissed her forehead before drawing her closer to his body. He whispered in her ear. "I'm not asking you to forget about your husband. He will always have a place in your heart. I'm just asking you to make room for me."

Elise fought back her tears. It was as if she was betraying Gabe, cheating on him. Yet, she knew she had to overcome her guilt. "Well, you're off to a good start with that kiss."

Carson released her. "I'll take that as a compliment, then. Goodnight, Elise."

"Goodnight, Carson."

Chapter 31

Melanie grabbed a cereal box from the cupboard and sat in her usual spot at the table, where a bowl, spoon, and a gallon of milk waited. "So, how was your date?"

Elise lowered her coffee cup from her mouth and picked up the buttered English muffin half from her plate. "Fine."

"Just fine?" The cereal avalanched from the box and overflowed onto the table. "Dang it." Melanie shoved fistfuls of cereal back into the box. She brushed what was scattered on the table off the edge and into her bowl.

"It was fine. The movie was good, and then Carson drove me home."

"Did you kiss him?"

Elise scoffed. "That's none of your business."

"Aw, you did. I can tell by the way your face is turning red."

Elise could feel the heat rising in her cheeks. She was sure she was blushing. "Mel, we're both adults. Besides, it's customary to kiss a date goodnight."

"I thought you said it wasn't a date. That you're just friends." Milk gurgled from the jug onto the cereal.

"We decided it was our first official date."

"Did I hear someone say they went on a date?" Janet entered the kitchen and poured a cup of coffee.

"Mom said it was an official first date." Mel spooned cereal into her mouth.

"Well, that's nice. Your mom deserves to go out once and a while." Janet winked at her daughter before sitting at the table.

"Are you going to marry him?" Melanie questioned with her mouth full.

"Mel, it was just a date." Elise sipped her coffee, refusing to discuss the topic any further.

Janet recognized the defensive tone in her daughter's voice. "Melanie, the bus will be here soon, so eat up." Her attempt to redirect her granddaughter's conversation failed.

"Well, I like him," Melanie stated before taking another bite of cereal.

Elise glared at her daughter. "You don't even know him."

"But I bet you do." Melanie teased.

"Enough. Eat your cereal. If you miss the bus, I'm not driving you to school. You can walk."

"Fine, then I'll miss my first hour. It's Math, and I hate it anyway." Melanie glanced at the clock on the microwave. She began shoveling in cereal as she picked up her bowl and headed toward the kitchen sink.

She was relieved to no longer withstand her daughter's inquisition and teasing. Elise looked up from her coffee and saw her mother staring at her. Tilting her head to one side, she sighed. "Not you too."

Janet shrugged her shoulders. "I didn't say anything." She defended, even though she was curious to know the details of her daughter's date.

"It was one kiss." Elise blushed, feeling the need to confess.

Janet watched the color rise on her daughter's face. "It must have been some kiss."

Elise smiled before looking down at the table. "It was."

"So, then you'll be seeing more of Carson?"

"I believe so. At least, that is his intention."

"I see." Janet sipped her coffee.

"But we're going to take it slow." She stared at her mother's face feeling a need to justify further. "He's a nice guy."

"You don't need to explain anything to me."

"Then why do I feel as if I do?"

"Maybe you're trying to convince yourself." Janet reasoned.

Elise brushed her mussed hair away from her eyes. "It's confusing. In my heart, I still love Gabe. But he isn't here and never will be."

"I think Gabe would want you to be happy." Janet began, offering a persuasive argument.

"I know in my heart he would, but it's strange. I feel as if I am cheating on Gabe." Elise stated, on the verge of tears.

"Then, as you said, take things slowly. Give your heart time to adjust to the change. Fall in love. Be happy again. It's what I want for you. It's what Gabe would want for you."

Gabe crossed the room and leaned over the kitchen table. "Listen to your mom, Elise. You deserve more than pining for me for the rest of your life."

"It's just hard." Elise wiped the tear from her cheek.

"It's a big change in your life, and change is never easy." Janet reached across the table for her daughter's hand.

Elise clasped onto her matriarch's palm and squeezed as if trying to absorb strength.

Janet grinned as she stared into her daughter's bloodshot orbs. "He seems like a nice guy. Give him a chance." She gave her daughter's hand one final squeeze before releasing it. "The choice will be yours. But take it from me; it's no fun growing old by yourself."

Melanie ran into the kitchen, grabbed her lunch from the refrigerator, and kissed both women on their cheeks. "The bus is waiting at the end of the driveway. Gotta go!"

"See you after school! Have a good day!" Elise yelled as she heard the door slam shut.

Chapter 32

Marge entered Elise's office just after lunch. "I think these are for you." She placed a crystal vase filled with roses and baby's breath on her desk. "There's a card." The employee assumed the bouquet was from Carson unless her boss had a mystery man she did not know about.

Elise stared at the red roses before looking at the photo of her and Gabe. She recalled when he had given her a single red rose and explained it was all he could afford. She looked at Marge, who loitered.

"I assume they're from Mr. Hunter." Marge dared to suggest.

Elise removed the card wedged in the clear floral pick and opened the tiny envelope. She glanced at it quickly before reading it aloud. "Elise, I enjoyed our first date. I look forward to many more. As always, Carson." She looked at the roses, leaned forward, and inhaled their fragrance. "Nice."

"So, you went on a date." Marge peeked out the office door to ensure the bookstore was void of customers.

"It was nice," Elise admitted.

Marge raised her eyebrows inquisitively. "Nice? Just nice?"

"We went to a movie, and he took me home." Elise blushed.

Crossing her arms over her chest, Marge tilted her head to one side and squinted her eyes in suspicion. "There's got to be more to it than that. I need details."

Elise looked heavenward and could not help but smile. "I found him to be polite. Our conversation flowed easily, and all in all, it was a pleasant evening."

"And . . ." Marge smirked.

Elise sighed, surrendering her admission. "He kissed me goodnight."

Marge slapped her hands together and smiled. "I knew there was more to the story. And how was that goodnight kiss?"

Elise's mouth fell agape. She was not one to kiss and tell.

The bell of the front door rang.

"Dang." Marge took one step outside of the office. "I want to hear more later."

Elise could hear 'Hello, can I help you find something?' echo as Marge walked away.

A twinge of jealousy pulled at Gabe's heart. "I wish I could have showered you with bouquets of roses too. He's the one, Elise. I just know it. He'll treat you as you should be treated and remain steadfast by your side."

It was challenging for Elise to focus on the stack of paperwork she needed to complete by day's end. She glanced at the vase of red roses and then at the photo with Gabe's smiling face contemplating her true feelings. Her phone buzzed. Her body jerked as if she had been caught doing something inappropriate. Elise looked at the displayed text from Carson.

'Hello, Elise. I hope your day is going well.'

She replied. 'Piles of paperwork to get through. Your roses arrived a short time ago. Thank you. They're beautiful.'

"Wow! Are those from Carson?"

Elise turned her phone over to hide the screen. She looked at the time on her computer screen. "My, this day has flown by."

Melanie tossed her bookbag on the small table cleared for her to do her homework. She read the card in the flowers. "Oh, they are from him. Nicely done, Mom." She patted her mother on the back.

"I didn't do anything." Elise swiveled in her chair to watch her daughter retrieve a snack from the cupboard. "He is just being kind."

"Face it, Mom, he's sweet on you." Melanie opened a bag of pretzel rods, selected two, and offered the snack to her mother.

"I think you're reading too much into this. It was just one date." Elise took a pretzel rod as her phone buzzed.

"Oh, is that him now?" Melanie teased.

"Probably spam." Elise left her phone where it lay. "Do you have any homework?"

"Just Math." Melanie scowled. "I know, I know. Get it done." She clicked on the lamp, plopped down in the chair, and pulled her book from the bookbag. "When is Carson going to tutor me?"

"I have yet to ask him. Maybe beginning on Monday?"

Melanie shrugged her shoulders. "Whenever."

With other items to check off her to-do list, Elise grabbed her phone and left her office. She read the text message, 'I have an early evening appointment. I'll call you later. Bye.' She sent a thumbs-up emoji before going behind the counter, which she soon regretted. "Slow afternoon for a Friday, Marge?"

"It's been steady since the roses arrived. Now, I want details about that goodnight kiss."

Elise groaned inwardly but decided to share a tidbit of the truth. "It was nice."

"Oh, I can only imagine." Marge chuckled.

The kiss weighed heavily on her mind. "The only person I was ever intimate with was Gabe. It seems a little awkward kissing someone else."

"Awkward? In a good way, right?" Marge pried.

Shaking her head slightly, Elise reflected. Was it awkward or just different? "I'm not certain. But in a way, it was just a moment in time that we shared."

Marge remained silent as she watched her boss stare at something in the distance that was not there. She decided to pull Elise back to reality. "Did you get all of your paperwork done?"

Her employee's question fell on deaf ears as Elise remembered why she had left her office. "Only two weeks until Christmas. We need to set a cut-off date for accepting special orders and post it on the website."

"We should make a sign for the counter, too," Marge suggested and quickly did so.

Several customers lingered in the store as closing time approached.

Marge retrieved her jacket and purse, pausing before she left. "See you tomorrow. Remember, I have Sunday off for a family Christmas party."

"See you." Elise looked in the direction of her office as she shut off the counter computer. "Mel, you want to help me close?"

Melanie was already at the front of the store. "Way ahead of you." She turned off the open neon light, locked the front door as the last customer left, and began turning off the lights while her mother cashed out the register.

~

Janet stared as the vase of roses was placed in the center of the kitchen table. "My goodness. Those look expensive."

"They're from Carson." Melanie boasted.

"They're lovely." Janet placed the platter of spaghetti on the table, accompanied by a bowl of green beans and a basket of garlic bread. "I hope you're hungry. I think I overdid it on the spaghetti."

"Leftover spaghetti is always good. I can take it to work tomorrow." Elise washed her hands in the kitchen sink. "Mel, wash up and come eat."

Janet leaned over the bouquet and inhaled the fragrance. "Lovely."

As Elise tucked herself into bed that evening, she took her father's bible from the nightstand drawer. She let the pages fall open to reveal the first rose she had received from Gabe. It was dry, quite brittle, and its petals' rich scarlet color had faded. It seemed silly to keep it all these years, but it was more than a flower. It represented Gabe's heartfelt confession of his love for her. She held the rose beneath the lamplight and rotated it between her forefinger and thumb. Elise wondered if the roses from Carson were intended to mean the same.

Chapter 33

Leading up to Christmas break, Carson came to the house and worked with Melanie at the kitchen table most school nights. Depending on his schedule, he sometimes joined the trio of women for dinner. Elise continued to monitor her daughter's Math grade, which inched toward improvement.

Elise worked the bookstore alone on Christmas Eve. The remainder of the special orders were picked up, and the last shopper left at three o'clock as she locked the door. As she shut off the open sign, a knock sounded on the door.

Tired and eager to go home, she intended to tell the customer the bookstore was closed. When she went to the door, Carson's smiling face greeted her. She opened the door. "I'm sorry, sir, the bookstore is closed." She smiled as she allowed him to enter.

"But I have a special order to pick up." Carson jested. "Actually, to deliver." He pulled a small box from his coat pocket.

She stared at the beautifully wrapped box.

"Since I have my family in town tonight and tomorrow, I thought I would drop this by."

"Aw, but your gift is under the tree at my house."

Carson raised his eyebrows up and down devilishly. "All the more reason to come and see you." He smiled. "Here, open it."

Elise accepted the small rectangular box, removed the bow and ribbon, and took off the wrapping to reveal a black velvet box. She looked into Carson's chestnut eyes, hoping he had not given her an expensive gift. Lifting the cover to reveal a sapphire, diamond, and white gold bracelet, her breath was nearly taken away. "Oh, my. It's beautiful."

"The sapphires nearly match the color of your eyes." Carson tried to read her thoughts. Was she pleased? Offended? He waited as she continued to stare.

"I've never owned something like this before. What if I lose it?"

"We can get it insured."

"Insured?" Elise continued to stare.

"Do you like it?" He ventured to ask.

"It's lovely but much too expensive."

"If you don't like it, we can return it, and you can pick something else." He suggested.

"No, it's beautiful. I'm just a little overwhelmed."

"Here, let me help you put it on." Carson took it from the box and fastened the clasps around her wrist. "Perfect."

Elise admired the sparkling diamonds and sapphires in the light. "It's gorgeous. Thank you."

"You're welcome." Carson wrapped his arms around her body, drawing her toward him. He pressed his lips to hers and kissed her gently. "Merry Christmas, Elise."

"Merry Christmas, Carson."

Gabe went to the chair where Petey slept. "Merry Christmas to you both." He traced his finger down the cat's boney spine. "You're getting thin, Petey."

Carson kissed her forehead before releasing her. "Are you ready to go home?"

"I just have to shut off the lights and cash out."

"I'll get the lights." Carson offered as he went in search of the switches.

Elise finished closing the register and walked Carson to the front of the store. "Thank you again for my beautiful present."

After a kiss goodbye, Elise let Carson exit out the front door. She shut off her office computer on her way out of the back of the store.

~

With Christmas break come and gone and school back in session, Elise stood in the kitchen doorway and admired Carson's patience as he explained a Math problem to Melanie.

"Bottom line, fractions are never divided. Instead, the second fraction is inverted, and then multiply the numerators and then the denominators. You can also simplify them by cross-canceling. That way, you don't have to reduce later." Carson went through the problem step by step and watched if Melanie's facial expression indicated she understood. "Now, you try this one." He wrote the problem on the paper and turned it toward her. Spying Elise in the doorway, he winked, hoping to finish tutoring soon.

Elise returned to the living room and scanned the free publisher's books she had brought home. Absorbed in a particular novel, she smiled as Carson's arms wrapped around her as he stood behind the upholstered chair. She felt his lips press against the top of her head before placing his chin on her shoulder.

"That must be a pretty good book." He whispered.

"It is. I plan to order a few and have the book in stock." She kissed his cheek. "Done tutoring?"

"For tonight. Mel has a much better grip on dividing fractions. She just needs a little more practice."

"Thanks for helping her. As of lately, the last person she wants to hear advice from is me."

"Ah, the defiant teenage years." He scowled as he released her and sat on the arm of the chair.

Elise set the book aside and shrugged her shoulders. "I guess, but she has a couple of years before becoming an official teenager. I think a change in her hormones is more to blame."

Carson nodded once. He noticed they were alone in the room. "Did Janet go to bed early?"

"She's reading in her bedroom." Elise stood. "Did you want to watch TV?"

"No, I have to go home, do some paperwork, and pack for a conference."

"Oh, that sure crept up quickly."

"Yes, I fly out tomorrow late afternoon and will be gone for a week."

"A whole week?"

Carson sensed her disappointment as he stood. "I'll stop by the bookstore on my way to the airport." He clasped her hand, encouraging her to rise, and led her to the door. "I'd take you with me, but I would be tied up in meetings all day. The evening dinners and guest speakers would be boring for you too."

Elise had little interest in investing and real estate. "True."

Carson turned and wrapped Elise in his arms. "When I get back, we'll have dinner together, just the two of us."

"Oh, sounds amazing." Elise detected a tone of teasing in his comment.

Carson knew he was in love with her but patiently waited for her to admit it to herself. Should he tell her the three little words on the tip of his tongue and risk her not conveying the same? "Well, my dear, I'll see you tomorrow." His kiss was gentle, tender. "Goodnight."

"Night." Elise returned to reviewing books but found her mind strayed from the task. "A whole week without seeing him."

~

Elise was busily stocking a shelf with an ample selection of the blind date with a book when Marge entered for her shift on Tuesday.

"Good morning. Oh, blind date. The customers always like getting a free book." Marge admired the display.

"I think they like it because their choice is a bit of a mystery." Elise placed the last book to fill the shelf.

"Are we putting them out early this year?"

"We have so many, I thought it would be a good idea to draw in customers." Elise looked toward the back door as she heard a knock. "Book order is here."

Even though it was a slow day customer-wise, Elise and Marge managed to check in the order and shelve the books.

Elise glanced at the clock. Melanie would be walking through the door soon. She looked at the woman who approached the counter. "May I help you?"

"Yes, I'm here to pick up a book I ordered."

"Your last name?"

"Brooks."

Elise scanned the shelf of special orders, located the book, and handed it to Marge to ring up. "Is there anything else we can help you with?"

"No, thank you."

The bell on the front door rang, drawing Elise's attention. Melanie entered with Carson towering behind her.

"Now, while I'm away, text me if you have a question. In fact, take a picture of the problem and send it to me." Carson instructed as Melanie went to the office for a snack. He grinned at Elise. She looked tired. "Busy day?"

"Not really, but we managed to stay busy," Elise admitted.

"I assume Mel went to your office."

Elise scowled. "Yes, why?"

"Is there someplace private where I can kiss you goodbye before I leave?"

Elise scanned the store as another customer entered. "It's not the best place, but it will do." She came around the counter, clasped his hand, and led him to the utility room. Once inside, she turned toward him.

Carson embraced her in his arms. His lips met hers, conveying his passion with the hope it would sustain her during his absence. When their kiss ended, he touched his lips to her forehead. "This will be the longest week of my life, but I promise to call you every chance I get."

Elise nodded. "I'm going to hold you to it."

Carson glanced at his watch. "I'm running late. Gotta go." Placing one last kiss on her lips, he left the bookstore.

As promised, Carson called often. Sometimes more than once per day. He even managed to help Melanie with a few Math problems.

When the wheels of his plane touched down on the tarmac to end his trip, Carson called Elise. "Are we still on for dinner tonight?"

Elise looked at the clock. It was nearly time to close the bookstore. "I'm sure Mom has something prepared, but I can let her know I won't be eating tonight."

"Great. I'll stop at the grocery store before I pick you up at your house. Then, we'll go to my place, and I'll cook a magnificent meal for the two of us."

"You can cook?" Elise was skeptical.

"Well, I only have a few select dishes that I've mastered. Maybe we could curl up on the couch afterward and watch a movie." He suggested.

"Sounds lovely."

"I'll be at your house at 6:30 and have you home by 10:00ish."

"OK. What's for dinner?"

"It's a surprise." He teased.

As promised, Carson directed his car into his date's driveway promptly at 6:30. His headlights flashed on the living room wall as he drove toward the house.

"Mom, Carson is here," Melanie announced before entering the kitchen and joining her grandmother at the table to eat.

"Thanks, Mel." Elise grabbed her coat and opened the front door before Carson knocked.

"Hi, Carson," Melanie yelled from the kitchen.

"Hello, Mel. Janet." Carson greeted them while standing outside the door.

"Bye, you two." Elise closed the door behind her and turned toward her date.

Carson cupped her face with his hands and kissed her. "I've missed you."

Elise smiled. "I've missed you too."

Chapter 34

With Elise inside the car, Carson slid into the driver's seat, clasped her hand, and brought it to his lips. After placing a kiss on her dainty fingers, he held her hand securely as he drove to his house. Within minutes, Carson directed his car into his driveway.

Elise stared at the illuminated lamps atop cast-iron posts as they drove toward the house, which looked like a model home from an architecture magazine. "Your house looks lovely."

"Thanks."

"It's on the lake?"

"Yes, it's an investment. Much too big for me." He stared at the mansion. Its outdoor lights projecting on its walls resembled someone telling a ghost story with a flashlight beneath their chin. It was a lonely place. Even though it was fully furnished, his footsteps echoed on the hardwood floors as he walked from room to room.

Carson drove into the three-car garage and parked.

Elise exited her side of the vehicle and waited while Carson retrieved the groceries from the trunk. He shifted the bags to one hand and unlocked the door. "After you."

Stepping inside the dark house, sensor canned lights turned on, causing Elise to look up.

"Let me take your coat." Carson offered before removing his and hanging both in a closet. "The kitchen is this way."

Elise followed, wide-eyed at the detailed architecture and designer furnishings. "Wow, your house is lovely."

"It was turn-key. The couple had lived here for a few years. The husband was a builder, retired, and the couple decided to sell everything and travel."

Elise stared at him, almost disbelieving his comment. "They just walked away?"

"Basically. The previous owners didn't want the responsibility anymore." Carson entered the

344

kitchen and placed the groceries on the granite countertop island.

Elise stood in the doorway and stared at the elegant Tuscany kitchen. She looked up at the vaulted ceiling, embellished with cross beams and candlestick chandeliers illuminating the room. The cooktop seemed to glisten within the well-lit, vented stone hearth. The cupboards were tall and topped with detailed trim. Elise assumed she would need a stepladder to reach the top shelves. The floor was an elegant yet simple tile. A magnificent island that could easily seat ten people was centered opposite the sink. It was embellished with natural wood paneling that matched the cupboards. Intricately carved corbels of grapes gave the illusion of supporting the granite countertop. The fireplace at the end of the room looked inviting. "This is the most beautiful kitchen I have ever seen."

Carson took a pair of wine glasses from the cupboard and glanced at her. He was pleased by her comment. "Like it, huh? It's the reason I bought the place." He retrieved forks and linen napkins. Carson took a bottle of wine from the grocery bag and uncorked it. "Shall we eat in the dining room? I've yet to use it. Never had a reason to do so."

Elise shrugged her shoulders. "Sure, I guess." She followed him to an adjoining rectangular room. One wall was covered with oil paintings of portraits staring back at her. It made her feel as if she was being watched. The table was quite long, with at least a dozen chairs on its perimeter. "They must have done a lot of entertaining."

Carson set a glass, fork, and napkin before opposite chairs. "Maybe. Would you like a glass of wine while I prepare our dinner?"

"I usually don't drink wine, but a small glass would be nice. Thank you."

He poured both servings, placed the bottle on the table, and handed her a glass. He offered a toast. "To a wonderful dinner and good company."

"Here. Here." Elise agreed as their glasses touched, filling the room with an enchanting ring.

"Make yourself comfortable. I'll be right back with our dinner." Carson set his glass on the table and went to the kitchen.

Elise glanced around the room, admiring the paneled walls, drapery, and furniture. She paused before each portrait and wondered if those captured within them were past relatives of the previous owner. An echo of Carson talking to himself with dishes clattering in the kitchen caused her to cringe. "Do you need any help?"

"No, I got it."

As she examined the last portrait, Carson entered the room carrying two plates of macaroni and cheese with fresh fruit. "My dear, your dinner is served." He set the plates on the table and held Elise's chair for her to sit.

Gabe examined the food. "Simple, yet elegantly presented. Nice job."

Elise smiled as she sat. "Looks delicious."

"I figured, who doesn't like mac and cheese?" He smiled as he sat across from her.

"Right. It's my favorite comfort food." Elise placed her linen napkin in her lap, took her fork, and scooped a portion onto her utensil.

Carson watched, yet to take a bite, as she ate the forkful. "Well?"

To Elise's surprise, it was delicious. She nodded as she savored the rich cheesy flavor. "It's excellent. My compliments to the chef." She raised her glass of wine, toasting his accomplishment.

Carson lifted his glass. "Thank you."

Their conversation throughout the meal was light and upbeat.

"Oh, I can't eat another bite." Elise placed her fork on the edge of her plate and the palm of her hand on her overstuffed stomach. "Thank you, it was delicious." She dabbed the corners of her mouth with her napkin. "Out of curiosity, you said you are an expert at a few select dishes. This is one of them. What is the other?"

"First, I didn't say I was an expert. I said I have mastered two dishes. The other is bologna sandwiches. But I offer various options – mayo, mustard, cheese, the usual." He smiled before shoveling another forkful into his mouth. Carson looked at the mound of mac and cheese still on her plate. "I guess you'll need a doggie bag." He sipped his wine before announcing. "I've got dessert too."

A chuckle bubbled from Elise. "Maybe later, thanks."

Carson finished eating, sat back in his chair with his wine glass in his hand, and stared at the beautiful woman across from him. Unnerved by his silence, Elise gathered her silverware and plate. She began to rise from the table to clear her dishes.

"Now," he began, "sit back down. You are my guest, not the maid."

"You have a maid?" She returned to her seat.

"No, but I have a cleaning lady," Carson admitted. "I'm too busy to maintain this house, and to be honest, I'm probably not the greatest housekeeper either."

Elise placed both elbows on the table and folded her hands beneath her chin. "I don't mind. After all, you cooked. It's only fair that I clean up."

"Not in this household." Carson rose, stacked her plate onto his, and went to the kitchen, leaving Elise alone at the table.

Unaccustomed to being waited on, she picked up the glasses and napkins, and entered the kitchen with the half-filled bottle of wine in her hand. Carson was loading the dishwasher as Elise stepped beside him and placed the items in her hands on the counter. "This really is an elegant kitchen."

"I'm glad you like it. Perhaps it will be yours someday." He regretted his comment as she shrugged her shoulders and stepped away.

Carson tidied the kitchen, refilled their glasses, and handed one to Elise. "I've got something I want you to see. Follow me."

Intrigued, Elise was a mere step behind him as he opened maple hand-carved French doors.

"I believe this will be your favorite room in the house." Carson turned on the lights to reveal floor-to-ceiling shelves containing books too numerous to count. It was a small room compared to the others. There was a fireplace on one wall. A pair of inviting wing-backed chairs before it. A small table on which to lay several open books for research was off to the side. It was topped with a lovely lamp.

Elise grinned. "You know me well." She toured the room, glancing at the titles on the spines, touching them reverently. "They left all of these too?"

"Yes. Maybe the books were just for show?"

Elise thought of Carson's visits to the store and the many books he had purchased. He could have read any of the books in the library instead of buying more.

Before Elise could get too wrapped up in her literary world, Carson offered. "You may borrow a book whenever you wish, but I thought we could watch a movie for now. What do you think?"

"Sounds good." Elise followed him through another doorway. "Another elegant room," she commented as she entered and saw a large, stacked-stone fireplace with a big screen TV above the mantel. The furniture was inviting with its overstuffed cushions. The oil paintings on the wall were of landscapes, her favorite.

"Would you like me to build a fire in the fireplace?"

"No, don't go to the trouble."

"It isn't any trouble at all." Carson picked up a remote, and with one click, the flames flicked around the artificial logs.

Elise laughed. "Nice."

"Thank you." He motioned toward an oversized chair with an ottoman. "Have a seat."

Elise hesitated, uncertain how to get into the chair. Finally, she sat on the edge and scooted to the back as gracefully as possible without spilling her wine.

Carson sat beside her. "Let's see what we can find to watch." He used a remote to turn on the TV and scan several channels. "There is too much to choose from these days. It's overwhelming, don't you think?"

"Yes, if you don't like what is on regular TV, then there are a bazillion stations, paid and unpaid, that specialize in something."

They agreed on a movie that neither of them had seen before. Within fifteen minutes of its start, Elise drifted off to sleep.

Carson retrieved a throw from the shelf beneath the coffee table and draped it over his date.

"I'm not certain how to take you falling asleep, Elise. Either I'm boring as hell, or you feel comfortable enough with me to go to sleep." He reclined next to her and continued to watch the movie. "Maybe it was the wine." Before long, he drifted off to sleep too.

Chapter 35

Melanie tipped the cereal box and filled her bowl. "Where's Mom?"

Usually a light sleeper, Janet would have heard her daughter arrive home last night and leave in the morning. So, she created a plausible excuse. "I assume she went to the bookstore early this morning."

Pouring an ample quantity of milk into the bowl, Melanie submerged her spoon and lifted a dripping mini pyramid of cereal into her mouth.

The back door opened. Janet and Melanie looked at Elise as she stepped into the kitchen. She was dressed in the same clothes she had on the previous evening.

Trying to avoid their inquisitive stares, Elise announced. "I need to take a shower." She hoped to slink to the bathroom without receiving any criticism about her arrival.

Melanie became saucer-eyed. She nearly choked on her mouthful of food. "You're just getting home?"

Elise exhaled as she stopped and looked at her daughter. "Yes, I fell asleep. We both did." She defended as she crossed her arms over her chest.

Janet sipped her coffee, refraining from comment. After all, her daughter was pushing forty years old. What Elise did in her private life was none of Janet's business.

Melanie narrowed her eyes, tilted her head to one side, and smirked as she shook her damp spoon at her mother. "Oh, sure. You both fell asleep. I know what that lousy excuse means."

Elise glared at her daughter. She placed her fisted hands upon her hips. "It's the truth, and anyway, how would you know what my 'lousy excuse' implies?"

"You know," Melanie smirked as she nodded her head.

"No, I don't know. Explain it to me." Elise put her hand on the table and leaned toward her daughter, waiting for her reply.

"You had sex with him."

Elise raised her eyebrows, questioning. "You're ten."

"Almost eleven," Melanie interjected.

"How would you know about sex?"

"The internet." Melanie submerged her spoon into her cereal for the next bite.

Elise shook her head and looked heavenward. "For your information, not that it is any of your business. We did not have sex."

"Why not?" Melanie ate the spoonful.

Elise stood up straight and crossed her arms over her chest. "I suppose we aren't ready for that part of our relationship yet."

"Well, I don't know what you're waiting for. It's not like the two of you are getting any younger." Melanie tipped her bowl to her mouth and drank the milk, placed her dishes in the sink, and went to dress for school.

Elise stood with her mouth agape. She looked at her mother, who was grinning.

"She's right, you know." To avoid commenting any further, Janet bit into her bagel, leaving cream cheese on her upper lip as she chewed.

Shaking her head, Elise retreated to the bathroom to shower before opening the bookstore.

~

Elise unlocked the back door of the bookstore and looked down at Petey, who had just celebrated his nineteenth birthday. The old feline greeted her with a pitiful meow.

"Well, good morning to you too, Petey. I know you're hungry." She began to hum as she turned on several lights, took a can of cat food from the closet, and dumped it into Petey's dish. Elise patted the feline on the head as he lowered it to eat. "There you go, you old cat." She continued to hum as she turned on her office computer.

Throughout the morning at the bookstore, Elise reflected on the previous evening spent with Carson. Unfortunately, each task took longer to finish than usual.

After lunch, Elise joined Marge behind the counter to review the special orders. Her mind drifted to the sensual feeling of waking in the arms of a man once again. She grinned.

"A penny for your thoughts." Marge pried as she noticed her boss staring at the same screen for several moments.

Distracted from her daydreaming, Elise looked at her employee as if she had been caught doing something naughty. "Just thinking about my dinner last night with Carson."

"Did the two of you go out?"

"No, he made dinner for me, mac and cheese."

"My favorite. Carson really knows how to spoil a gal, doesn't he?" Marge chuckled.

"It was delicious." A faraway look blanketed her vision as Elise grinned. "We watched a movie afterward. Well, he watched it. I fell asleep."

Marge dared to inquire. "So, did you spend the night?"

"Unknowingly. I blame the mass quantity of carbs I ate. Oh, the wine may have had something to do with it too. I must admit, though, it was nice waking up in Carson's arms."

Marge nodded as she became a little dreamy-eyed. "That secure feeling." She set aside a special-order book. "I'm happy for you."

"Thanks."

"He's a nice guy." Marge picked up the next book and brought up the order on the computer screen.

"I think so too."

"And so do I." Gabe reiterated as he went to a shelf, looked back at Elise, and knocked a book to the floor.

Marge's body jolted. "Dang ghost." She walked to the end of the aisle and picked up the book.

Elise leaned over the counter. "What is the heading on the chapter?"

"Preparations Complete." Marge closed the book, reshelved it, and joined Elise. "How did you know the book lay open at a chapter?"

"It seems every book that falls to the floor lands at the start of a chapter. So, I assumed it was the same."

"Strange, don't you think? It's as if the ghost is trying to tell us something."

Elise's phone dinged. She retrieved it from her pocket and read the text, 'I had a great time last night. It was nice not sleeping alone and waking with you in my arms. Can't wait until we have 'dinner' again.' Elise grinned from ear to ear.

"You're smiling like a cat that just caught a mouse." Marge teased.

"Not our cat. Petey is too old. Besides, when he does catch one, all he does is play with it. If you must know, the text is from Carson. He said he had a good time last night." Elise typed in her reply. 'Last night was nice, and your mac and cheese was delicious.'

"What does Mel think of him?"

"She likes him. She says he's hot." Elise thought for a moment. "He is patient with her, especially when tutoring her in Math."

"I've gotta agree with her. Carson is hot." Marge shrugged.

"She gave me the third degree when I arrived home this morning."

"Well, she's a little too young to understand what goes on between a man and a woman."

"That's what I assumed." Elise chuckled. "She accused me of having sex with Carson. When I asked her how she knew about it, Mel said she learned about it on the internet."

Marge shook her head. "There's too much dang information kids can find online these days."

A customer entered the store, drawing their attention and ending their topic of discussion.

~

Spring flowers were in full bloom, and the weather was unseasonably warm.

Carson inhaled the hearty aroma as he entered the house through the back door. "Smells delicious." He carried a colorfully wrapped present and several helium balloons. He looked at Elise, who was busy helping Janet in the kitchen. "Where's the birthday girl?"

Melanie entered the room. "I'm here."

"Well, happy birthday. How does it feel to be eleven years old?" He smiled as he handed her the bouquet of balloons. Elise took the present from his hand and placed it on the counter.

"No different than being ten." She admitted.

"Mel, why don't you put the balloons in the center of the table. It will make a nice decoration." Elise suggested.

Gabe realized his little girl was transforming into a young lady before his eyes. "Happy birthday, Mel. I'm blessed to be here to witness another of your milestones."

"I'll just put the rolls in the oven to bake, and dinner should be ready in ten minutes," Janet announced as she removed the roast from the oven and put the risen rolls inside to bake.

"Janet, you're going to too much trouble. I could have taken everyone out for dinner." Carson put his arm around Elise's shoulder and hugged her.

"Oh, it's no trouble. Besides, I know how you like a home-cooked meal." Janet placed a hearty platter of pot roast with potatoes and carrots on the table. Elise added a basket of freshly baked rolls. They sat, bowed their heads, and said grace. The food was passed around family-style.

Carson placed his fork on the side of his plate. He pulled a warm roll apart and smothered half with butter. "Janet, you're going to spoil me. The roast is delicious." He took a bite of his roll. "Mmm...homemade rolls too. My compliments to the chef."

"Thank you." Janet cut the tender meat on her plate with the edge of her fork.

Elise looked at her mother. "She spoils me too and always has a meal waiting for me when I arrive home from the bookstore."

With appetites satisfied, Carson offered to help clear the table. Janet brushed his assistance aside. "The dishes can wait. It's time for cake, ice cream, and presents." She placed a homemade cake before her granddaughter.

"Oh, my favorite flavor – chocolate."

After a chorus of 'Happy Birthday,' everyone enjoyed the tasty dessert followed by opening presents.

"Thank you, everyone." Melanie ate the last bite of cake on her plate.

~

As the school year neared its end, Carson arrived one evening to tutor Melanie.

Elise and Janet tidied the kitchen of dinner dishes while Carson and Melanie began to review for a test. Eavesdropping, Elise listened to the lesson while she dried the dishes.

"Carson, are you doing anything Wednesday night?"

Elise placed the washed platter in the cupboard and looked at her daughter, curious about the posed question.

"I've no plans." He admitted.

"No appointments?"

Carson checked the app on his phone. "No, none."

"Do you want to go to my spring choir concert?"

He glanced at Elise, who displayed a sympathetic cringe. "Sure. What time?"

Melanie looked at her mom. "What time, Mom?"

"It begins at 7:00, but you need to be there at 6:30." She stepped behind Carson's chair and placed her hand on his shoulder.

Carson covered her hand with his and squeezed it tenderly. "Sounds like a fun evening. I'll come and pick the three of you up, and we can go together." He rotated his arm to bring Elise beside him. "Now that's out of the way, we need to study." He patted Elise on the rump as she turned to leave the room.

Melanie looked down at her review sheet and smiled.

~

Still dressed in his suit for work, Carson arrived early to pick up his three dates. He entered through the back door of the open garage. "Hello, is everyone ready?"

Melanie entered the kitchen wearing a lovely dress. Her flaxen hair curled and pulled back from her face. Her deep blue eyes looked at Carson, anticipating a compliment.

"Mel, you look lovely."

Gabe smiled. "Beautiful, just like your mom."

"Thank you. Mom curled my hair."

"She did a wonderful job. You look beautiful." Carson complimented as Elise and Janet entered the room. "And the two of you look lovely too."

"Thank you." They said simultaneously.

Elise went to Carson, raised up on her tiptoes, and kissed him. "You look pretty snazzy yourself."

He pretended to blush as he straightened the sleeves on his suit coat. "Oh, this old thing."

They arrived at the school in ample time. Melanie reported to her classroom while everyone else found a seat in the gymnasium. Beginning with the kindergarten room through the fifth grade, each class took their turn to sing the three songs they had practiced in music class.

Melanie smiled from ear to ear as she joined her concert guests after the concert.

"Well done, Mel." Elise hugged her daughter.

"You sang beautifully," Janet added.

"Good job. I think ice cream is in order, my treat." Carson announced.

~

"This is my last Math test this year. Yeah!" Melanie was eager for summer vacation.

"Then let's make sure you do well." Carson encouraged. "Let's start with this problem." He pointed to a problem while writing a note and pushed it toward Melanie. As she read each word, her eyes enlarged. She looked at Carson, ready to squeal with delight. He put his finger across his lips, requesting her silence. He turned the note over, wrote another message, and pushed it toward her again. Melanie read it and nodded, unable to keep a smile off her face.

"You understand, right?" He stated as if referring to the Math problem and winked.

"Yes."

Carson tucked the note into his pants pocket, ensuring Elise would remain ignorant of his intention. "Next problem." He winked.

~

On the last school day, Elise, Carson, and Janet watched Melanie cross the stage and accept her fifth grade graduation certificate. They waited outside the school as the applause echoed from the hallway as fellow students clapped-out their upperclassmen, a respectful dismissal ending their elementary education.

In the following weeks, Melanie glanced at her mother's left hand whenever Elise returned home from work or after spending the night with Carson.

Much to her disappointment, the old wedding ring remained, as did her dad's wedding band on the chain around her mother's neck.

After a hectic summer Saturday at the bookstore, Elise glanced at the clock. "Almost closing time." She toured the store, straightened shelves, and put wayward books in their proper place.

The bell of the front door rang a minute before closing time.

"I'm sorry, we're closing soon. Is there anything I can help you find?" Elise came around an endcap, locked the front door, and turned to see Carson holding a bouquet of red roses in one hand and a book in the other.

He smiled. "I certainly hope so."

She grinned. "Are those for me?"

"As always." He leaned forward, placed a gentle kiss on her lips, and handed her the bouquet. "And so is this."

Accepting the book, Elise read the title. "It's not a new title. In fact, it isn't one I'm familiar with at all." Elise went behind the counter and laid the roses down. She intended to run the sales report for the day and cash out.

"There is an inscription inside." He encouraged.

Elise opened the cover, turned the blank page, and discovered a small black velvet box inset in the book's pages. She read the adjacent page aloud. "I love you with all my heart. Will you marry me?" Elise's mouth fell agape. She looked at Carson. "Are you serious?"

He nodded. "Yes."

She lifted the lid of the box to reveal a diamond ring. Her breath caught in her throat. "It's beautiful." Elise stared at his askance, handsome face, and tried to smile. She thought of Gabe's proposal, her wedding, and how her life had changed drastically when he died. Then the unexpected happened, she was pregnant. Her mother, and best friend, remained by her side throughout it all, including Melanie's birth. If she married Carson, she assumed she would move into his house and cast her mother into a life of loneliness. Would Melanie want to move into Carson's house? His proposal was like a pebble thrown into an aquarium filled with water, causing waves until they dissipated into calmness.

"There's so much to think about. I mean, I have my daughter and mom to consider."

Gabe shook his head. "He's the one, Elise."

Carson ran his hand through his thick curly hair pulling it away from his forehead. "I get it. This is an unexpected change. You need time." He grinned. "At least that isn't a no."

"What are you waiting for? I'm dead. I'm not coming back. Say yes, Elise." Gabe chided.

"I really want to say yes, but there is so much for me to consider." She looked at the ring. Its facets sparkled under the light. "It's lovely."

"You've got to be kidding me." Gabe stormed. "There's nothing to consider. He loves you. I'm quite certain you love him too. Go, live happily ever after."

"We can have a long engagement?" Carson offered it as an option.

Elise closed the ebony velvet box and book, unable to meet his gaze. She opened the register drawer to count the money. Flustered by the fork in the road she was facing, Elise slammed the drawer shut. "Oh, this can wait until the morning." Elise picked up the roses and book. "I have to shut off the computer in my office." She turned off the store lights on her way, with Carson following. "Oh, dang, it's pizza night. I have to pick one up on my way home." She placed the items on her desk while she closed a document and logged off her computer.

Carson glanced around her office, seeing it for the first time. He stared at the framed photo on her desk. "Is this you and your first husband?" The man's face in the picture looked vaguely familiar.

"Yes."

Carson scowled, searching his mind as he picked up the photo to examine it closely. "How did you say he died?"

She glanced at Carson, struck by his prying question. "He was in an accident while riding his motorcycle home from work."

"Yes, he was looking at his cell phone when he ran the red light." Carson continued to stare, recalling the incident in his memory.

Elise scowled. "How did you know?"

Carson looked at Elise, uncertain if he should reveal the truth. He placed the photo back on her desk.

"How did you know?" She repeated.

"Because I was driving the car that hit your husband."

"I knew he looked familiar." Gabe spread his fingers on his palms and looked heavenward. "He held my hand and stayed with me until the police and ambulance arrived."

Elise collapsed into her desk chair.

"It was an accident, Elise. He wasn't looking where he was going. I tried to stop." He attempted to hold her hand, but she yanked it away from his grasp. "After the collision, I called 911 and stayed with him until the police and ambulance arrived."

"And what did I tell you, Carson? What were my last words?" Gabe wished he could be heard.

Carson looked at the photo again. "His last words were 'take care of her.'" He looked back to Elise, who had yet to speak.

Gabe scowled as he read his wife's mind. "Oh, no, you don't, Elise. You aren't going to back out of this now. I'm tired of seeing you grow old by yourself. Someday Janet will die, Mel will leave home, where will you be? You'll be alone. Sorry, not happening." Gabe marched out of the office, went to the aisles of books, and began throwing book after book onto the floor.

Carson turned and stared out the office door. "Is someone in the store?"

Elise sprung from her chair and ran toward the books as they flew from the shelves. Carson followed and stood dumbstruck as he stared at the airborne novels.

"How about this one, Elise. And this one. Have you gotten the message yet?" Gabe continued to rifle the books from the shelf one after the other.

"What's going on?" Carson continued to watch.

"It's Gabe." Elise picked up one of the books from the floor.

"Your dead husband?" Carson looked at the scattered books as more continued to fall.

"Yes, he is always near, as if he is watching over me." Elise picked up the book closest to her. "This is how he communicates." She read the title. "Closing A Chapter."

The books stopped falling.

Elise continued to pick up each open book. "Beginning Again, Come What May, For Better Or For Worse, The Wedding." She picked up the next two books. "The Stars Align, Making The Decision." Taking a deep breath, she whispered, "Oh, Gabe." A tear cascaded down her cheek as she looked at the ceiling and took another deep breath. She turned around. Carson was gone.

Chapter 36

Elise entered the house with the book under her arm, a pizza in one hand, and the vase of roses in the other.

"Another customer loitering after hours again?" Melanie set the plates on the table, opened the box, and put two pieces of pizza on her plate.

"Not exactly." Elise's reply was a mere whisper. She placed the flowers on the kitchen table and walked away with the book in her hand.

Janet paused as she unscrewed the cap on the gallon of milk and looked at her daughter.

Melanie sensed something was wrong. "Mom?" She watched her mother disappear through the kitchen door and into the hallway.

"Eat your dinner, Mel." Janet set the glass of milk before her granddaughter and followed Elise into her bedroom. With a slice of pizza in hand, Melanie followed.

Elise, yet to remove her coat, sat numbly on the edge of her bed. She stared at the book in her hand.

Janet stood in the doorway. "Are you OK?"

With tears streaming down her cheeks, Elise looked at her mother.

Melanie peeked around her grandmother, squeezed through the doorway, and entered the room. "Mom, what's wrong?"

"I don't quite know. Nothing, yet everything." She ran her hand over the cover of the book. "Carson proposed."

Melanie's eyes widened, and she grinned. "Yes! That's great, Mom." Her smile faded as she stared at her mother's sullen face. "But why aren't you happy?"

"It's complicated."

Janet interceded in the conversation. "How? He loves you, and you love him, right?"

Elise glanced from Melanie to her mother. "I just need some time to think things out."

"What's to think about?" Janet pressed.

"Listen to your mother, Elise." Gabe insisted.

"I don't know if I can marry him." Elise brushed a tear away from her cheek.

"Why?" Janet and Melanie said simultaneously.

"I don't know if I can forgive him."

"Forgive him?" Janet sat on the bed next to her daughter. "For what?"

"For killing Gabe."

"What are you talking about, Mom. He killed Dad?" Melanie took another bite from the slice of pizza.

Elise took a deep breath. "He was involved in the accident that killed your dad."

"It was Gabe's fault. He ran the red light." Janet reasoned.

"He ran the red light because he was answering the text I sent him. Carson recognized him in the photo on my desk and realized who he was. He said he called 911 and stayed with Gabe until the police and ambulance arrived."

"Elise." Janet placed her hand over her daughter's splayed fingers on the book. She wrapped her arm around her waist and hugged, hoping she would see reason.

"I was the catalyst of the fateful accident," Elise said numbly as the guilt from the past settled upon her shoulders once again.

"It wasn't your fault. It wasn't Carson's fault either. It was an accident." Janet sighed. "This is an opportunity for you to be happy if you choose to take it."

Elise looked at her mom. "But I was happy with Gabe."

"And he's gone."

Elise nodded as she wiped away another tear as it trickled down her cheek.

"You deserve to be happy. Go, Elise. Go and get him." Gabe encouraged, though he knew his voice was unheard. "Make the decision to change your life."

Elise rose and tucked the book into the crook of her arm. "Go ahead and eat without me. I'm going out."

Determined to end her emotional turmoil, she drove to Carson's house, parked the car, and shut off the engine. Uncertain what she would say, she sat for a moment composing her thoughts.

"Come on, Elise. You can do this." Gabe coaxed.

Lifting her chin, she went to the front door with the book in her hand.

~

Carson had hoped to spend the evening celebrating his engagement. He canceled the reservation at the restaurant and settled for a frozen meal from his freezer. The microwave beeped as he uncorked a bottle and poured himself a glass of wine.

He sat in the lounge chair, turned on the TV, and stabbed his fork into the man-size portion of goulash. Carson blew the steaming forkful to cool it and paused as the doorbell rang. Ignoring what he assumed was a salesman or religious minion trying to convert sinners, he dropped his fork into his food as he changed the channel.

The doorbell rang incessantly.

Not wanting to be disturbed, Carson placed his meal on the side table and marched to the front door. "I need to post a damn 'no loitering' sign." He flung the door open with gusto, ready to whiplash whoever was on the other side, but his agitation turned to apprehension as his heart skipped a beat, and he looked into Elise's bloodshot eyes. "Hi." He spied the book reverently held in her hands before her. Was she turning him down? Returning his ring?

Elise burst into tears. She looked down at the book in her hands, unable to speak.

Carson lowered his gaze to the limestone porch trying to avoid her rejection. Her arms wrapped around his neck. She pressed her body to his, burying her face under his chin. Instinctively, he wrapped his arms around her, drawing her to his body. He interpreted her closeness as a positive sign. "Does this mean 'yes'?"

Elise nodded her head in affirmation.

Carson beamed with delight as he lifted her body from the porch, rotated, and shut the door behind them. "Then why are you crying?"

Elise took a deep breath to calm herself. She needed to speak her mind, her heart. "This is a big step for me. For most of my life, I've loved Gabe and only Gabe. I've never let him go, maybe because I know he is always beside me. By committing to you, I feel as if I'm saying goodbye to him. It's hard."

"But I'm not asking you to say goodbye." Carson reached for her arms, pulled them away from his neck, and took the book from her hand. "Please, believe me, it was an accident. I stayed with Gabe until the paramedic pushed me away. He loved your dearly, as I do. I truly believe he would want you to be happy."

She nodded.

"Do you forgive me?"

"There's nothing to forgive. It was an accident." Elise took a deep breath. "Thank you for staying with Gabe until he received medical attention."

"I didn't want him to be alone." Carson brushed away a tear from Elise's cheek. "This is supposed to be a happy occasion. So, if we do this, I think a proper proposal is in order."

Elise took a step back as she watched Carson remove the ring from the ebony velvet box. He dropped the book next to his feet, knelt on one knee, and looked into her sapphire eyes.

"Elise, will you marry me?"

She cupped her hands over her mouth before removing them. "Yes."

Carson glanced at the wedding ring on her finger. "Then let's do this. Let's put your ring on your necklace with what I assume is your husband's wedding band. Does that work for you?"

Elise nodded as she watched him slip her wedding ring from her finger and place the engagement ring in its rightful place. She unclasped her necklace. Carson strung the ring onto the chain and fastened it on his fiancé's neck.

"I love you, Elise." He wiped the dampness from her cheek and lowered his lips toward hers.

"I love you, Carson." She whispered before their lips touched.

Gabe smiled. "I knew you could do it, Elise."

Unbeknownst to the kissing couple, a beam of light appeared from the foyer vaulted ceiling and illuminated the floor where Gabe stood. He glanced one last time at Elise and Carson. "I guess that's my cue. I wish you both a blessed marriage, one filled with happiness." He turned, paused, and looked back. "Don't think I won't be watching. Elise, a part of my heart will always be yours. See you on the other side when your time comes." His spirit elevated into the beam of light and disappeared as he passed through the ceiling.

Chapter 37

The couple opted for a small ceremony in early Autumn. They pledged their lives to each other in the backyard of Carson's lakefront home.

"Is this my room?" Melanie stepped to the foot of the queen-size bed. "It's enormous."

"Yes, let's just hope you can keep it clean," Elise stated. "For now, you'll be staying with Grandma while we're away on our honeymoon."

"It's lovely, Elise. The three of you are going to be very happy here." Janet added.

"Mom, there are plenty of bedrooms. Carson and I agreed that you may move here too."

"I appreciate your thoughtfulness, but I'm fine where I am. However, I insist that Carson invite me to dinner. I want to try his mac and cheese."

Carson peeked his head into the room and stood behind Elise. "I promise, Janet. When we return from our trip, it will be the first meal I make, and you will join us for dinner." He wrapped his arms around his bride's waist and nuzzled her neck.

~

After the return of the honeymooning couple, Janet joined the trio for a grand dinner of mac and cheese. She agreed with Elise. It was delicious. Carson offered a copy of his recipe, which Janet eagerly accepted.

Elise arrived at the bookstore early the following day. After turning on the computer in her office, she looked at the photo of her and Gabe and grinned. She pulled a framed picture from her bag and placed it next to the other photo. The new image was of her and Carson. It captured their happiness while embracing on the beach during their tropical honeymoon. She grinned. There was indeed room in her heart for both men.

Thank you for reading

Leaving You

Behind

If you have a moment, please leave a review at the
store where you bought it or on Goodreads.

For additional information about the author, signings,
and her books, please visit

www.BrendaHasseBooks.com

To sign up for the author's newsletter, please visit

www.BrendaHasseBooks.com/newsletter-sign-up

CPSIA information can be obtained
at www.ICGtesting.com
Printed in the USA
JSHW021519080722
27705JS00002B/11